A
PERFECT
STRANGER

BOOKS BY SHALINI BOLAND

A
PERFECT
STRANGER

SHALINI BOLAND

bookouture

First published as an Audible Original in November 2021 by Audible Ltd.
This edition published July 2022 by Bookouture.

An imprint of Storyfire Ltd.
Carmelite House
50 Victoria Embankment
London EC4Y 0DZ
Uniter Kingdom

www.bookouture.com

ISBN: 978-1-80314-356-9
eBook ISBN: 978-1-80314-355-2

PROLOGUE

ANNIE

Despite the dark, bloated clouds, the hammering rain and this god-awful rattling truck, today is the first day I feel anything approaching happiness. I make the sharp turn down the lane that leads to our cottage and think contentedly of the three loaded shopping bags in the back under the tarp. David's going to be so happy when I show him all the goodies I've bought. The only items the little convenience store didn't have were avocados, but they're an extravagance anyway, so maybe it's just as well. David and I have been struggling financially for months. Things were looking extremely bleak. Until now.

'Mummy, is the new man going to help make dinner?' My four-year-old is strapped into his car seat next to me, kicking rhythmically at the glove box. I've given up asking him to 'please stop doing that' and, anyway, I can barely hear his kicks above the sound of the rain.

'No, George. Daddy and I are going to cook tonight. The "new man" is called Jonathan and I think he has to go to work.' George is referring to our lodger, Jonathan Dean. He's the chef at a hotel in the next village. He's also the reason I'm in such a good mood. Earlier today, Jonathan moved in and paid us a month's

deposit and a month up front in cash to rent our spare room. So, for the first time in ages, David and I actually have more than two pennies to rub together. Jonathan's references were impeccable and it was endearing that he seemed to be so grateful to us. He's newly divorced with two children and it sounds like he's had a rough time of things. Plus, he struck up a great rapport with George, who now fancies himself as a mini chef.

'Mummy, can I help make the dinner?'

I glance across at my little brown-eyed son, at his straw-coloured curls darkened by the rain. He's the spitting image of his father. 'Yes please. That would be lovely. You can set the table if you like.'

The cottage comes into view at the end of the lane. Today, it's just a dark, drizzly shape with a few smudged outbuildings next to it. A cluster of leafy trees overhang the barn and garage, dripping and swaying in the late summer storm.

'But, Mummy, I don't want to set the table. I want to do the cooking like the chef man.'

'His name is Jonathan.' My attention is taken by the sight of the grey cottage door swinging open. My first thought is that it's David coming out to help unload the groceries. But then the door slams violently shut.

'Mummy, I want to do the cooking, not set the table!' My son tugs at my arm.

'Yes, yes, okay, Georgie. Course you can help Mummy with the cooking.'

'And Daddy can cook too.'

'Yes and Daddy.' But I'm not really listening any more. I pull up on the drive, as close as I can get to the path. The front door has swung open again, but there's no one standing in the doorway. I realise the door has been left open and is banging in the wind. If it keeps swinging and banging like that, it's going to come off its hinges and that would be a hassle and expense we can do without.

Did I leave it open? No. I wouldn't have been so careless. Maybe it was the lodger. His car isn't out front. He must have gone out. I'll have to remember to tell him that the front door needs a firm push in order to be closed properly. If I can hear it banging from here inside the truck, then surely David must be able to hear it from inside the house? Why hasn't he come along to close it?

The windows of the cottage are dark, streaked with rainwater. I shiver and suddenly get a bad feeling. 'George, can you stay here for a minute while Mummy goes to check something?' I tuck my damp brown curls behind my ears and take a breath.

'I need a wee.' He's wriggling in his seat.

I give a sigh and tell myself that I'm worrying over nothing. David has no doubt gone out the back to check on the chickens, or maybe he's in the garage. Thinking about it, he's probably the one who left the front door open. 'Okay then, Georgie, come on. Let's go in. We're going to get very wet though. We'll have to run!'

I unclip my son from his car seat and we sprint for the house. I leave the shopping in the truck. I'll come back for it once the rain eases – or maybe David will get it for me. George dashes to the loo as I stand in the hall and call out to my husband.

There's no reply.

Although it's only five thirty, the cottage is dark and shadowy. I switch on the hall light, but nothing happens. I switch it off and on again before accepting that the bulb has gone. I don't think we have any spares. So annoying that this has happened after my shopping trip – I could have bought a replacement if I'd known.

'David!' I try again, not really expecting a reply. There's no sound or light coming from any of the downstairs rooms. My husband is obviously outside. He'll be soaked when he comes back in. George and I are already dripping and we only ran a few yards. My vision blurs. I blink the rain away from my lashes.

My son reappears from the cloakroom.

'Did you wash your hands?'

He nods and holds them out for me to inspect.

'Good boy. Let's go upstairs and get out of these wet things.' I click on the landing light. Again, nothing happens. Must be a fuse. Or maybe the storm has knocked out a power line.

'It's dark, Mummy.'

'I know. We'll have to be careful on the stairs. Hold my hand.'

We walk up together and go into his bedroom where the light doesn't work either. In the gloom, I help him change into dry clothes – a long-sleeved T-shirt and joggers – and I towel-dry his hair. George finally shrugs me off and digs his Batman torch out of his toy box. He starts flashing the bat signal onto his walls.

'Are you going to stay and play here for a minute while I get changed?'

He looks up at me. 'And then we'll do the cooking?'

'Yes, definitely.' I give him a wink, but now I'm worrying about the fridge and freezer defrosting if the power doesn't come back on. What if all that food I've just bought goes bad? 'Stay in your room, George. I don't want you tripping down the stairs in the dark.'

'Okay, Mummy.'

I leave his room, closing the door firmly behind me. We really should get a stair gate. Maybe that can be rectified now that we have a little money to spare. I push at the door to our bedroom, pressing the light switch out of habit, irritated when the darkness remains. The door won't open properly for some reason. There's something in the way. Maybe my dressing gown has fallen off the hook again and got caught under the door. But as I push once more, the door thuds against something. Something that feels large and heavy, like a piece of furniture.

I realise my heart has started to pound quite loudly and uncomfortably. I'm not sure why. There's a prickling sensation down my back as though someone is watching me. Sweat gathers at my armpits. I swallow and freeze before plucking up the courage to turn around. But the small landing is empty. I'm being silly.

I take a breath and squeeze myself through the gap in my bedroom door. Luckily, it's just about wide enough. I peer down at the dark shape that was blocking the door, but I can't quite make sense of it.

And then, all of a sudden, I can.

'David? David!' I clamp my mouth shut. I don't want George coming in and seeing... this. I can barely look myself. Am I here? Is this real?

My husband is lying face-up on the bedroom carpet. His eyes are open, but he's not looking at me. He's staring up at the ceiling. But I don't think he can see the ceiling. I don't think he can see anything. Because there's an obscene dark line across his throat. His throat has been cut. My husband... David... is dead.

ONE

EMILY

Josh lets go of my hand as we leave Green Gates preschool. He looks so cute in his short-sleeved checked shirt and cargo shorts, his chubby little cheeks pink from the sun despite the fact that the preschool staff are rigorous about applying sunscreen and making sure the children all wear hats. Josh's best friend, Ivy, is showing him her dance moves, her two black plaits swinging wildly and Josh is laughing his head off, trying to copy her, but not quite getting it.

'That boy's got moves.' Ivy's mum Luanne slides her sunglasses off her head and onto the bridge of her nose. She takes Josh's hands in hers and starts dancing with him. I shake my head and grin at their antics.

Luanne Cassidy is one of my best friends. We met at ante-natal classes three and a half years ago and we try to socialise at least once a week. She's the nicest, smartest person I know, works in finance and is filthy rich, with a gorgeous, charismatic husband, Troy, who's a stay-at-home dad. Troy usually does the preschool runs, but Luanne left work early today for a dental check-up, so was able to collect her daughter.

'Wish I was three again.' Luanne lets go of Josh and puts a

manicured hand on her hip. 'Playing with friends all day and dancing in the street. Handed snacks whenever you're hungry.'

'Carried when your legs get tired,' I add.

'No tax returns.'

'Or having to empty the bins.'

'Although I would miss alcohol...'

'You wouldn't need it.' I point to our children who are now jumping around crazily on the pavement like drunk pixies. 'And it's not fair to mention alcohol.' I place a hand on my five-months-pregnant belly and give my friend a mock glare.

'Oh, yeah, forgot you can't drink.'

'That's okay. The thought of alcohol makes me queasy anyway. In fact, the thought of most food and drink makes me ill at the moment.'

'You poor thing. Do you still feel up to coming tomorrow?'

'Tomorrow?' I frown, cursing my memory, which seems to have gone AWOL lately.

'After work... The trial at my health club? They have a great antenatal yoga class we could do.'

'Yes, I'm definitely still up for that.' There's no way I'll be able to afford membership at her swanky club, but it'll be nice to pretend for a while. 'My sickness isn't usually too bad in the evenings, so I should be fine.'

'Great. I'll pick you up tomorrow just after six thirty, on my way home from work.'

We take hold of the children's hands and cross the busy main road, waving our thanks to the cars that slow down. We're both parked down a side street. It's one of the last roads in the area without double yellows, but I'm sure the council will be out with their paintbrushes soon to rectify that.

'Such a cute car, Em.' Luanne spreads her hands wide to emphasise her point. I always tease her about her wild hand gestures, but I like how expressive she is. She's talking about my nearly new ice-blue Mini Cooper, parked halfway down the road, the paintwork gleaming in the sun.

'It's not exactly a Jag,' I reply, eyeing her sleek four-by-four that's parked further up. But I do love my little car.

My husband, Aidan, sells prestige cars for a living and he hooked Lu up with her brand-new Jaguar I-Pace earlier in the year. My Mini was a total extravagance – Aidan had a small Lotto win and treated me. I told him he should use the money to pay off our debt. But he said he wanted to do this for me and he managed to get a really good deal. In the end, I was persuaded. I work hard as a doctor's receptionist and figure what's the point in working if you can't enjoy life every now and then. Doctors' receptionists get a bad rap, with a reputation for being standoff-ish. But I get a *lot* of hassle in my job – especially from rude patients complaining about the long waiting times. Don't blame *me*! I can't help the fact that there are too many patients and not enough doctors.

Luanne gives me a nudge as Josh chatters away to Ivy about the blanket fort they made at preschool this afternoon. It's such a serious conversation – they look like they're having a business meeting – that Lu and I can't help smiling. I'm overtaken by a surge of love. How lucky am I to have this beautiful boy as well as another little bundle on the way? I place a protective hand on my bump. Sure, things aren't perfect. Aidan and I still can't afford to buy our own home or take any holidays abroad, but we're both working hard and if Aidan can just get a few more big sales this summer, maybe we'll be able to finally start paying off the credit cards.

At the thought of said credit cards, my feeling of well-being pops like a soap bubble and my shoulders grow heavy. I bite my lip as we reach the Mini, trying to banish guilt from my thoughts.

'You okay?' Luanne puts a hand on my arm.

Her question brings up all sorts of worries, but I can't get into any of it now. Not here on the pavement in front of our children. 'Yeah, I'm fine.'

'You sure?' She frowns.

'Just the usual stuff.' I smile and shrug, trying to get back to how I felt a few moments ago.

'Like?' she pushes.

'I guess I'm feeling guilty about having such a nice car when we can't really afford it.'

She nods and then flips her sunglasses back onto her head, fixing me with her dark-brown eyes. 'Look, Em, you own the car, so enjoy it, otherwise you may as well not bother. If things get too tight, moneywise, you can always trade it in for something else.'

Her words are blunt, but she's right. 'Thanks, Lu. Don't know what I'd do without you talking sense.' Although it's easy for her to say when she has zero money worries.

We hug goodbye and Josh and I get into the Mini and make our way home through the rush-hour traffic. Green Gates preschool is in Parkstone, but I live and work in Ashley Cross, just over a mile away. It's not exactly a cheap area in which to rent, but it's so lovely with its bars and boutiques, coffee shops and restaurants all set around The Green, a small wooded park with a playground. My heart lifts every time I see it. I can barely believe we live here.

My dream is to be able to afford our own character property here one day. Our current house is a rental – a tiny eighties box that we've tried to make the best of, opting for a fun, contemporary vibe with our décor. Our landlady, Izzy, is lovely and has kept our rent frozen for the past three years and was understanding on the couple of occasions we've been late with it. I just hope she never decides to sell the property. Well, not until we're in a position to move, because there's nothing else in our price bracket in this area.

I pull into our narrow drive behind Aidan's navy Audi.

'We gonna see Daddy now?' Josh pipes up from the back.

'Yes, we are, Joshy.' I hope my husband is in a better mood today. He's been grumpy all week. Maybe it's because it's his birthday on Friday and he's going to be thirty-five. I can barely believe it myself. We met in our teens and now we're practically middle-aged. I pray he's not having some kind of midlife crisis.

As soon as I've undone Josh's seatbelt, he slips out of his car seat and runs up to the front door. I grab mine and Josh's bags off the passenger seat, lock the car and follow my son, suddenly realising that I'm nervous about going in and seeing Aidan. I love him, of course I do, but he's just not himself at the moment.

I unlock the door and step into the narrow hallway with its large rectangular mirror and slim console table complete with artfully arranged candles that are too expensive to ever burn. Josh runs into the kitchen and then the lounge.

'Daddy!' he cries.

My heart sinks when I find Aidan in there sprawled on the grey corner sofa, glued to his laptop, his work suit crumpled. Aidan always seems to be on his phone or laptop these days. I can't seem to pry him away. The blinds are half closed and the light from the screen illuminates his face, making his features appear almost unfamiliar. He looks up and gives a half-hearted smile.

'Hey.' I return the smile brightly, pretending not to notice my husband's dishevelled appearance and downhearted mood. Maybe I can cajole him out of it. 'It's warm in here. How was work?'

'Okay,' he replies.

I walk over to the blinds and wrestle with the cheap metal slats as I attempt to open the window. My dream is to have painted wood shutters. They're so beautiful and they're also perfect for bright summer mornings because they block out all the light. But I don't know why I'm even thinking about them, because I'm more likely to fly to the moon than be able to afford them. Having finally eased open the window, I turn back to my husband. 'Any sales today?'

'There's a couple interested in the black Lamborghini, but I think they're time-wasters.'

'You never know. Maybe they're serious.'

He shrugs and lifts Josh off his lap. 'Sorry, mate, I've got to finish this. Give me half an hour and then we'll play, okay?'

Josh starts pulling at Aidan's trousers and I can tell that Aidan's getting wound up. I intervene. 'Come on, Joshy, let's go make dinner.'

'No. I want to play with Daddy!' Josh thrusts out his lower jaw and clings on to his father's leg.

'If you come and help me now, we can make one of those blanket forts in your room later.'

His eyes light up. 'Can we?'

I nod and look at my husband for some kind of acknowledgement, but his eyes are already back on the screen.

Once Josh has had supper, been bathed and been tucked up into bed, I return to the living room to find my husband in exactly the same spot, his eyes still on his laptop, only this time he's swigging from a beer bottle. There were no further offers to play with his son this evening, but thankfully I kept Josh occupied with the creation of a sprawling and complicated fort made out of dining chairs and sheets. I also gave in to Josh's request to sleep in his fort tonight, so we pulled his mattress onto the floor and dragged it underneath the den. We also had to take photos so he can show Ivy tomorrow.

Aidan hasn't emerged from the living room all evening. I could just leave him to it, but I'm irritated by his lack of involvement with Josh today. I have a quick debate with myself about what to do. Should I say something and risk an argument, or let things lie and end up stewing all night?

'What's going on?' I stand in the lounge doorway with my arms crossed over my chest. My heart is thumping.

'Going on?' He looks up absentmindedly from his screen. 'Nothing. Why? Does Josh still want to play?' He puts his laptop down on the sofa and makes to stand up.

'Josh is in bed.'

'Already? What's the time?'

'Seven.'

'Oh, sorry, I lost track. I...' Aidan shrugs and sinks back into the sofa. He blinks and closes the laptop. Gets to his feet. His eyes are bleary and bloodshot. He doesn't look well.

'Aidy, are you okay?'

'Yeah, I'm—'

'And don't say you're fine when you're obviously not.'

His shoulders slump. 'Sorry. I really meant to play with Josh. I wanted to. I just got sidetracked.'

'With what?'

'Work stuff.'

'Is that all?' I stare at him until he finally looks at me directly. I perch on the end of the sofa and he sits back in his original spot. 'What's been bugging you these past few days? You've been moody and... weird.'

'Thanks a lot.' He raises an eyebrow.

'You know what I mean.'

'There is something I want to talk about, but I don't think you're going to like it.'

The thumping in my ribcage grows louder as I wait for him to continue.

'Thing is, I'm not happy in my job, Em. I haven't been for a while. I actually... I don't want to do it any more.'

'Oh.' I don't know what I was expecting him to say, but it wasn't this. I swallow down a mixture of panic and relief. 'What don't you like about it? Have you been looking at other jobs?'

'I don't like anything about it. I need a change.'

'From sales?'

'The whole thing. Work, money, all of it. I'm fed up with it all.'

I shift closer and take his hand, concerned about Aidan's worries, but relieved that his mood isn't anything to do with *me*. With *us*. 'Everyone gets fed up with things, Aidy. It's life. It's how it is. Some days are good, others are...'

'Shit.' He finishes my sentence.

'Yeah. Exactly. But you shouldn't do anything rash. Just because you're fed up with it this week. Maybe it's just, I dunno, a phase. You always used to love your work and you're so good at it. Clients love you.'

He curls his lip. 'Not any more. I've lost my spark. My *thing*. This isn't a new feeling. I've been thinking about it for weeks.'

'So... what? You want to change your career?' This doesn't feel right. Is he telling me the truth? I stare at his troubled face as he looks down at his lap. Selfishly, I'm panicking. The only reason we can afford our modest lifestyle is because of Aidan's work. My salary barely covers Josh's preschool fees.

'Sorry, Em. I know this is probably a shock. I know it's not what you want to hear, which is why I haven't spoken about it. I was hoping it would go away. But the feeling in my guts is worse than ever. I want to change everything – career, lifestyle, the lot. Maybe even move somewhere new.'

'*What?* No. I like our lifestyle. I mean, sure, if you want a new career, that's fine, but you won't just quit your job, will you? You'll take your time to think about what you want to do next and how... viable it is? We don't have too many other options at the moment.' I place my hands on my bump to emphasise the point. But Aidan just looks at me with this almost pleading expression that makes me nervous.

'Mummy, I don't like the fort. It's scary.' Josh walks into the living room in his pyjama shorts, his face flushed, his short hair damp with sweat.

Aidan gets to his feet. 'I'll sort him.'

'You sure?'

He nods and takes Josh's hand. 'Come on, mate, let's get you back to bed.'

I watch them go, dwelling on my husband's revelation. Shell-shocked. I should support him wholeheartedly. I don't want him to be unhappy. But instead, I feel a wave of dark resentment followed by a gnawing anxiety that our lives are about to change. And not for the better.

TWO

DANI

As the endorphins kick in, I begin to feel much more positive about everything. Spin classes with Felix are always so uplifting. I think it's down to his incredible energy and also the music he plays. Plus, he pushes you just enough that you feel like you're working hard, but not too much that you want to collapse. Although *all* the instructors at Porter's health club are really good. That's what you pay for – premium classes with the best instructors in luxurious surroundings.

The club has a laid-back modern vibe with a state-of-the-art gym, two pools, a spa, access to classes and personal trainers and several bars and restaurants. And, as my friend Louise likes to say, the membership fee is expensive enough to keep out the plebs. Lately it's become my second home, so I'm certainly getting my money's worth. My husband, Marcus, is a member too, but he's so busy with work that he's hardly ever here. I got him a personal trainer, but that only lasted a week before he told the poor man to eff off. Marcus doesn't appreciate being told what to do, even when it's for health reasons.

I glance across at my gym buddies, Louise Parr and Victoria Butterworth. They're fully focused on Felix, probably trying to impress him with how fit and motivated they are. I smile to myself at Louise's perfect pout and her fake boobs thrusting forward, her blonde waves pulled back into a swinging ponytail. We've all got crushes on most of the male instructors, but especially on Felix, with his perfectly sculpted abs and chiselled cheekbones. Not to mention his gorgeous dark-brown eyes. Although he's about a decade younger than all of us and probably poor as a church mouse. Not that I would ever cheat on Marcus. The thought of it makes me shudder. Not so sure about Louise though. I reckon she'd be up for a no-strings fling with Felix if the opportunity arose, although if Steve ever found out...

The class ends too soon and we dismount our bikes. Louise, Vicky and I leave the studio together and we walk over to the water fountain to top up our water bottles. Here at the club, the three of us are the subject of a lot of gossip – some of it quite malicious. But that comes with the territory of being blonde, beautiful and married to three of Poole's richest men. If people got to know the real me, they'd realise I'm not what they think. But people see what they want to see.

I met Vicky about four years ago at a charity dinner at the sailing club where she and her husband, Ted – who works in the city – were seated at the same table as me and Marcus. The four of us hit it off straightaway and spent the whole night laughing so loudly I thought we were going to get kicked out. Of course there was no chance of that, as I discovered later that Vicky was head of the charity's planning committee. She and Louise were already good friends and with my looks and husband credentials I was quickly welcomed into their clique.

Befriending Vicky and Louise marked the start of me feeling more comfortable and accepted in my new life as Mrs Danielle Baines. Marcus and I had only been married a few months and I was quite overwhelmed by the money and the lifestyle and the nonstop social occasions. It was so far removed from my previous life as a barmaid at the Seagull, one of the roughest pubs in Poole. I first met Marcus five years ago when he, his younger brother Alex and his dad came into the pub to celebrate his dad's birthday. The Seagull used to be his local, so he knew most of the clientele. But he spent the whole night talking to me. I fell hard for him. We'd only been seeing one another for a few months when he proposed.

Although Marcus was already successful by the time I met him, he comes from humble beginnings and started out his career washing cars. He built his business up during his twenties and thirties and now at the age of forty – almost ten years older than me – he owns a huge showroom selling new and used prestige vehicles. After we married, I quit my job and we moved into a beautiful harbourside house in Lilliput. Basically, all my dreams came true. Well, *nearly* all my dreams.

'Hi, Dani. It *is* you, isn't it?'

I turn to see a familiar-looking woman with shoulder-length caramel-coloured hair, wearing an unattractive oversize grey T-shirt over cheap black leggings. She's a little puffy and sweaty, but she's pretty and has a nice smile. She's standing next to a beautiful black woman who's giving us the once-over and doesn't seem too friendly. I've noticed her around the club a few times.

'Hi,' I say uncertainly.

'Emily Graham.' The woman gestures to herself, her smile faltering. 'Aidan's wife. My husband works for your husband at the showroom.'

'Oh, right. Hi, how are you?' Now I remember. She's nice, but always too eager to please. And no wonder I didn't recognise her. It looks like she's piled on the pounds.

'I'm fine, thanks. Just here with my friend Luanne, having a trial session. This place is gorgeous, isn't it?'

I nod and smile at Luanne, who gives a lukewarm smile in return. I'm used to this response. Most people are intimidated when I'm with my friends. Unfortunately, Louise and Vicky don't do anything to help matters. They give Emily and her friend their classic dismissive smiles that only help to reinforce our cliquey reputation. I guess you'd call us 'mean girls' if you didn't know better. But I'm really not like that. At least, I try not to be.

'Have you done any classes yet?' I ask, trying to be friendly. 'I can recommend Felix's spin class.'

'Oh, yeah, Felix is hot,' Luanne drawls with a grin in our direction. Okay, maybe she's not as intimidated as I thought.

'I've just had an induction session and now we're going to a yoga class,' Emily gushes, her eyes wide like a doll's.

'Great. Hope you enjoy.' I take a swig of water, wondering if she'll be able to afford the membership fees. Marcus pays his sales staff a good rate of commission, but not *that* good.

'Thanks. Anyway, nice to see you.'

'You too.' The girls and I head down the elegant winding staircase towards the locker rooms.

'I definitely think Emily should do the spin class rather than the yoga,' Louise says when we reach the bottom. 'Bit of a porker, that one.'

Vicky giggles.

'Louise!' I chide, joining in with their laughter. I glance up the staircase and am unnerved to lock eyes with Emily, who's watching us. We both redden and look away. I'm sure she wouldn't have heard us all the way down here. But even so, I do feel like a complete bitch.

THREE

EMILY

Bellingham's wine bar and brasserie sits slap bang opposite The Green, just a couple of minutes' walk from where we live. One half is a laid-back restaurant serving wood-fired pizzas and other rustic fare, the other half is a wine and cocktail bar with exposed brick walls and lots of wood and glass, leading out into a verdant courtyard that I've managed to hire for the evening. It's buzzing in the bar tonight and that's partly down to me.

After Aidan dropped that bombshell on Wednesday about wanting a change of lifestyle, I decided that instead of worrying, I should be proactive and try to make him realise how lucky he is. That our life is actually pretty bloody great. Maybe a change of employer wouldn't be a bad thing, but to up sticks and move away, well, it's just too drastic. This is our home. Our friends are here. *Everything* is here.

So I'm making plans to show him just what he would be missing by leaving. Starting with a surprise birthday party tonight. I invited everyone I could think of. His work colleagues have come, as well as his school friends from Poole and the joint friends we've met over the years. And, of course, our best friends, Luanne and Troy.

'What time's he arriving?' Troy asks, his deep voice blending with the thump of the bassline from the DJ, who's playing a summery Ibiza club mix.

I glance at my watch. 'Should be about ten minutes or so. I told him to meet me here for a birthday drink and a pizza.'

'Nice one.'

Luanne leans into her husband and they gaze at one another adoringly before having a kiss. I love the pair of them, but it does make me nauseous the way they're always all over one another. Okay, maybe that's just jealousy speaking. Luanne with her flawless caramel skin and Troy with his broad frame and dark eyes. Like this perfect super couple.

'Oi, cut it out.' I nudge Luanne and roll my eyes.

'What?'

'You two! Snogging like a couple of teenagers!'

They pull apart and smile at me, bemused but unrepentant. I grin to show I'm only joking. I wish that Aidan and I could be like that again. Like we used to be when we were younger and couldn't keep our hands off one another. I tell myself that it's because Lu and Troy's relationship is newer. They'd only been together a year when Luanne fell pregnant with Ivy. Whereas Aidan and I have been a couple for over sixteen years.

'Did you manage to get Aidan that jacket?' Luanne asks.

'I did. It arrived this morning. Talk about cutting it fine! I thought I was going to have to print out a photo of it to put in with his birthday card.' I take a sip of my tonic water. Aidan told me not to buy him anything extravagant for his birthday. But that felt mean, so I pushed the boat out and bought him a Reiss jacket that I saw him admire on a TV show. He'll love it. I just won't tell him what it cost.

'Hey, Emily!' I feel a tap on my shoulder and turn to see a fresh-faced blonde woman and a sporty-looking guy in a tracksuit. It takes me a couple of seconds to place them before it comes to me. Dom and Sarah Parr are a couple Aidan and I met out at Ringwood lakes a few summers ago. We'd signed up to do this wakeboarding course and had a hilarious but fun few weeks messing about on the water. In my case, mostly falling in. They're a lot younger than us, but we really clicked at the time.

'Sarah! Dom! I'm so happy you could make it. Sorry for the short notice. It was a last-minute thing.'

'No worries. It's lovely to see you. Thanks for inviting us.' Sarah gives me a hug and I wonder why I've left it so long to keep in touch. 'It must be over a year since we last caught up.' Her eyes dart down to my rounded stomach.

'Got another one on the way,' I confirm, having found that people are reluctant to say anything in case it's not a pregnancy bump.

'Congratulations,' she and Dom chorus.

'Sarah's pregnant too,' Dom announces proudly. 'Our first.'

It's only then that I notice her own neat bump. I congratulate them in return before introducing them to Luanne and Troy, all the while trying to keep a watchful eye on the door for Aidan. I finally spot him outside on the pavement. He's had a haircut and is wearing his favourite grey suit. He looks so handsome.

He's just about to open the door when he stops short and turns around. There's someone getting out of a taxi behind him. It's his boss's wife, Dani. As Marcus is Aidan's employer, I had to invite them both, but I can't see any sign of Marcus with her. I'm actually a little surprised she's got the nerve to show her face after being so snooty towards me at the health club yesterday. Okay, well, maybe not her, but her friends were downright bitchy. I'm sure they were gossiping about me and Lu afterwards.

Aside from running into Dani and her clique, the health-club trial was just what I needed – a real chance to relax and unwind. Luanne was right, the antenatal yoga class was the perfect de-stresser. The only problem with the whole evening was that it made me want to join even more, but that's a pipe dream because there's no way we could afford the membership.

Outside on the pavement, Dani says something to Aidan. He frowns in response. I hope she remembers that this evening is supposed to be a surprise. Now, along with the frown, Aidan is shaking his head. Dani puts a hand on his arm and says something else. My heart judders for a moment. I wish I knew what she was saying. I watch her. She looks so well put together, her platinum hair gleaming, her pale-green dress fitted in all the right places. I wonder where her husband is. Whether he'll show up or if she's come here tonight on her own.

I turn to my friends. 'Aidan's here.'

Troy stands on a chair and raises his voice without any trace of embarrassment. 'Hey, guys, Aidan's about to come in!'

All our friends congregate around me. There must be around forty of us in total.

Aidan holds the door open for Dani, who walks in first. She turns to thank him and I'm mentally urging her to get out of the way. Finally, she steps aside as Aidan walks through the door, a dark scowl marring his features.

'Happy Birthday!' everyone yells, but I don't join in because I realise that I might have misjudged things. Aidan puts on a confused smile, but his taut jaw and hooded eyes tell me everything I need to know.

I watch as his friends and work colleagues surge forward to wish him a happy birthday. He chats to them in turn as they pat him on the back and pump his hand, kiss his cheek and hand over gifts and cards. I hang back, giving him time to get over the surprise. Perhaps that's all it is. Perhaps it's all absolutely fine and I'm simply overreacting to his earlier frown. After all, it probably is quite a shock.

I realise Dani's standing next to me at the bar. She's on her own, ordering a glass of Perrier with a twist of lime. I should say something. Be polite, even if she's not. 'You not drinking either?'

I comment, raising my glass of tonic water. 'Driving or pregnant?'

She turns to look at me and I see sheer disdain in her eyes that almost makes me take a step backwards.

I catch my breath. That was rude of me. Maybe she simply doesn't drink.

'*What?*' she snaps.

'Uh, sorry, I... I just noticed you're not drinking either.' I point to my glass but realise that this woman has no interest in me or my conversation. The atmosphere between us crackles with negative energy. I try to remain civil. 'Marcus not joining you?'

Dani takes her Perrier from the barman and hands him a five-pound note, telling him to keep the change. 'Sorry, did you want another drink?' she asks me with zero enthusiasm.

'No thanks, I'm fine.'

She sips her sparkling water. 'Marcus had a meeting. He said to say sorry he couldn't make it.'

'Oh. That's a shame.' I grit my teeth, wanting to move away from this awkward conversation. 'But it was good of you to come anyway.'

She softens for a moment. 'How was the yoga class?'

'Yeah, it was good, thanks. Relaxing.' I rest my hands on my bump, thinking back wistfully to how much I enjoyed it and how I'd love to attend the class regularly. How lucky Dani is.

She glances down at my hands and notices my bump, her eyes widening slightly, but she doesn't comment on it. 'Anyway, I can't stay long. Just here to say a quick happy birthday. Marcus said Aidan's one of his top salespeople.'

I nod, realising that she's here out of obligation rather than actually *wanting* to be here. And then I remember that Aidan may be a great salesperson, but that's all about to change, as my husband wants to leave and get a new career. My phone vibrates. I take it out of my bag and put my drink on the bar. It's a message, but nothing I want to deal with right now, so I put it back in my bag and try not to think about it.

I'm not sure what else to say to Dani. I've run out of small talk. I gesture to my husband, who's sitting at a table opening a birthday card, which is obviously something hilarious if the laughter from his friends is anything to go by. 'I better go see Aidan. I haven't even said hello yet.'

'Sure, of course.' She waves me away as though dismissing me and I weave through the crowd. Although, judging by the look he just flashed me, I wonder whether talking to my husband is going to be any less uncomfortable than my conversation with Dani.

'Happy birthday.' I manage a smile as our friends part to let me through. Aidan gets to his feet and plants a brief kiss on my lips. 'Thought we'd all surprise you.' I don't know why I'm stating the obvious. My cheeks feel hot and my throat is dry. I realise I've left my tonic water over by the bar, but I don't want to retrieve it as that would mean another awkward conversation with Dani.

'I thought we were supposed to be having a quiet drink and a pizza,' Aidan snaps in my ear, so only I can hear him.

'I wanted to do something nice for you. Cheer you up. There's a buffet out the back. I reserved the courtyard.'

I notice Troy and Luanne attempting to usher everyone outside. Bless them for helping out. I suddenly feel like this whole evening was a big mistake. Instead of cheering Aidan up and making him appreciate things, this party with all these people wishing him well has exacerbated his bad mood. He may be smiling on the outside, but I can tell it's all faked. His whole body is rigid, his expression forced. 'It was a nice thought, Em, but I'm really not in a partying mood at the moment. I thought you would have realised that.'

By the way they're eying us, I can see a few of our guests

have caught some of the conversation. 'Should we find some-where quieter to talk about this?'

Aidan shakes his head. 'There's nothing to talk about.'

'What do you mean?' I can feel my temper rising, my face heating up and my body tensing. 'I've just arranged this really nice evening for you and you're giving me grief. I can't win.'

'Everything all right, Em?' I turn to see Luanne at my side, her dark eyes full of concern.

I smile and force out a little laugh. 'What? Yeah, it's all good. Aidan's hungry though, so I think we'll go through to the courtyard.'

'Most of us are out there already.' Luanne sighs and sips her cocktail. 'It's gorgeous. Loads of twinkly lights and tropical plants. Feels like being abroad. They've got the outdoor pizza oven going too. The food smells amazing.'

'Come on, Aidy,' I cajole. 'Let's enjoy ourselves and get something to eat.'

He gives a brief nod and we weave through the packed bar and out into the balmy evening air. Luanne gives me an enquiring look, but I just roll my eyes and shake my head, the tight feeling in my throat getting worse.

The rest of the evening passes with Aidan and I barely saying two words to one another. He's putting on a good show with his mates, laughing, drinking, eating and being the life and soul of the party, although it looks like he's avoiding Dani, which doesn't surprise me if he's thinking of handing in his notice. She doesn't stay long anyway. But I'm more concerned with the fact that Aidan doesn't speak to me, doesn't even look my way. I alternate between anger and anxiety, but I, too, have to put on an act for our friends and it's exhausting. I'll be relieved when the night is over. Although then I'll have to face my husband. And that's not something I'm looking forward to.

FOUR

DANI

I unfocus my eyes so that the view out the taxi window is nothing but a blur of trees and buildings. Being this close to midsummer, it's still light outside, which makes it feel doubly strange. What an awful evening that was. Really uncomfortable and awkward. I could kill Marcus for making me go. And he could have warned me that it was supposed to be a surprise party. Trust me to run into Aidan outside and open my big fat gob: *Happy birthday, thanks for inviting me to your party*. He gave me this confused look and that's when I knew I'd put my size-five Jimmy Choos in it. What an idiot.

And then his smug pregnant cow of a wife thought I was pregnant too. I mean, the cheek of the woman. I didn't even realise she was expecting until I saw her cradling her belly. Explains why she's put on the weight. But maybe I'm being hard on her. After all, I did ruin her husband's surprise party. She had every right to be snotty with me. I was going to apologise, but then she just stomped off. Wouldn't even accept a drink. I only ended up staying for an hour or so, chatting to a few of Marcus's employees. But they've all got their opinions of me and it's tiring trying to prove them wrong.

I slump into the back seat. I cannot wait to get home and get into some comfy clothes. The only problem with being Marcus Baines's wife is that you have to keep up a certain standard. I feel as though wherever I go, I'm representing him. Don't get me wrong, most of the time I love dressing the part. It's every girl's dream to have a huge walk-in wardrobe and a personal shopper. But sometimes I wish I could go out without the make-up and the designer gear. Without the towering heels and acrylic nails.

Marcus tells me I look beautiful whatever I'm wearing. He's not a domineering kind of guy. He's kind and sweet. I'm lucky. No, it's the wives you have to dress up for. They're the ones you have to impress or intimidate or whatever. Honestly, it's all so exhausting. I actually can't wait to get home to have a shower, climb into our huge super-king-size bed and wait for my gorgeous husband to get home.

Finally, the taxi turns off Sandbanks Road into Bayview Road and pulls up outside our gates. I buzz down the window and key in the code, inhaling the warm, salty breeze off the harbour as it cools my skin. I leave the window open as the gates swing wide and the taxi driver makes his way along the leafy drive. But I get a shock when I'm confronted by a row of cars parked haphazardly outside the house.

What the hell?

I don't recognise any of the vehicles. Marcus's black Porsche Taycan isn't among them, but then he always parks his pride and joy in the garage. He said he had a meeting tonight, so I wasn't expecting him to be home. Unless the meeting's here. That must be it.

The taxi driver interrupts my confusion with a request for his fare. I give him cash and step out onto the grey block-paved driveway. I pause outside our huge cedar-wood front door, not wanting to have to engage with yet more people tonight. Doesn't look like I have much of a choice though. I reach into my bag, pull out my compact, flip it open and gaze at my reflection in the tiny round mirror. *Not too bad*. I apply a slick of lipstick and a dab of powder, smooth down my hair and open the door.

As I stand in the expansive marble-floored hallway, laughter spills out from the main living room to my right. Male laughter. A lot of it. From here, I can see straight in through the open door, but there's no one on the sofas. Perhaps they're at the dining table at the other end of the room. I frown. It doesn't sound like a business meeting. Marcus likes to socialise, but it's generally the two of us as a couple meeting up with friends or family. He's not a man who often has 'the lads' over. I know he used to party hard, but I'd thought those days were behind him. At least that's what he told me before we got married. Not that I'd mind. It's just a bit out of the blue. Plus, I'm so not in the mood for this tonight.

I should go in and show my face, say hello. But, for some unaccountable reason, the thought of it fills me with anxiety. I tell myself not to be such a daft cow. I straighten up, smooth my dress over my hips and walk down the hallway towards the living room.

The lights are dimmed and there's a haze of smoke and strong aftershave. As I walk in, I see half a dozen men in shirt-sleeves glance up at me from around the dining table that's littered with glasses, bottles, pizza slices, playing cards and poker chips.

'Dani!' Marcus gets to his feet, comes over and kisses me on the lips, putting his hands on me in a proprietary way that I don't like.

'Your missus is fit.'

I glance over to see a youngish guy in his mid twenties with fair hair and stubble give me a wolfish grin. I don't return the smile. Marcus would usually flatten anyone who spoke to me like that in front of him.

'A little respect, Jonesy. That's my wife, Dani.'

'Lucky you,' the man murmurs.

I give them a vague unenthusiastic smile without making eye contact. 'Can I talk to you, Marcus?'

The men give a low jeer indicating that they think my husband's in the doghouse. They're right.

I walk out of the living room, without checking to see if Marcus is following me and head to the kitchen at the opposite end of the house. It's my favourite room – a vast, light area of white-and-grey marble with pale wood cabinetry and gold fittings. But the star of the show is the turquoise harbour which twinkles and ripples beyond the ten-metre expanse of glass sliding doors. Above the ocean, an endless blue sky on the cusp of darkening.

'You okay?' Marcus's tanned face is flushed with alcohol, his dark-blue eyes a little bloodshot, but he's still annoyingly good looking, his cropped dark hair slightly greying at the temples. 'How was the party?'

'I thought you had a meeting.'

'Yeah, I did. Finished early, so I invited the boys round for a poker night.'

I raise an eyebrow at his use of the phrase 'the boys'. It's not something he's ever said to me before. 'You could've come to the party instead. It was so boring. I hardly knew anyone there. And then I come home to find you're having a lads' night in.' I dump my bag on the island and pour myself a glass of sparkling water from the Quooker tap.

'Oh... yeah... I suppose I could've come. Sorry, wasn't thinking.'

'And thanks for the heads up – you never told me it was supposed to be a surprise party. Safe to say, I think I ruined the surprise.'

'A surprise party. Was it? Sorry, babe, I didn't realise. His wife sent the invitation by text. I just skimmed it. Think it was all really last minute.'

'Well, I'm not going to any more of those things on my own, okay?'

'Okay, no worries, babe.'

'How long are they staying?' I jerk my head in the direction of the living room.

'We might be quite late. Is that okay? Got a good game going.'

I shrug one shoulder. This isn't what I was expecting. 'Didn't even know you played poker. I wanted us to have an early night.' I press myself up close to him and slide my hand beneath his shirt. Maybe I can persuade him to get rid of them early.

'I can't, Dani.' He takes my hand away and kisses my forehead.

'Fine.' I step away, hurt and frustrated. 'Who are those blokes, anyway? I've never seen any of them before.'

'I work with them.'

'Work with them where? All your showroom staff were at Aidan's party.'

'Not all of them. The business is expanding. I've been taking on some new guys. Gotta get to know them, you know?' He glances up at the kitchen units. 'We got any Doritos and dip?'

'Top shelf of the pull-out larder.'

'Brilliant.' He walks over and pulls out a couple of packets and a tub of salsa dip. 'Anyway, I better get back to the game, okay?'

I nod, realising that Marcus's attention is no longer with me. It's in the living room with his new work buddies. I glance up at the clock to see that it's only nine. Although it's early, the energy has drained from my body like water down a plughole. 'I'm going to bed.'

'Okay, babe, sleep well. I'll be up later.' He winks and leaves the kitchen.

I watch him go and suddenly feel like crying. Instead, I pour myself another glass of water and take it upstairs to our master suite. I draw the heavy silk curtains, strip off and crawl into bed. But I'm unable to relax while there are strangers in my house. Strangers who are keeping my husband away from me. I'm surprised I haven't seen them before. I'm always popping into the showroom, so I know all his staff by name. And he's never brought any of his other staff home to play poker.

Are they really employees or work colleagues? Or did my husband just lie to me?

FIVE

EMILY

Aidan and I walk home in near silence, side by side but not touching. I really want to have things out with him, but I'm conscious that Lucy from next door is back at the house babysitting for Josh. She's only fourteen and I don't want her to have to witness Aidan and me in the middle of an argument. So I keep my mouth shut. I doubt Aidan's current silence is down to any consideration of Lucy's feelings; I think he's just concentrating on staying upright. He had a lot to drink tonight.

Thankfully, the walk home is short and there aren't many people around at this late hour. Just the odd taxi whizzing past and a skinny fox trotting down the street, unconcerned by our presence.

Back home, Aidan goes straight to the downstairs loo. I go into the lounge where Lucy's already on her feet. She's such a sweet girl, long limbed and naturally elegant, her pale hair pulled into a careless bun on top of her head. It's just her and her mum, Fran, next door. Fran's a solicitor who works long hours and is constantly feeling guilty about not spending enough time with her daughter. But, from what I can tell, the two of them have a great relationship. The kind of love and mutual respect I hope I'll be able to have with my kids once they're older.

Lucy gives me a sleepy smile. 'Hi, Emily. Did you have a nice party? Did Aidan enjoy it?'

'Yes, thanks,' I lie. 'How was Josh? Did he go to sleep okay?'

'He was an angel. He came down a few times, but I sat with him for a while and he eventually fell asleep around eight.'

'Ah, thanks so much, you're a star.' I hand her three twenty-pound notes. 'I'll walk you next door.'

'That's okay, you don't have to.'

'I want to.'

After seeing her safely into her house next door – a pretty semi-detached cottage with bags of charm – I dawdle back up her path, along the pavement and back towards our house. I stand outside the front door for a moment, gathering my thoughts and my strength. Are Aidan and I about to have an argument, or will he decide to go straight to bed? I'm not sure which would be worse. I don't feel mentally prepared for an argument, but I think a night of angry silence would probably be worse.

I take a breath and go back inside, closing the door behind me. Aidan's halfway up the stairs. He turns.

I wrap my arms around myself, trying to think of what to say. 'Aidan...'

'Look, Em, I'm really tired. Think I'm gonna go to bed.'

'You're going to bed?' I grit my teeth, willing myself not to say something I might regret.

'We can talk tomorrow,' he offers.

'Fine.' I turn away and march into the living room, imagining slamming the door behind me, but not quite bringing myself to do it.

I hear his footsteps. But rather than fading away up the stairs, they're growing louder. He comes into the lounge, an unreadable expression on his face. 'What's the matter?'

'I know you're mad that I organised the party, but I was just trying to do something nice!' I yank off my heels and plonk myself onto the sofa, the soles of my feet throbbing.

Aidan loosens his tie and walks off.

'Where are you going?'

'I need some water. I'll be back in a minute,' he calls back morosely.

I listen to the squeak of the tap and the whoosh of water. He always turns it on with too much force so that water splashes everywhere. There's a pause and I picture him gulping down a glassful. There's another whoosh as he tops it up again. Then his unsteady footsteps as he returns.

'I got you this.' I proffer a shiny black box tied with a metallic white bow. I know it's the wrong time to give him his birthday present, but I can't help myself. If I'm honest, I'm trying to make him feel guilty. Trying to get him to realise he's being an arse.

Aidan takes a couple more gulps of water and sets his glass on the coffee table. I wince at the clatter it makes. He looks at my gift and then lowers his gaze to me, giving me a vague drunken stare. 'Thanks. I'll open it tomorrow, okay? I really need to go to bed now.'

'Aidan! It's your birthday. I got you something nice. The least you can do is open it!' I feel like crying, but I bite the inside of my cheek instead.

'Okay then, thanks.' He sits down heavily on the sofa and takes the gift. I feel no joy in giving it to him now. I wish I hadn't bothered buying the damn thing. But I guess there's also a small part of me that hopes he loves it. That he'll appreciate the thought that went into it and apologise for being an ungrateful bastard.

Aidan fumbles with the bow. He's growing impatient, so I help him slide the ribbon off the box. He removes the lid and folds back the tissue paper. The jacket sits there, beautifully folded, far nicer than anything else he owns. He sets the box down on the sofa and lifts out the garment, holding it up for a moment before draping it back over the box.

'Well?'

'It's the one I said I liked.' His voice is quiet yet thick with emotion.

'Yes.'

Aidan bows his head and closes his eyes.

'What's the matter? Don't you like it any more? Aidan, what is going on with you?'

He sucks air in through his teeth and opens his eyes. 'You'll have to take it back. Get a refund.'

'So you *don't* like it?'

'Of course I like it, but that's not the point!'

I stand up and cross my arms, outraged by his tone. By his ungratefulness. 'So why don't you tell me what *is* the point?'

'You don't get it,' he mutters. And then he glares at me. 'Have you seen our credit-card bills lately?'

'Yes. I know we're broke, but one jacket isn't going to make a difference. It's your birthday and you've been so down lately that I wanted to cheer you up.'

'By arranging expensive parties and buying designer clothes? That's not the way to cheer me up!'

'So what should I have done? A sandwich on a park bench and a T-shirt from Primark?'

'To be honest, yes. That would've been perfect.' Aidan slumps back against the sofa as though he wishes it would swallow him whole. He closes his eyes.

'Aidan, things aren't that bad, are they? Dani told me you're their top salesperson. Surely that means you must be raking in the commission. We'll pay the cards off soon enough.'

Reluctantly he opens his eyes again. 'Please, Emily, I'm still quite pissed and I'm really tired. I don't think it's a good idea to talk about this right now. We should go to bed.' He heaves himself to his feet.

'Wait. Just tell me what's going on. I'll get a refund on the jacket if you want, but you can't keep shutting me out and refusing to talk. If things are as bad as you say they are, then we'll make a plan. A budget. We'll stick to it, okay? I hate that you're not talking to me about this stuff. You just keep giving me these looks like everything's my fault!'

Aidan runs a hand through his newly cut French crop. I think to myself that that haircut probably cost at least forty quid. He sets his generous mouth into a hard line. 'Fine, if you want the truth, I'm losing my job. I got made redundant, okay?' His eyes are wide, his mouth now twisted with emotion and then his face goes slack, like all the air has gone out of his body.

'*What?* You're joking. When did you...? I mean how long...?' I get to my feet. My heart starts thumping and my mouth is dry. I can't tell if it's concern for my husband, concern for myself, or anger that he's kept this huge secret from me.

'Marcus told me on Monday. He's given me a month's notice.'

'I don't understand... Dani said you were one of their top guys, so why would they let you go? Why did she even bother showing up tonight? No wonder Marcus didn't come with her. I'm so sorry.' I take a step towards my husband, wanting to give him a hug. But he flinches away from me, so I stop where I am, hurt by his rejection. 'Surely you can reason with him. What excuse did he give for laying you off?'

'Just said he's cutting back. Something about business not being as good as it was.'

'Is he making anyone else redundant, or just you?' Alarm bells are ringing in my brain.

'I don't know. Just me, I think.'

'But that's not right. Not if you're making good sales. It makes no sense. You really need to speak to him again.'

Aidan pushes his fingers against his forehead. 'There's no point. It's true, I used to make good sales, but lately I've been missing my targets and—'

'What about if *I* talk to Marcus? Appeal to him. Beg him to give you another chance.' Even as I'm suggesting it, I know that will never happen.

'*What?!* No. No way! How do you think that will look? My wife having to talk to my boss because I can't sort out my own mess?'

'Okay, yeah, sorry.'

Aidan shakes his head. 'Look, Emily, it's a done deal. And I want out of a sales career anyway. I'm sick of the stress.'

'Why didn't you tell me any of this earlier? We could have talked it all through.' My mind is racing with panic. With all the implications that his revelation will mean for our lives.

'I didn't want to worry you. You're pregnant. I can't have you getting high blood pressure like last time. And now I've managed to stress you out anyway. I've messed everything up. I'm sorry.' He bows his head and I realise my husband is crying.

This time, I cross the room and put my arms around him, letting him sob quietly onto my shoulder. My body feels stiff and uncomforting. I'm not cut out for this. I'm not one of those warm, soft wives who cluck around their husbands. I'm a firm believer in just getting on with things. At least, I used to be. This Aidan-losing-his-job situation has thrown me. I'm not sure how to... be.

After a moment he pulls away and drags the back of his hand across his eyes. 'What a mess. Sorry, I've drunk too much and let it all get on top of me. I'll be all right in the morning. Well... kind of all right.'

'We'll work it out, Aidy.' I say the words, but I have absolutely no idea how this will work out in practice. 'I'm sorry about the extravagant party and the expensive jacket. If I'd known you'd lost your job, I'd never have—'

'It's okay.' He sniffs. 'It's my fault for not saying anything earlier. But, Em, we really will have to stop spending. And you know we won't be able to afford to live here any more.' He gestures to the room, the house.

My stomach dips. Aidan is right. If he doesn't have a job, there's no way we'll be able to afford the rent and bills for a house in Ashley Cross. Not on my salary. In fact, we won't have enough for a house anywhere. My mind jumps to what this might mean for us – a poky flat, jobseeker's allowance, housing benefits, all those government handouts that I never in a million years thought we might have to rely on. What if we don't even qualify because I have a job? We won't be able to afford child-care. Aidan will have to stay home and look after the kids while I work. Troy does the stay-at-home-dad thing willingly, happily. But Aidan...? He'll hate it. He won't be happy. If he doesn't want to work in sales, then what *does* he want to do?

'Emily.' He puts a finger under my chin and tilts my face up to his. 'I really am sorry.'

I nod, not trusting myself to say any more on the matter. Now is not the time to air all my worries about what we're going to do next. I'll force myself to wait. Come up with a plan. 'It's okay. Let's go to bed now and we can sort things out tomorrow.'

Aidan's shoulders sag with relief. 'So you're not leaving me then?'

'Leaving you? No, of course not, why would you even think that?'

'Because I'm not what you signed up for. I'm a total failure.' He gives a bitter laugh.

I tut and roll my eyes. 'People lose their jobs all the time. It's nothing to do with failure. It's to do with life sucking. We'll be okay.'

But as we climb the stairs together, I can't seem to quell the spiralling sensation in my stomach. Why is this happening? How am I going to bear giving up our little house, selling my car, leaving my friends, taking Josh out of preschool, having a new baby while living in an unfamiliar – and more than likely grotty – area?

'I love you, Em,' Aidan says as we reach the top of the stairs, his voice breaking a little.

'Love you too.' I give him the warmest smile I can muster, but it's all for show. Inside, I'm devastated by his news. Losing his job is one thing, but saying he wants a complete change is scaring the hell out of me. I don't want our lives to change. Not like this, not when it's change for the worse.

I cradle my bump and try to keep calm. I can't allow myself to dwell on all these negative thoughts. I need to stay positive. This could be a good thing. *It'll be fine. We'll be fine.* We have to be.

SIX

People always underestimate me. They think I'm just a regular guy from a regular town with a regular job. But that's my super-power. I look so normal. Like any other person. Okay, so maybe I'm above-average looking, but I play down my looks like every-thing else. The other mistake they make is that they don't think I'm intelligent. Just because I don't talk about highbrow issues or dress a certain way. Just because I don't use big words. Well, let me tell you, big words are often an idiot's way of trying to impress you. And I'm no idiot.

SEVEN

DANI

Marcus is in the kitchen drinking milk straight from the carton. He chokes as I walk in, catching him in the act, and waves the carton at me. 'I was just finishing it off, okay? Look, it's empty.' He drops it into the bin theatrically.

I don't say anything. Just walk straight past him, open the fridge and start taking out the ingredients for my grapefruit smoothie. I plan to make it and head out onto the terrace without talking to my husband. He's still in my bad books after last night.

As an added fuck-you, I made sure to look especially sexy this morning. Just so he knows what he's got to lose. I'm wearing a super-short, low-cut white dress and tan wedge heels, toe rings and an ankle bracelet. I also used the curling wand to create loose Bardot-esque waves through my normally poker-straight hair and made my eyes dark and smoky, adding flicky eyeliner for good measure.

I can tell it's worked. Marcus comes over like a puppy dog and puts his arms around me, resting his chin on my shoulder. 'Don't be mad, Dan.'

'The living room stinks of cigarettes.' I slip out of his arms and dump the smoothie ingredients onto the quartz chopping board on the island and take a sharp knife out of the drawer.

He follows me over. 'We didn't smoke any cigarettes. Just cigars.'

'Cigarettes, cigars, same difference. I could smell it on your breath when you came to bed at God knows what time in the morning. How can you be so perky? You should be knackered, at your age,' I can't help adding.

'Cheeky cow.' Marcus flicks a tea towel at the back of my legs, but I deftly bend out of the way, stifling a grin.

'Well, it's gross. You know how hard it is to get rid of that smell. Couldn't you have gone outside to smoke? Have you forgotten we've got Carrie, Alex and the kids coming over this evening? You know what Carrie's like about smoking. She'll probably turn around and go home as soon as she catches a whiff.'

'Don't break my balls, Dani. I'm sorry, okay. And, anyway, we're having a barbie outside in the sunshine. We won't be anywhere near the lounge. If Carrie does kick off, we can blame the smell on the barbecue charcoal or something.'

I know I sound like an old nagging shrew, but I can't help it. I've woken up in the most irritable mood, which isn't at all like me. I'm usually really laid-back – it's one of the qualities Marcus loves about me. Yet lately I've been really grumpy about everything. I glare at him. 'It's not just the smell; you've left it in a right state and Karen isn't in again until Monday, which means I'll have to clean up the mess myself.'

'So give Karen a call. See if she'll do a couple of hours this morning. Tell her we'll pay double time.'

I consider it for just a couple of seconds. 'No. It's Saturday. She's got two young kids. I'm not guilting her into coming in on her day off.' Our cleaner is the loveliest woman, who keeps our home gleaming like a palace. She's been with us for two years now and I'm constantly telling her she's never allowed to leave us. I don't want to do anything that might give her cause to hand in her notice.

'Fine.' Marcus sniffs and rearranges his shorts. 'I'll give you a hand before I go into the showroom, all right?'

I give him a begrudging nod. 'You can make a start while I have my smoothie on the terrace.'

'Okay, your highness.' Marcus gives me an exaggerated curtsey and I can't help giggling.

'Shut up, you wally.' I start chopping the ingredients for my smoothie.

He grins and swaggers out of the room, pleased with himself now he's got me to smile. But I'm not forgiving him that easily.

I drop the chopped ingredients into the blender and give it a few quick pulses before pouring the mixture into a chilled glass. Then I grab my sunglasses, head outside and make myself comfortable on the rattan corner sofa, gazing out across the harbour. It's only eight thirty, but it's already warm out here. I sip my smoothie and start mentally planning what I need to buy for this evening's barbecue. Marcus and Alex will want to cook the meat themselves, it's just down to me to buy it and get everything else prepared. I love having my little nieces and nephew over. I think I enjoy their company more than the adults.

'Nice out here this morning.' Marcus comes outside to join me, a glass of orange juice in his hand.

'I thought you were supposed to be tidying the living room.'

He tuts. 'Yeah, I will. I'll do it later. Gotta get to the showroom. Oversee the guys switching the cars around before we open. If I'm not there, they'll end up pranging them.'

I knew it would be down to me to clear up last night's mess, but I don't say anything else. I decide that I'd rather keep the peace and have my husband adore me than have him go off to work in a mood. 'You'll get back early though, right? For the barbie.'

'Yeah, course. I thought I'd take a long lunch break too.' His eyes twinkle. 'Take my gorgeous wife out to the Boat Shack.' The name belies the fact that it's the most expensive and exclusive restaurant in the area. It only opens when the weather's good because it's situated at the end of a jetty and looks like a basic beach bar. But the chef is world class and it's almost impossible to get a table. Marcus looks at me expectantly, waiting for me to squeal in excitement. But I don't.

'Marc, that would've been amazing, but I can't today.'

He frowns. 'What do you mean you can't? I've just rung Terry and asked him for a favour. I wanted to make it up to you after last night.'

My heart drops. 'That's so thoughtful, babe.' I put a hand on his arm, but his face remains stony. 'I'm meeting Vicky today.' The lie trips off my tongue too quickly, but he won't like the real reason I can't have lunch with him.

'Reschedule.'

I chew the inside of my cheek, realising that he won't understand, but knowing that I absolutely cannot meet him today. 'I really can't, I'm sorry.'

'Is this about last night?' he snaps.

'No. No, of course not. It's nothing to do with that. It's just...' I think quickly. 'I promised Vicky we'd meet up. She's having some kind of crisis with Ted at the moment. I'm her best friend. I can't let her down.' I pray she'll forgive my lie about her and Ted. My cheeks are hot and my heart is hammering. I hate lying to my husband. It's not me; it's not *us*. Marcus and I have a great relationship, but my appointment today is something that he just doesn't get. And, believe me, I've tried to make him understand.

'I thought *Louise* was Vicky's best friend. Why can't she talk to Louise about Ted instead of dragging my wife away?' The crease in Marcus's forehead grows deeper.

'Louise is great when you want to have a laugh, but she's not so good on the deep chats. I'm really sorry, Marc, but Vicky's a good friend. You know I don't have that many friends these days – all my old friends think I'm too posh for them now that I've got money. They're jealous. I can't afford to piss Vicky off too. She needs me.'

'What about me? I need you too.'

I give him a pleading look.

My husband throws his hands up in the air. 'Fine. I'll cancel the Boat Shack. Terry won't be happy with me.' He stands up and stalks back inside.

It's not like Marcus to be so tetchy. Of course I feel bad that he's gone to all that trouble to get us a table. But I didn't think turning down his lunch invitation would make him quite so upset. Maybe he's just hungover from last night. Or maybe there's something else going on. Or maybe I'm overreacting and everything will be fine.

EIGHT

DANI

Selena Mallick's house is like a doll's house; everything about it is miniature and exquisite – a lot like Selena herself, a five-foot-nothing Anglo Indian with perfect features. Selena's my nutritionist and she lives just off Poole Quay in what used to be a worker's cottage, back when people were *all* five foot nothing. I'm not super tall – only five foot four – but I still have to duck my head when going through her front door. Makes me feel like Alice in Wonderland. Whereas she glides from one room to another without any such inconvenience. At least I remembered not to wear heels today.

Maybe I should have gone to lunch with my husband instead of coming here, but Selena is always booked up weeks in advance, so if I'd missed my appointment, goodness knows when I'd be able to get another one. And I'm still a little annoyed with Marcus for making me go to that party on my own last night while he decided to play poker with his new friends, or *work colleagues*, or whoever the hell they are.

'So lovely to see you, Danielle. Come in.' I've told Selena to call me Dani, but she never does, so I've given up asking. I'm pretty sure her own name is never abbreviated either. I can't imagine her as a *Lena*. Marcus would probably call her *Sel*. I stifle a laugh at the thought. She's so not a *Sel*. Selena returns the smile, thinking it was meant for her.

I follow her into the little room at the front of the house with its leaded windows and inglenook fireplace. Even the sofas are tiny – more like oversized armchairs. She looks like a child seated on grown-up furniture. But her voice is warm and rich and serious, not childlike at all.

The first time I visited Selena I was taken aback that she works from home and not from an office. With her reputation, I'd assumed she'd be wearing a lab coat and glasses and welcoming clients into some swanky high-tech building. But she told me she likes people to feel comfortable rather than intimidated and, as all her clients are through recommendation only, she feels perfectly safe inviting them into her home.

When I originally told Marcus I was going to see a nutritionist, he showed no interest whatsoever. Back then, I had all these hopes of him coming with me. Of us embarking on a healthy eating regime that would change everything. But he said there was no way he was eating all that hippy shit – his words, not mine. He added that he worked damn hard and looked forward to a nice drink and some decent food when he got home. He wasn't going to be made to feel guilty over what he ate. It's always been a sticking point between us and that's why I couldn't tell him that I was choosing to come here today rather than have lunch with him. It would have made him even angrier.

'How have you been since I last saw you?' Selena crosses her petite legs, pen poised over her notepad. She's old-school, writing everything out with a pen and paper rather than using technology. She says the act of writing out the words helps her to remember all the important details.

'I'm okay, I suppose. I've been drinking the smoothies every morning and eating the steamed vegetables, whole grains and white fish. I've stuck to the diet really well.'

'Yes, I read all that in your questionnaire. But how are you in yourself?'

'Um, good. It's only been six weeks since my last visit, so I guess it's early days.'

We spend the next hour discussing the inner and outer workings of my body. Selena must really love her job because she just oozes interest in every minute detail. At the end of our session, we namasté – I always feel so fake doing it, but it would be rude not to – and she says she's encouraged by my progress. She adds that she'll send my updated diet plan in the mail and we make another appointment for eight weeks' time.

On the walk back to the car, I feel tired but happier, more positive. I definitely feel loads more healthy since I started visiting Selena. It's just so disappointing that Marcus won't come along too. I used to enjoy nice food as much as my husband, but I've changed my ways over the past couple of years. I've had to resort to giving Marcus healthy food by stealth. Selena gave me a few hints and tips for how to upgrade his diet so he won't notice.

The drive back from Poole is frustratingly slow. I break it up with a visit to Waitrose where I do a massive grocery shop for this evening, including a lot of healthy alternatives. And I add lots of treats for the kids – lollies, magazines, water pistols and pool toys. I also pop to the butcher, greengrocer and florist. I don't think it's possible to physically stuff anything more into the boot of the car.

Finally, after battling through yet more weekend traffic with the air con cranked up to eleven, I turn into Haven Road and my heart lifts as the harbour comes into view studded with pine-tree-covered islands and multi-coloured boats and paddle boarders gliding about the silver water. As I make a right onto Sandbanks Road, I pass families and couples strolling along the wide pavement and picnicking on the narrow beach while dogs splash in the shallows. I buzz my window down to inhale the warm, briny air, catching the high-pitched hum of motorboats and jet skis and the carefree laughter of locals having drinks on their balconies and terraces.

Finally, I'm driving up Evening Hill, the sun dappling through the trees. Almost home, excited to start preparing for the barbecue. I love having family get-togethers. Family is what life is all about, if you ask me.

Just as I'm wondering to myself what time Marcus will be home, I hear a car horn blaring up ahead as some idiot overtakes a cyclist, ignoring all the vehicles on my side of the road and almost causing an accident. The cyclist has mounted the pavement, but appears to be fine, thank goodness. I slam on the brakes and come to a stop, my heart pounding. By some miracle, the car behind manages not to rear-end me and I stop millimetres short of the car in front. The offending dickhead drives past us in a black Porsche Taycan just like my husband's, a deep bassline thumping from his speakers. And I realise it *is* my husband's car!

I flash my lights and wave frantically. Marcus is usually such a careful driver, so I can't think what can have got into him to be so reckless. Unless it's some kind of emergency. He could have been killed or killed someone else. As the car gets closer, a flash of sunlight through the trees illuminates the driver's face and I see that it's not my husband at all. It's a rough-looking man and he's flipping us all off as he drives past. I double-check the number plate and see that it's definitely Marcus's Porsche. But who's the guy driving it? Has he stolen my husband's car?

NINE

EMILY

I step in through the front door with a sense of dread and gloom. Josh and I have just been to the swing park on the green. After Aidan's bombshell yesterday, all I actually felt like doing today was staying in bed. But it's Saturday – the only day of the week when it's just me and Josh. Aidan works Saturdays and he still has a month left before his job finishes. It's a little strange that he's carrying on there after being made redundant, but apparently Marcus is giving him the opportunity to earn some more commission before he leaves, which I suppose is something.

Josh and I usually go somewhere far more adventurous and exciting than the park, like the play trail at Moors Valley, or visiting the animals at Honeybrook Farm, making sandcastles on the beach, or building dens in the forest. But today all I could manage was a walk round the corner to our local green. Not that Josh minded one bit. He loved it. We took a little picnic and he played with friends while I chatted to some of the parents, pretending that everything's rosy. Pretending I was just another yummy mummy without a care in the world.

And now we've come back home to a place that suddenly looks and feels completely different. What I once thought of as a stepping-stone to our perfect pad has now become the perfect pad we're about to lose. Talk about a change of perspective.

'Are you hungry?'

Josh nods. 'We can have an ice lolly now.'

I laugh. 'It's teatime. You're having cheesy pasta and broccoli.' His lower lip wobbles, so I quickly change the subject. 'Did you have fun playing with your friends today? You were so brave going right to the top of the climbing frame.'

Thankfully, all thoughts of ice lollies are forgotten as Josh starts recounting his time at the play park. He follows me through to the kitchen, which must have originally been a tiny space, but benefits from the later addition of a small dining conservatory. A couple of years ago I upcycled a cheap pine dining set by painting the chairs and table legs bright colours so that the room is now a cheerful and welcoming space rather than the dated eighties disaster it was when we moved in. My son sits at the table and chats away while I prepare his supper. The tangy smell of cooked cheese turns my stomach, so I throw the conservatory doors wide open to try to get some fresh air in. I'll be glad when this morning-sickness stage is over. Although today it feels worse than ever.

I sit with Josh at the table, nursing a mint tea while he eats. He's rubbing his eyes and yawning as the food goes into his mouth, down his T-shirt and onto the laminate floor. Glancing at the clock on the wall, I realise that Aidan should have been home from work a while ago.

'Finished?' I ask.

Josh nods and yawns loudly.

'You sleepy now?'

'No.'

'What about a nice splashy bath?'

'No.'

He really should have a bath after his day at the park and his cheesy-pasta-covered face and top, but I don't have the energy to insist. He'll be fine, I'll run a flannel over his face. He can have a bath tomorrow morning instead.

'How about some nice quiet time in your room before bed?'

Josh pulls angrily at his T-shirt and shakes his head. He's perilously close to reaching the Defcon-2 stage of overtiredness and I can't cope with a meltdown from my son right now. Not when I'm so close to having one myself.

'Well, it's bedtime soon, but how about we watch some *Postman Pat* first?'

'Yes. Pat.' Josh nods and plugs his thumb into his mouth. We leave the messy kitchen behind and head to the living room where I settle him onto the sofa under a blanket before slipping his favourite DVD into the player. I'd lay bets on him being asleep within ten minutes. I slump next to him on the sofa as the familiar *Postman Pat* opening credits roll.

Now that my son is calm, a knot of dread returns to my gut. Aidan should be home any second and we said we'd discuss things properly this evening. Talk about what we're going to do next. What he wants to do with his life. Will he want to retrain? Go to college? Be a stay-at-home dad? How will we adjust?

The TV characters' voices are infiltrating my brain, making it hard for me to think properly. I watch Pat's shiny red van travelling across the countryside. If only everything was as simple as it is in fictional Greendale. Glancing across at my son, I see his eyes are already growing heavy. I close my eyes too and attempt to tune out the TV. Start on some of those deep-breathing exercises I learned in Wednesday's antenatal yoga. Inhaling deeply, expanding the air in my stomach and breathing out all the tension. In and out, slow and steady.

It's no good. My mind is itching and fizzing with stress. Too many thoughts and worries flying along my brain's synapses. Lights switching on and off, buzzing like a faulty fluorescent tube. What can I do to calm down, to make this anxiety go away? Aidan says he wants a change of lifestyle, but I think he's simply lost his mojo. I open my eyes and sit up straight. Of course. It's obvious. He's lost his job, so he feels like he's no good any more. He needs a boost. If he were offered another job, that would give him back his confidence.

Maybe we don't have to change our life after all. Maybe wanting to change careers was simply his knee-jerk reaction to being made redundant. Wounded pride. Anger at being rejected. I grasp eagerly at this possible lifeline. All I have to do now is find another job that's perfect for him.

I reach forward to pick up my iPad from the coffee table and start tapping in a search for local recruitment agencies. To my left, Josh is already fast asleep, his mouth hanging open, his faint whiffling snores making me smile. It's early for him to be asleep already, but it can't be helped. I'll just have to be prepared for him to wake at the crack of dawn. I reach for the remote to turn off the TV, but then I change my mind. It's kind of soothing to have this gentle children's programme playing in the background. Instead, I turn down the volume a notch and get back to my online search.

After a while of scrolling and searching through several sites, I've bookmarked a few sales opportunities that sound really good. Jobs that Aidan could do with his eyes closed. The basic salaries aren't that great, but the rates of commission look pretty decent. I also have the brainwave that he might like to train as an estate agent. I think that would be perfect for him. Plus, it would get us closer to our dream of buying our own place.

I notice the time at the bottom of the screen – it's almost six o'clock already. Aidan should have been home over an hour ago – the dealership closes at four on Saturday. Maybe he's gone for a drink after work. I check my phone, but there are no missed messages or calls. I try his number, but he's not picking up. I try it again. And again. Finally, I tap out a text:

Hey, everything okay? Are you still at work?

I stare at my phone screen, waiting for a reply, but it remains stubbornly blank.

Now that we're several episodes in, the theme tune to *Postman Pat* is starting to grate, so I turn off the TV. The silence is heavy. Josh isn't snoring any more; his head droops against a fluffy cushion. I get to my feet and carry him upstairs to bed, hoping that by the time I come back down, I'll hear the key in the lock and Aidan will be walking through the front door. I really want to show him the jobs I've found. I just have to hope he's open to the idea of applying for one of them.

I peer out of Josh's bedroom window. The road outside is quiet. No sign of Aidan's car yet. I close the blackout blinds and tiptoe out of the room, starting to get annoyed that Aidan didn't think to message me to let me know he'd be late home. He must realise I'm worrying about him. Especially after the state he was in last night.

The next half hour sees me caught in a loop of looking out the lounge window, checking my phone messages and then telling myself to stop worrying. It's a pointless circuit that's getting me nowhere.

I go into the kitchen to make a cup of tea that I don't want, purely to distract myself. But I'm now at the stage where I'm beginning to imagine every single terrible scenario it's possible to imagine. Aidan has been in a car accident; Aidan is so depressed he's tried to kill himself; Aidan is having an affair with another woman – with Luanne, or a work colleague, or his boss's wife, Dani. Aidan has got into a fight with Marcus and has been arrested.

I tell myself to calm down. To stop being so dramatic. The reason he's late home is probably something completely innocuous. Like he got stuck with a client and couldn't get to a phone. Or his car broke down and his mobile ran out of battery. But it's been over two hours and given what's happened...

Do I start ringing his friends to check whether they've seen him? Or is that over the top? What about the hospitals? The police? What if something really has happened to him? What if I'm already a widow? I can't be a single mum. How will I raise a three-year-old and a newborn all by myself? I just can't! Of course I can. Other people do it, they manage and I will too. But I don't want to manage! I want my husband. I want Aidan. I don't care if he has no job. We can be poor together. Please let him be okay.

This is ridiculous. I need to do something to stop myself from spinning out. I'll call Luanne, she'll know what to do.

Steam is pouring out of the kettle's spout, but I ignore it and reach for my phone. Scroll through to Luanne's number. But before I can tap the phone icon, I hear the sound that I've been praying for all evening. The sound of Aidan's key in the lock. *Oh, thank goodness.*

I take a breath. I know I should be relieved and I am. But anger is bubbling up too. Fury that he's put me through the wringer like this. Instead of rushing out into the hallway, I get back to making my tea. Getting a mug out of the cupboard, unscrewing the lid of the tea caddy and pulling out a teabag. I'm acting on autopilot, my ears straining for my husband's voice, for an apology. Waiting for him to come and find me.

The front door slams shut and his keys jangle excessively. His footsteps sound erratic and heavy. This doesn't sound like Aidan. I have a prickle of apprehension. I put the kettle down and walk hesitantly out of the kitchen.

I'm relieved to see it *is* Aidan. He has his back to me and is struggling to take off his jacket. He's swearing and stumbling around like a crazy person. I realise he's drunk.

'Aidan!' I hiss. 'What are you doing? Why didn't you call?'

'Emily!' he cries, looking up with a dazed expression, oblivious to my tone.

'Shh, you'll wake Josh.'

'Josh!' he repeats, nodding sagely. 'Where's Josh? Where's my little superhero?'

'Where were you?' I can't bear to see him struggling with his jacket any more, so I help pull his arm out of the sleeve and drape the discarded garment over the banister. 'Where've you been?'

'Went to the Bricklayers with Jez.'

'You mean this whole time you were in the pub around the corner? I've been worried sick.' I stride back into the kitchen, my fury spiking at his thoughtlessness. 'I called, I messaged, I thought you were hurt or depressed. I thought...' I clench my fists and turn to face him.

Aidan throws his arms around me and I get a faceful of beer breath, which makes me gag. 'Aah, Em, you were worried about me. You're a good wifey. A good mum.'

I ease myself out of his drunken embrace. 'You said you'd be home by half four. That we'd talk about everything. It's almost seven. I thought you'd been in an accident.'

'No, I'm fine, I'm fine. But I don't wanna talk about any of that stuff.' He bats the air with his hand. 'Talking's rubbish. Let's just relax, yeah?'

This is hopeless. I'd been waiting to have a serious conversation about getting him a new job. I've bookmarked six or seven really good ones that I found online. But there's no point talking to him while he's like this. He's even more drunk than he was last night. And yet, even though I know it's pointless, I can't stop myself at least mentioning it.

'I found some interesting jobs for you today.'

He ignores my statement and I can't tell whether it's deliberate or because he's just not focusing. 'You hungry? Shall I go to the chippy? I'm starving.'

'There's some cheesy pasta left over in the oven. You might have to heat it up.'

'Mmm, cheesy pasta. Yes please.' My husband staggers

across the kitchen to the oven and lifts out the spotted red-and-white baking dish. He scrabbles in the cutlery drawer for a spoon and starts shovelling the pasta into his mouth. 'So good.'

Is this what my life is reduced to? Feeding cheesy pasta to grumpy males. As soon as I have that thought I immediately take it back. Josh is my world and Aidan is too. Only it doesn't feel like that right at this moment.

Within moments, the dish is empty. Aidan plonks it on the top of the cooker and gives me a thumbs-up followed by a sad stare. 'Sorry, Em.'

I shrug. 'At least you're home now.'

'Yeah. Home.' He massages his forehead and I hope he's not about to cry again. But he snaps out of it and runs himself a glass of water, gulping it down. 'Aah, that's better. How's my little Josh-man?'

I take my tea and sit at the table. 'He's asleep. We had a busy day at the park.'

'Yeah? And how's our little bump?'

I put my hand on my stomach. 'Fine.'

'What about you? You mad at me? You're mad at me, aren't you? I can tell because of your flary nostrils and because your mouth goes all small.'

'Thanks a lot! No, I'm not mad. Just annoyed that you didn't let me know where you were. I was worried. Imagining all sorts.'

'Sorry.' He comes and sits next to me. 'Sorry, Em. Didn't mean to say that. Am I forgiven?' He takes my hands and starts stroking my fingers.

'I know you're stressed about losing your job, but you can't go out and get drunk every night. That's just going to make everything ten times worse.'

'Not every night. Just *two* nights.' He holds up two of his fingers in front of my face. 'Two.'

'Okay. Fine. Two nights. Just don't let it turn into every night.'

'Okay, Mum.'

I grit my teeth and get to my feet.

'Sorry, sorry.' He grins and winces, holding his hands out as though to ward off my irritation.

'Glad you think this is funny.'

'No. No.' He drops his smile. 'I'm sorry. I am, I really am.' Now he looks as though he's about to cry again. I'm not sure which is worse – drunk-arsehole Aidan or drunk-crying Aidan.

It's too early to go to bed, but I don't think I can take a whole evening of this. I stand up, unsure of what to do with myself. And then I sit back down again. I should be more understanding. It must have been a shock for him to lose his job. No wonder he's going a little bit off the rails. 'Don't worry, Aidy. We'll be okay.'

He bows his head.

'Aidan, are you okay?'

'It's not what you think,' he mutters.

'What isn't?'

'Everything. It's all my fault.'

'Of course it isn't. Lots of people get made redundant when it's not their fault.'

He snaps his head up and fixes me with a stare, his eyes bright and pleading.

'Aidan, what is it?' I start to get a sharp, uncomfortable feeling behind my rib cage.

'Em, there's something I have to tell you.' He pauses. 'Something you won't like.'

TEN

DANI

I park my red Range Rover Velar in the drive for now and hurry into the house.

'Hello!' I listen for a moment. 'Marcus!?'

He comes striding out of the kitchen in white linen shorts and a blue Hawaiian short-sleeved shirt – his standard barbecue outfit. 'Hey, babe, have a good day? How was Vicky?' At least he seems to have forgotten his spurned offer of lunch. His face falls when he sees my expression. 'What is it?'

'I just saw someone speeding down Evening Hill... in your Porsche.'

Marcus loses his troubled expression and waves his hand dismissively. 'Oh, yeah, I got one of my employees to take it over to Lovetts for a quick service.'

I raise an eyebrow. Marcus doesn't normally let anyone drive his precious car. Not his employees. Not even me. 'Well, I really don't think whoever that was should be driving your car. It'll be a miracle if it's not totalled already. He nearly caused a massive accident. And when I saw it wasn't you behind the wheel, I thought—'

'It'll be fine.' I'm sure Marcus thinks I'm exaggerating.

I scowl, setting my handbag down on the large glass console table.

Marcus gets an unfamiliar defensive look in his eyes. 'Well, I didn't have time to take it to the garage myself, did I? Not with Alex and Carrie coming round later.'

'Who *was* that bloke anyway? I didn't recognise him. You know he gave me the finger as he drove past. Little shit.'

'He's new, don't worry about it. I'll have a word.'

'Well, I don't think he should be working for you. Especially not in the showroom. I wouldn't trust him with any of your cars. He's a boy racer. I wouldn't be surprised if he's gone to pick up his mates for a cruise round town.'

'Relax, I'm training him up. He'll be fine once he's got the hang of things. Did you get the shopping?'

'It's in the car.'

Marcus rubs his hands together. 'Come on, then, let's bring it in.'

'Can you bring it in, Marc? I need a cold drink. I'm really shaken up after that near miss.'

He gives my arm a rub. 'You'll be all right. Anyway, you met Jonesy already, remember? He was here last night.'

'*What?*' And then it comes to me. He was the young guy with the wolfish grin. The one whose eyes raked over my body without caring that my husband was in the room. '*Jonesy?* Who exactly is he anyway? What does he do?'

'I told you, I'm training him up to work in the showroom. Don't worry about it, Dan.'

'Well, I don't like him. He was way out of line last night. Hitting on his boss's wife. That should be a sackable offence.'

Marcus tuts. 'I'll have a word with him.'

'Hmm.' I give a little shudder and decide to change the subject. 'You gonna bring those groceries in? It's hot out there. We need to put the meat and fish in the fridge.'

'I'm going, I'm going. Did you get the steaks from the butcher?'

'Yes.'

'And the—'

'*Yes* and the gourmet lamb sausages.' I try not to roll my eyes.

'Excellent.' He rubs his hands together again. 'I was telling Alex about those sausages and he reckons the ones he gets from the farmers market are much better. But I told him he hasn't tasted anything until he's tried these.'

'You shouldn't be eating all that meat, Marcus. Let me draw you up a healthy-eating plan. Just try it for one month and you'll wonder why you didn't start sooner. It'll give you loads more energy and—'

'I've got plenty of energy, thank you very much.'

I shake my head and let it go for now. I wish he'd take it more seriously. He acts like healthy eating is a joke, but it's not.

I go through to the kitchen and pour myself a glass of cold water, gazing out at the harbour. It looks so tranquil and calm, all blue and sparkling and unconcerned with human troubles. Sometimes I feel like I'd like to sink into all that blueness, dissolve into the water and float away.

Marcus puffs into the kitchen carrying about six bags of shopping at once. He dumps them all on the island. 'Looks like you bought the whole supermarket, Dan.'

'You know me, I like to treat the kids.'

'They're lucky to have such a generous aunty. Oh and you'll be pleased to hear I cleaned up the living room. It's not exactly up to Karen's standards, but at least I gave it a go.'

I put a hand to my heart and drop my jaw in pretend shock. 'You never?'

He nods, smiles and buffs his nails on his shirt. 'You better check it though – cleaning's not exactly my thing.'

I walk around the shopping-bag-strewn island and give him a kiss. 'I'm sure it looks great.'

'So am I out of the doghouse?'

'For now. But I'd be even happier if you tried my new eating plan. You'll love it, I promise.'

Marcus's smile drops. 'God's sake, Dan, can you please stop going on about it? Can't we just enjoy a nice barbecue tonight without going on about health and diets and whatnot?'

'Fine.' I clench my fists and try not to let my frustration show. But it's not easy.

ELEVEN

EMILY

I sit in the kitchen listening to the hum of the shower above. Aidan said he had something to tell me, but then he added that he needed to clear his head. So he downed a strong coffee and went up to have a shower, leaving me here wondering. Stewing. Aside from losing his job, what else could it be? I push away that other possibility. The one I can't even let myself imagine. No. Whatever it is, it can't be that. We'll deal with whatever it is together.

My stomach gurgles and a wave of nausea sweeps up my gullet, filling my mouth with saliva. I'll be so happy when this morning sickness finally goes for good – although I don't know why it's even called morning sickness when it can strike at any time. I haven't eaten anything this evening, but the thought of proper food isn't at all appealing. I take a packet of cream crackers from the cupboard, breaking one in half and munching on it to stem the sickness. It works, for now.

The shower has stopped. I hear the creak of Aidan's footsteps across the floor. This house has almost no soundproofing. You can hear everything in every room. I'm used to it though. I like it. Makes me feel closer to everyone. Like there are no barriers or secrets. I wonder again about what it is my husband wants to tell me. I'm also wondering about the job opportunities I've bookmarked on my laptop. Will any of them appeal to him? Will he even want to look at them?

I sit at the table and go into a daze. The summer evening light still floods the conservatory, a warm breeze wafting in through the open door. The sound of birdsong and distant laughter. The smoky scent of a neighbour's barbecue.

'Hey.' Aidan appears in the kitchen, his hair damp. Dressed in grey jersey shorts and a creased white T-shirt, he's still bleary-eyed, but at least he seems to have sobered up a little.

'Hi.' I catch the lemony scent of his shower gel. It's a smell I normally love, but right now it activates my morning sickness. I swallow saliva and try not to gag.

'Sorry about before. I was being a real dick. Not letting you know where I was, drinking too much. I've sobered up now. Still a bit drunk, but my head's clearer. I'm not... I'm...' He sits opposite me, rests his chin on steepled fingers.

'You're not what?'

'I'm not sure how to tell you this. I wish I didn't have to. Ah, I wish I were a better person.'

My stomach lurches. What the hell is he about to tell me? It doesn't sound good whatever it is. 'Aidan, you're scaring me.'

'Sorry, sorry.' He runs his hand over the top of his head, a gesture he always does when he's worried or nervous.

I have the feeling that whatever Aidan's about to say, it's going to be something I don't want to hear. I'd like to remain in the dark for a good while longer because once he says whatever he says, there'll be no way to unhear it. I actually feel like I want to clamp my hands over my ears and start singing *la-la-la* to block it out.

'You know I told you that we couldn't afford to stay here any more. That I wanted a change of lifestyle. A completely new start. And I told you that I'd lost my job.'

I nod and try to remember to breathe. Try to ignore the rising nausea.

'Well, that's only partly true.' He leans back and flexes his fingers in front of him, examining them like they're the most fascinating things he's ever seen. But I suspect it's because he doesn't want to look at me.

'Which part isn't true?' I score the top of the table with my fingernail, making a series of tiny parallel lines in the soft wood. My heart thumps. Our unborn child senses my unease and shifts uncomfortably, so I stop picking at the table and rest a calming hand on my belly instead. I can no longer tell if the shifting sensation is the baby's discomfort or my anxiety.

Aidan clears his throat. 'There's more to the house move than just us cutting back.'

'Like?' Only moments ago, I didn't want to know any of this, but I'm already starting to grow impatient with these cryptic sentences. *Just tell me already*.

'Well, I didn't exactly lose my job.'

'*What?* What do you mean? Why would you lie about that?' He's still not looking me in the eye. His face is pale and he's chewing his lip. 'Did you quit, is that it?' I have to admit, I never suspected this. Perhaps he was worried I'd try to talk him out of it. He's probably right, but even so...

'I didn't lose my job or quit my job, but I won't be able to stay there.'

'Why not?'

'Just...' He holds out a hand. 'Can you just be quiet for a second and let me tell you?' He says the words almost desperately.

I clamp my lips together, offended, but acquiescent.

'It's humiliating to admit this, but the truth is I owe money.'

I open my mouth to ask if he's talking about more credit-card debt. But then I remember that he asked me to be quiet, so I swallow my words.

'I'm in trouble, Em.' Now he looks up at me, his eyes connecting with mine, almost pleading. 'This isn't something that's going to go away. I've tried to find a way out, but there's nothing I can do.'

My nausea is returning with a vengeance. I try to focus on my breathing. Much as I'm horrified and confused by what my husband is telling me, I'm also trying my hardest not to throw up all over the table. I get to my feet. 'Let me just...' I get up to grab another cracker and start chewing on it, bringing the packet back to the table with me.

'Morning sickness?'

I nod.

His eyes narrow. 'I've probably made it worse. Stressed you out.'

I shake my head briefly – a mistake, as it makes me feel worse. I need to stay still, concentrate on my breathing and on the blissful dryness of the cracker.

'We can talk about all this other stuff later,' he offers. 'If you're feeling bad.'

'No, just give me a minute to get this under control.'

We sit in silence as I chew. I should be worrying about Aidan's revelation. But this sickness is debilitating. I rush from the kitchen and into the downstairs loo where I throw up bile and cream crackers, my body juddering and heaving, my hands trembling. A moment later, Aidan passes me a glass of water, which I use to rinse my mouth. I retch a couple more times before standing up, wobbly, but a little better.

'You okay?' Aidan puts a hand on my back. 'Sorry, stupid question.'

'No, I do feel much better. Let's go back to the kitchen.' I press the toilet flush and wash my hands.

'Are you sure?' Aidan looks more wretched than I feel.

'Yeah.' I walk back towards the dining table and sit in the

same chair as a moment ago, my head clearer. 'So, what kind of trouble are you in?'

'I've been stupid. Really stupid.' He pauses and pulls at the neck of his T-shirt before resting his hands on the back of the dining chair.

'How much money do we owe? Can we get a loan to pay it off?'

'It's all gone too far for that. I've been...' He looks out at the small rectangle of garden and then turns back to look at me. Whatever he's trying to say, it must be pretty bad because he absolutely does not want to tell me. His expression is hunted. I should feel more apprehensive. Instead, I'm just relieved that my sickness has passed.

'I've been gambling online. It's been going on for months. I'm still doing it now. I owe thousands – too much to ever hope to pay off. We're in deep shit.' He takes another breath and fires out the rest before I've even had a chance to take in what he's saying. 'I borrowed money to try to win it all back, but the guy I borrowed from, he isn't a nice person. He's realised I can't pay him, which means I'm in danger. Which means *we're* in danger.'

I can't comprehend what he's telling me. It sounds too *out there*. Like something from a movie. Not something that would happen to *us*, a normal car salesman and a doctor's receptionist with a young family. 'Gambling?' I say stupidly. 'You've been gambling? Online?' I think back to all those hours he's spent glued to his laptop and phone. Telling me he's dealing with clients when in reality...

'I know.' He holds his hands up. 'It sounds so seedy. It sounds so bad. It *is* bad.' His mouth stays open as though he's going to carry on talking. But then he shuts it again. A sheen of sweat has appeared on his forehead and upper lip.

'How did you start...? I mean, why did you even...?'

'I don't know, I... it was stupid. I saw one of those ads where they offer you a free twenty quid to have a go. And I thought, that sounds like a laugh. Wonder if I'll win anything. And I did. I tripled my stake money. And it was so easy. So addictive. I'm such a cliché. And now I've let you all down. I've ruined everything.'

'Why didn't you tell me before it got to this stage? We could have done something. Got you some help.'

'It's embarrassing. Humiliating. I thought I'd be able to win it back and then you'd never have to know. But it just kept getting worse and worse. And I borrowed more and more. And now I only have a few weeks' grace before they do something really bad.'

'Who? Bad, like what?'

'They didn't specify. But they know about you and Josh. I don't think we're safe here. We need to get out of town.'

I stare at my husband, the gambling addict, who's telling me our lives may be in danger.

I should feel something – fear, fury, anxiety, *something*.

But instead I am completely numb.

TWELVE

It's not often you can get paid good money for doing something you love. But that's where I am right now. I. Love. This. Job. The adrenalin rush, the tingle in my fingertips, my heightened senses. The anticipation that this is going to be the best one yet.

They don't even know I exist and yet I'm already having conversations with them in my head. Long, deep conversations where I try out different tactics to see how they'll respond. I'm constantly honing and refining my methods. Testing out which personality I should use to get the best results. I realise none of that is necessary. I know it will ultimately make no difference to the outcome. But it's all about job satisfaction.

And I can tell I'm going to get a lot of satisfaction out of this particular job.

THIRTEEN

EMILY

I squeeze my eyes tight for a moment, hardly able to believe that it's all true. But shutting out the world won't help, so I snap my eyes back open.

'Are you okay?' Aidan is staring at me as though I might do something drastic like run away or slap him.

'Show me the sites.'

'What?' He frowns.

'The online gambling sites. Let me see them.'

'*Really?* Why do you want to see them?' His face flushes a deep crimson.

'Are you still doing it? Still gambling?'

'I... I've got no credit. So, no.'

'But if you had credit, you would? What were you doing when I saw you on your laptop this week? You told me you were working. Is that true? Or were you gambling?'

He doesn't answer right away, which is an answer in itself. Finally he speaks. 'I was just... I was looking to see if there were any sites I'd missed that might give me some freebies. I know I shouldn't have done it, but I just thought if I could get some credit, I could start to win some of it back. I could—'

'No.' I cut him off. 'You have to promise me you won't do it any more. Those games are rigged. No one wins. Not in the long run. I thought everyone knew that. You *must* know that!'

'I do know that. Believe me, I do. But something else takes over in my brain. It's like a cloud blocks out the rational part of my mind. I... I know I have a problem.'

Something occurs to me. 'When Dani told me that you're one of their top sales staff, was she telling the truth?'

'What? Yeah, I'm good at what I do.'

'So, you are earning a lot of commission, but you're gambling it away?'

Aidan doesn't reply.

'Instead of putting your earnings towards your family, you've been—'

'I've always made sure I kept enough back to pay the rent and the bills.' His chin juts out. 'But, yes, I know. I'm a terrible husband. A terrible person.' He puts his head in his hands.

'And when we had that Lotto win and you bought my Mini?'

Aidan nods. 'It wasn't the Lotto, it was gambling money. I got on a winning streak. Although technically the lottery is still gambling. It's just more acceptable I suppose.'

I nod, trying to take it all in.

We spend the next hour or so sitting side by side on the sofa in the living room and I make him show me all the sites he's used. We go through and deregister his details from all of them. At least I hope that was all of them. I only have Aidan's word for it. And I suppose there's nothing to stop him signing up again at any time. Despite his promises that he's going to stop, I realise he'll have to get help. Join a support group or something similar. But one thing at a time.

I'm suddenly extremely hungry. I want cold toast, butter and marmite. Lots of it. Before going into the kitchen, I pop upstairs to check on Josh. His little body is stretched out on his bed, one arm flung over his head, his covers lying in an untidy heap on the floor. It's warm up here, so I leave him be and don't bother re-covering him just yet. I'm glad he's young enough not to understand how badly his daddy has messed up. I can only hope that we'll be able to fix it so that we can put all this behind us and he never has to find out.

Back downstairs, I sit in the conservatory at the dining table with a cup of mint tea, waiting for my toast to pop. Aidan leans back against the kitchen counter. He's tired and looks half drunk, half hungover, but at least he's staying to face me, rather than sloping off to bed. I briefly gaze out at the twilit garden, already nostalgic for our home. 'How long exactly will we be able to stay here?'

'I've got just over a month until I have to pay the amount in full. But we should leave way before then.'

I turn back to face him. 'What do you think would happen if we stayed? Brazened it out. Called the loan shark's bluff. Would they really get violent? Do people actually do that?'

'I wouldn't really want to take the risk.'

'No, I suppose not.' I think about the gangster movies and TV series we've watched together – *Lock Stock*, *The Sopranos* and others whose titles I forget – but surely our situation would be nothing like that, would it? My toast pops and I get up to take it out of the toaster, leaving it on the side to cool down.

'You and Joshy are worth more than money to me,' Aidan says softly.

I give a silent snort. It's a pity he didn't think about that when he was gambling everything away. But that's not fair. I'm not exactly perfect either. 'What about some kind of payment plan? If you're still earning good money at the showroom and you stop using the online sites, then we should be able to give the loan guys a decent chunk each month. How much do you actually owe?'

Aidan swallows. 'You don't want to know.'

'Just tell me.' The air between us is thick with the weight of lost cash. My mind conjures up lurid images of twenty-pound notes being eaten by virtual fruit machines, poker tables, roulette wheels and other brightly coloured, shiny games that I've never even heard of.

He dodges the question. 'I've tried to get an extension and I've asked if they'll accept instalments, but it's gone too far for that. They won't listen any more.'

'Right. Okay. But how much are we talking about? Twenty grand?'

He doesn't reply.

'Thirty?'

A long silence hangs between us until he finally gives in. 'Eighty-three.' Aidan has the grace to look down at his feet.

'*Eighty-three thousand pounds?*' I have to stop myself from swearing out loud. Eighty-three thousand may as well be a million because there's no way we'll be able to raise anywhere near that kind of money. To think that I was worried about not being able to afford to live in Ashley Cross any longer. Yesterday, that scenario was the end of the world. Turns out things can always get worse.

I briefly think of contacting my parents, but I dismiss that idea almost as soon as I have it. If they chose to, my mother and father could probably get hold of that amount of cash for me. But I know without a shadow of a doubt that they would never entertain the idea. Not even if my life depended on it. They'd end up convincing themselves that I was overreacting or being dramatic.

'Please say something,' Aidan prompts, his eyes wide and scared. 'I know it's an insane amount of money. It's all just got out of hand.' He paces back and forth, shaking his head. 'I've ruined everything, I know that, I'm sorry. I know you were hoping we'd eventually be able to buy a place of our own and have a better life. I promise you I'll do everything in my power to get us back to that, but right now...' He stops pacing and inhales deeply. 'Right now, the most important thing is to keep us all safe.'

I realise that compared to keeping my family safe, my dreams are inconsequential. I have to get my head around the fact that moving away is our only option. But quite how far we'll have to move is another matter.

All this talk of moving is bringing another matter to the forefront of my mind. A problem that I was hoping and praying would somehow go away of its own accord. Right now, it looks as if my prayers might have been answered, although not in the way I'd been hoping – leaving everything I know behind is not what I wanted, even though it's probably our only option. But that's something I can't think about right now. With any luck, I'll never have to think about it again.

I decide there's no point going ballistic over the amount of money Aidan owes. The actual amount makes little difference if we can't afford to pay any of it back. Anyway, my doctor says she's slightly concerned about my blood pressure. She's instructed me to avoid stress and stay calm – ha! So instead of allowing myself to get worked up, I try to focus on the practicalities. 'What exactly is the plan? You said we were safe for a few weeks, but what happens after that?'

'Like I said, we're going to have to leave here.'

'Surely they'll find us. Track us down somehow. They're not going to forget about that amount of money.'

'They won't find us. Not if we leave the area.'

I feel my blood pressure rising again. I try to slow my breathing, but it's not working. My stress levels are rocketing. I place my palms on the table and take a few gulping breaths.

'I'm sorry, I'm sorry!' Aidan comes over to where I'm sitting. He puts his arms around me and tries to give me some comfort, but my mind is spiralling and my body is hot and tingling. 'Please try to calm down, Em. I don't want you or the baby getting ill. We'll be together and so we'll be fine. We'll work it out, okay?'

'Will we?' My voice sounds far away.

'Yes,' he replies decisively. 'I'm sorry I've had to put this on you, but I'll sort it out and you won't have to worry about anything. I'll deal with it, okay? All you have to do is stay calm and look after our baby, okay?'

I nod and try to relax my shoulders. 'Okay.' I must admit, I do feel a tiny bit better now that Aidan is being more decisive. 'So I suppose I'll have to leave my job?'

Aidan sits in the chair next to me. 'Yes.'

'And have you got any idea where we'll go?'

'Not yet. But I'll work something out.'

'We've got no money. I think there's about fifty pounds in my current account at the moment.'

'We can sell the Mini – sorry, I know how much you love that car. Mine will have to go back to the leasing company. We can also advertise a lot of our stuff on Gumtree. Try to scrape as much cash together as we can. But I'm sure we'll be able to get jobs soon enough.'

'Not without references.' I feel like I'm the voice of doom every time he makes a suggestion, but one of us has to be practical, realistic. I just didn't realise that person would be me. I'm normally the optimist in tricky situations.

'We can get cash-in-hand work,' Aidan says.

I nod, trying to quell the panic in my gut. 'Can't we just, I don't know, go to the police? Tell them about the guy who's threatening you?' Even as I ask, I know this won't be an option.

'No. Trust me, that will only make things worse.'

'But maybe they'll put us in that witness protection thing.'

'But they might not. They might not take it seriously. And if these guys find out I've gone to the police...' Aidan's face loses its colour.

'What about going abroad?' I have visions of Greece or

Spain. Somewhere warm by the beach. A simple whitewashed cottage that we could live in rent-free in return for bar work or waitressing. As soon as the image comes to me, I know it's a ridiculous fantasy. We'd more than likely end up camping on the side of a dual carriageway or in some baking-hot, urine-smelling apartment with breeze-block walls.

'I did think about going abroad, but everywhere is so expensive. Plus, we'd need tickets and new passports, which we can't afford – I checked and ours are all out of date; it costs a fortune to renew them.' Aidan wipes his brow and I notice his hands are trembling.

'So somewhere in the UK then?'

Aidan nods. 'We just need to figure out where.'

I start to consider places that might be suitable. Parts of rural Wales are supposed to be quite cheap to live, plus it's beautiful there. But I'm not a country person. I like the urban lifestyle – cafés, hustle and bustle, shopping centres. Although I realise I may have to compromise. A lot.

And then it hits me.

I might have an idea. A really good one.

FOURTEEN

DANI

'Wash your hands!' Carrie calls out for the fifth time this evening – I've been counting. My sister-in-law is a germaphobe, which must be quite stressful when you have three young children. She's fighting a losing battle. With their hair still damp from the pool, Portia and Amelie are doing handstands on the lawn while periodically running over to the buffet table to help themselves to snacks. Carrie has told them to use the outside tap before they eat anything, and she also has a bumper-pack of antibacterial hand wipes that she keeps waving in their direction. I'd be more worried about the possibility of them throwing up after their combination of handstands, cartwheels and junk food.

'Shall I take him?' I hold my arms out for my gorgeous, dark-haired eight-month-old nephew Jack. Named after Marcus and Alex's father, he's a real bundle of energy and this is the first time he's stopped crawling and exploring since my in-laws arrived an hour ago. Thankfully, the swimming pool is walled off in a separate part of the garden, so we don't need to worry about any accidents.

'Would you?' Carrie looks relieved. 'He's getting heavy these days. And he's so demanding.'

As I take him into my arms, Jack graces me with an enormous smile that melts my heart. I give him a big kiss on the nose and he laughs so I do it again.

Carrie leans back into the garden sofa and tilts her perfectly made-up face up to the evening sun. She's a part-time beautician and everything about her is shiny. From her chestnut-coloured waves and dewy skin to her French manicured nails and expensive veneers. 'You're so lucky not to have any kids.'

I bristle slightly at her dismissal of her children, even though I know she doesn't really mean it. 'Your children are adorable.' I bounce Jack on my knee, pretending to let him fall onto the floor, which starts him laughing his head off.

'Honestly, you should enjoy your freedom while you can. It all changes afterwards. No more leisurely lunches and nights out. I mean, I guess you could get a nanny, but I wouldn't trust them to do as good a job. And you can kiss that beautiful body of yours goodbye. I've never managed to get my figure back properly. I wasn't too bad after the girls, but Jack wrecked it.'

'Carrie, your figure is amazing.' I'm specifically staring at her fake boobs.

She winks one eye open, sees me looking and grabs hold of them. 'What, these? They were my consolation prize from Alex.'

I grit my teeth. She doesn't need a consolation prize. She's already won the jackpot. My sister-in-law closes her eyes again, seemingly relaxed. But she has some kind of sixth sense, snapping them open when the girls come over for more crisps. 'Wash your hands!'

Alex and Marcus are standing over the grill, novelty aprons on, knocking back the beers while they discuss the merits of gas barbecues over charcoal. When they stand together like that, you can tell they're brothers with their tan skin, dark hair and blue eyes. They're both well built, but neither of them is particularly tall. Alex is probably five foot nine, to Marcus's five foot seven and a half. The half is very important to my husband.

I love how the two of them get on so well. Alex runs a local construction firm and is almost as successful as Marcus. But there's no rivalry between them. They help one another out whenever they can. They take pride in each other's achievements. And they both built up their businesses from nothing.

When Marcus and I first got married, I offered to help out at the showroom. Told him I could help in the office answering phones, that kind of thing. But Marcus said that I was his princess. He didn't want me to worry about the business side of things. He just wanted me to enjoy life and look after the home. We already have an army of employees who keep the house nice – a cleaner, gardeners, pool and hot-tub maintenance, decorators and the list goes on. So what is there left for me to do?

'Okay, everyone, the sausages are done!' Marcus turns to me. 'Don't worry, Dani, I've done you a corn on the cob like you asked, but you don't know what you're missing out on here. Grab yourselves plates and come on over.'

'What about the steaks?' Carrie asks.

'They'll take a bit longer,' Alex replies.

I'm still playing with Jack, so Carrie offers to bring mine over. I sing a few nursery rhymes to my nephew while I wait. First to come over to the table with their plates loaded up are my nieces, who position themselves on either side of me and Jack, their little bodies pressed up close to mine.

'Can you do handstands, Aunty Dani?' six-year-old Portia asks.

'I used to be really good at them when I was your age, but I haven't done one for ages.'

'Jack can't do them,' four-year-old Amelie says, kissing her brother's chubby cheek.

'You'll have to teach him when he gets older.' I blow a raspberry on my nephew's tummy, which has him dissolving into giggles.

'He can't even walk,' she says seriously.

'Or talk,' Portia adds. 'He just makes cute noises, except when he's crying.'

'All righty then!' Marcus and Alex join us at the table.

'I'll put some of my potato salad on your plate, Dani, okay?'

I've tried Carrie's potato salad before and it's absolutely delicious, but I have to be good and stick to my diet. 'That's okay, I'll just have some of the lettuce and cucumber, thanks.'

'What's wrong with my potato salad?' Carrie puts a hand on her hip in mock outrage, but I can tell she's actually offended.

'Come on, Dan, a few mouthfuls won't hurt you.' Marcus takes a forkful and starts chewing. 'Bloody lovely this is, Carrie.'

'Cheers, Marc.'

'Go on then. That would be lovely.' But I feel like crying. How am I supposed to stick to my diet with all this pressure? It's like being a teenager again and pushed into smoking and drinking.

Aside from potato-salad-gate, the rest of the evening is actually really nice. The kids are sweet as pie and my in-laws are fun. We laugh a lot and I get a warm, wistful feeling. It's almost perfect.

The four adults sit around the fire pit watching the sun set over the harbour, an extravagant display of red, orange and turquoise, gradually fading to lavender and indigo. Meanwhile Jack falls asleep in my arms and the girls are growing snoozy in front of the TV where they've been watching *Frozen* on a loop. Once the conversation grows sparser, Carrie stretches and stands, pulling a fairly drunk Alex to his feet. 'Taxi's on its way, Al.'

Marcus and I help them gather their things and rouse the children and we finally wave them off. We sleepily clear up the food from the garden and kitchen, deciding to leave the rest until tomorrow.

'That was such a lovely evening.' I take Marcus's hand and lead him up the oak staircase.

'Alex agreed that my sausages were the best.'

'You and your bloody sausages.' I grin and poke my husband in the ribs.

'What? He's my younger brother, I have to keep him in his place. It's all about respect.' Marcus grins. He puts an arm around me and brings me in close for a kiss. I oblige and lead him into the bedroom, start unbuttoning my dress and kick off my shoes.

'You're very tempting, Dan, but I'm too tired. Another night, yeah?' Marcus pulls away.

My good mood evaporates into the night. I stand here feeling a hopeless, hollow pit in my stomach. Aware of the huge empty house around us. Disappointment catches in my throat. 'You're too tired?'

He gives a nervous smile. 'Yeah. That's okay, isn't it? To be tired?'

I don't reply, scared of what I might say. But I think my face is expressing it perfectly.

Marcus is going down the route of pretending he hasn't noticed. 'Let's go to bed.' He reaches for my hand, but I move it out of his grasp. 'Come on, Dan.'

The longer I stand here silently fuming, the more likely it is that we're going to have a blazing row. I could soften my face, drop my shoulders and take my husband's hand. Give him a break. A pass. We've had such a lovely evening that it seems wrong to let these emotions sweep my body and ruin everything. But I'm powerless to stop them.

'Dani, what are you doing? Are you okay?'

'No. I'm not okay, Marcus. I am not. Okay.'

He holds his hands up to ward off my cold fury, but it's like I'm unleashing something that can't be put back in its cage. My frustration is like a physical thing. A hot tear slides down my face and I clench my fists by my side.

'Do you even care how I feel?'

He scowls, realising that I'm not going to be appeased with soft words. 'What kind of a question is that? Of course I bloody care. You're my wife, aren't you?' He takes a breath and mutters, 'Do I care.'

'Aren't I beautiful enough, is that it?'

'Now you're being ridiculous. You're bloody gorgeous. You know you are. Wouldn't have married you otherwise.'

'So why won't you sleep with me?'

'Because I've been working all day and I've had a skinful of alcohol and I'm knackered!' His face is red and he's really pissed off now.

I should stop this, apologise and we should go to bed. But I can't keep this emotion at bay. 'Sorry I haven't turned out to be the wife you thought. Not like mother-earth Carrie. You must be so disappointed in me.' I can hear the sneering, petulant tone in my voice and it sickens me, but I need to know what he really thinks. I have to goad him into admitting it.

'What? *No!* Why would you even say that?'

'Yes, you are. You can admit it, Marcus. I didn't turn out to be a good bet.'

'What is wrong with you tonight? It's not like you had any alcohol, so I can't blame it on that.'

'You know what's wrong.' I reach forward and start unbuttoning his shorts. 'And you know how you can help to fix it.' I slip my hand inside his boxers and start kissing him.

Marcus responds for a few seconds and then removes my hand and steps back. 'Dani, you're acting like a madwoman.

Let's just go to bed and forget the last ten minutes ever happened, all right?'

'What's mad about wanting to sleep with my husband?' I let out a frustrated growl. 'How are we supposed to have a baby when you won't even sleep with me? When you won't eat healthily or cut down on your drinking and smoking? You know it's not good for your sperm count!'

'This!' Marcus yells. 'This is exactly why I don't want to sleep with you at the moment. Because you're obsessed! I feel like some kind of sperm machine. You don't want to sleep with me for *me*. I'm just a means to an end!'

His words are like a blow to the chest. 'That's not true! You told me you wanted a family too. You said you couldn't wait to have children with me. But because I'm not as fertile as perfect Carrie, you won't even try. Is this why you're inviting work colleagues to the house and staying up late? So you don't have to come to bed while I'm awake?'

'What? No! Of course not.'

'Well, I think it is. You're avoiding me. You just admitted it. You said you don't want to sleep with me!'

'I didn't mean it. I just meant—'

'You know those blokes are just a bunch of users. They're only here because you're rich and they think they can take advantage of you. But you'd rather spend time with them than try to make a baby with your own wife! You refuse to change your diet to give us more of a chance to conceive. You're smoking cigars, drinking. You won't even consider IVF—'

'Because I've seen how hard it is on couples. How stressful it is. I don't want that for us.'

'So what about adoption?'

'Sorry, Dani, but I don't want to go through that either. Social services poking their nose into our lives, checking out if we're good enough.'

'And what about what *I* want?'

'I'm doing everything I can, Dani.'

'*Are* you? Are you really? Because it doesn't look like that from where I'm standing!'

He grits his teeth and glares at me.

My heart is pounding and my hands are shaking. Marcus and I have been trying for a baby for almost three years now, but this is the first time we've really argued about it. Really said how we're feeling.

'You have no idea, Dani. You have no idea what I do for you.'

'So why don't you tell me then?'

His face shutters.

'Thought not.' I turn on my heel and march across the landing.

'Where are you going?' He sounds fed up and exhausted now, the fight gone out of him.

'The guest suite.'

'Ah, don't be like that, Dan.' I hear him come after me, but I don't turn around. 'You know I can't sleep without you in the bed. I need my little wifey.'

I keep walking, but I know I'm going to cave in. I can't resist my husband when he apologises.

'Dani...' He takes my hand and turns me around. 'You know I love you and I can promise you now that it'll all work out.'

'You can't promise that.'

'I can. Now come to bed.'

I scowl, but I can tell he's not buying it. He knows he's winning me round.

'Look, if it will make you happy, I'll start your horrible diet tomorrow.'

I shove his shoulder. 'It's not horrible!'

'Okay, I'll start your delicious, amazing diet tomorrow. Okay?'

'Okay,' I mutter.

'Good. Now that's sorted, will you come to bed, woman? I'm falling asleep on my feet here.'

I nod and let him lead me into our bedroom where we have sleepy, beautiful make-up sex. And I let myself dare to hope that this time might be the time I get pregnant.

FIFTEEN

EMILY

Aidan walks into the kitchen with a tired-looking Josh in his arms.

I'm sitting at the dining table sipping tea and nibbling on some toast. I've been up since six, my mind whirring with plans. 'The kettle's just boiled.'

'Cheers.' He runs a finger down Josh's cheek. 'Hey, mate, want some cereal?'

He points to my plate. 'Toast.'

'With jam?'

He shakes his head. 'Marmite like Mummy.'

'Here.' I hold out a half slice and he wriggles out of his father's grasp and comes over to sit on my lap where I feed him the rest of my toast. He's warm and smells all sleepy, still wearing his crumpled pyjama shorts and T-shirt. I kiss his head and feel suddenly thankful that he's too young to be affected by what's going on in our lives.

'Did you sleep okay?' Aidan puts a pan of porridge on the stove.

'Not really. You?'

'I got about an hour or two.'

Josh slides off my lap. 'I go inna garden?'

'Okay, Joshy.' Once I've helped him slip on his canvas shoes, he runs outside and sits on his plastic tractor, then starts pedalling furiously across the grass.

Aidan makes himself a bowl of porridge and slots a couple more slices of bread in the toaster. There's a strange atmosphere hanging between us, which isn't exactly surprising. I wish more than anything that we could have a normal Sunday. It's sunny and warm outside. We could have gone for a family walk, popped into some shops, grabbed a coffee and met up with Lu, Troy and Ivy. Instead, we're drawing up plans to flee our home. I almost laugh at the absurdity of it all.

I briefly considered asking Luanne and Troy for a loan, but then they would have started asking questions and the whole situation would have become even more complicated. Especially as it would take us years to pay them back.

Aidan stands at the kitchen counter buttering his toast while his porridge cools. 'How are you doing this morning? With everything, I mean.' He turns to face me, his skin pasty, his eyes bloodshot. Hungover and stressed.

'Still a bit stunned I suppose.'

He nods. 'I'm really sorry, Em. About all of it. This is not how I saw our lives going. I've basically ruined it, haven't I?' He brings his breakfast over and sits next to me. We gaze out at our son in the garden rather than look at one another. From the corner of my eye, I see Aidan taking a few spoons of porridge. The thought of it turns my stomach. Thankfully, he lays down his spoon for a moment.

I didn't tell Aidan my idea last night because I didn't want to get his hopes up. Instead, I messaged my godmother, Bianca, and asked if I could drive up to see her today. She said she'd love to see me, so I've arranged to meet for an early lunch at a pub just outside Bath, which lies about halfway between here and her house in Gloucestershire. I was quite prepared to travel all the way to her house, but she said she fancied the drive.

'Are you okay to look after Joshy today?' I turn to my husband.

'Uh, yeah, I guess.' He seems taken aback. 'Why? What are you doing?'

I swallow. 'I just... I'd like to spend a few hours on my own, if that's okay. Processing everything.' I don't like lying to him, but I hope he buys it.

'Oh. Okay. Course.' His right leg is jiggling under the table and I know he's completely unnerved by my desire to be alone. I suppose he expected us to spend the day together discussing our next move, which would have been totally logical. Maybe he's scared that I'm going to leave and never come back.

I take his hand and look him in the eye to try to reassure him. 'Don't worry. I'll be back this afternoon.'

'Yeah, sure, no problem.'

My gaze drops and I notice that Aidan's porridge has started to congeal in the bowl. I try not to look at it.

The drive to Bath is uneventful, aside from a few unscheduled stops to throw up by the side of the road. Ever since Aidan's revelation, my morning sickness has returned with a vengeance. And I can't seem to get the sight and smell of Aidan's porridge out of my head.

I arrive at the Riverside Inn twenty minutes early. The pub garden is packed and I'm about to turn around and see if there's any room inside instead when I spy my godmother sitting away from the general hubbub at a table under a large sun umbrella, sipping her drink and studying a laminated menu. She's found a spot right by the river, away from the car park and kids' play area. Trust Bianca to get the best table going. I make my way over.

She glances up as I approach, flipping her Jackie O sunglasses up onto her head. 'Look at you, beautiful girl! You're positively blooming. Pregnancy suits you.'

'Hi, Bianca. Thank you, but I know I look awful. I barely slept last night and I have shocking morning sickness. I'm deep in what's known as the grotty stage of pregnancy.'

'Well, I'm sorry to hear it. But when you get to my age, you'll have a new definition of what looks grotty.'

'Rubbish. You look stunning as always.' I take a seat opposite her and she pushes a glass of mineral water in my direction.

'I got you some water and ordered you a sandwich like you asked for. But they have a really lovely menu here if you want to change your mind?'

'A cheese sandwich is perfect.'

Bianca is in her late fifties, but she still looks absolutely incredible with her svelte figure and ash-blonde hair – like a toned-down Joanna Lumley. She's twice divorced with no children, which is a shame, as I think she would have made a great mother. I told her that once and she strongly disagreed. *It only seems that way to you because you see me so infrequently. I'm really not cut out for it, darling. Too selfish.*

My own parents were and still are, this golden couple who live a charmed life. Before retiring, Dad was a commercial pilot and Mum was part of the cabin crew. They met, fell in love and travelled the world, partying and living it up before Mum fell pregnant with me. Apparently I ruined their fun. They would tell me this often, before adding that they were only joking. But I knew they weren't joking. Another 'joke' they love to have with me is not to expect an inheritance because they have every intention of blowing the lot on enjoying life.

Fine by me.

Just after I was born, they bought a place close to where Aidan and I now live, in the leafy suburb of Lower Parkstone. It was a lovely, big, characterful house near the golf course –

looking back, it was the kind of place I could only dream of owning now as an adult – where they did plenty of entertaining when they were home, which wasn't that often. For most of my childhood, I was left in the care of a string of au pairs and child-minders who ranged from unexpectedly lovely to completely disinterested and – in one case – scarily psychotic.

My parents retired to Spain as soon as I left school at sixteen, figuring I was finally old enough to look after myself. By that time, I was already with Aidan, of whom they had absolutely no opinion. *If he makes you happy, Emily, then by all means go out with the boy.* They sold the family home when they moved to Spain, which meant I had to get myself sorted with accommodation. Luckily, Aidan convinced his parents, Marion and Phil, to let me move into their council house with him. But it was awkward – I could tell they didn't think I was right for their son. They still don't, but they put a brave face on things for the sake of Aidan and Josh. I couldn't wait for us to move out and get our own place together. I ended up staying with his parents and younger sister, Michelle, for just over a year until Aidan and I could afford to move out and rent our own place – a tiny bedsit in Upper Parkstone.

The one wonderful constant all through my childhood and beyond was my mother's best friend and work colleague Bianca Friedman, my godmother. She lives in Gloucestershire these days, but I speak to her on the phone most weeks. She fills me in on how my parents are doing because I rarely talk to either of them and, whenever I do, it's always *me* calling *them*. They just about made it to my wedding, but they've only met their grandson twice. First when they had to come over to the UK for my grandfather's funeral. And second, when they flew over for their friends' twenty-fifth wedding anniversary. But Bianca always made a point to keep in touch with me over the years. I'm not sure how someone so lovely could even be friends with my parents.

'Have you been waiting long?' I ask.

'Not at all.'

'You were lucky to get a table.'

'Luck had nothing to do with it. I made a reservation over the phone.'

That's Bianca all over – organised. 'Good thinking. I didn't realise it would be so busy.' I glance around at the crowded garden – the couples and extended families, the dogs and kids. There are several new arrivals hovering at the edges, trying to spot a free table but knowing there's no chance. 'How have you been, Bee? Any updates on your new man?'

She pulls a face and sips her drink. 'Total disaster. Turns out he was the most boring man in the universe.'

I can't help laughing at that. 'Oh no, I'm sorry.'

'Such a bloody waste because he was gorgeous and he was also pretty good in bed. But the conversation was an absolute snooze-fest. I wanted to gag him half the time – and not in a good way.'

'So...'

'Yep, gave him the old heave-ho. I felt a little guilty because the poor darling was besotted. But no woman should have to suffer two hours on the merits of a Makita drill versus a Bosch. Besides, I'm going to be sixty next year.'

'You're not!'

'I am. So I don't want to be saddled with a dud for my twilight years. I want stimulation and excitement, thank you very much.'

'Don't blame you.' Although part of me is wondering how much stimulation and excitement she'd be prepared to put up with. Would being threatened by loan sharks and having to flee your home count as excitement?

'Okay, darling, what's wrong?' She stares at me with a critical eye as a young lad brings out our order – an impressive cheese and salad sandwich on wholemeal bread for me and a chicken Caesar salad with no dressing for my godmother.

'What makes you think something's wrong?'

'Oh, I don't know – maybe texting me late on a Saturday night to ask if I'm free the next day for lunch. That was a bit of a clue, sweetie. Plus, you've been twisting and playing with your fingers since you got here, which is a dead giveaway. You always used to do that as a little girl when you were anxious.'

I flush and look down at my cheese sandwich. 'Sorry. And, yes, you're right.'

'It's fine, darling.' She reaches across and gives my hand a squeeze. 'So, tell me what's up. I hope it's nothing to do with that gorgeous husband of yours. He's still treating you well, isn't he?'

'Yes, Aidan's treating me well...' I pause.

'But?'

And then it all spills out. Everything. The whole unvarnished truth about Aidan's predicament. This is why I didn't want him to come with me today, because he would have felt embarrassed and humiliated. I would have had to spare his ego and downplay everything. But I needed to tell Bianca the truth, because she can spot a bullshitter a mile away. I finish my story, but end by saying, 'I'm not here to ask for money. Please don't think that.'

She doesn't say anything for a few moments. Just gazes out over the river. 'Hmm, that's quite a pickle you're in.'

I hope this confession hasn't been too much for Bianca. I hope I haven't turned her away from me. I feel the sting of tears behind my eyes, but I can't let her see them. I've always prided myself on being strong around her. On not letting my emotions show, because I want to impress her. To show her that I'm self-sufficient and tough like she is. I guess she's always been my role model, my surrogate mother. I wish Bianca really *were* my mother. How lovely would it be to have a mother who cared?

'I'm sorry to lay this all on you,' I add. 'But I didn't know who else to talk to.'

Bianca gets up from her seat and comes and sits next to me. She takes my hand in both of hers and kisses me on the temple. 'Do you have an idea of what you might need from me?'

'Well...' I take a breath. 'I know this sounds cheeky and please say no if it's not possible and I won't be at all offended, but... might one of your properties be available for us to stay in for a while? Just until we can get sorted with new jobs and, well, I suppose new identities. I'm not sure how we're going to manage everything, to be honest. But if we could just have a few months' breathing space out of danger, we can figure something out. It's just that with me being pregnant and with having Josh...'

My voice is becoming hysterical. I need to calm down. Bianca has never seen me lose it before. I really don't want her to think I'm a basket case. But I'm already regretting asking her. It feels so mercenary. I feel like a user. She's looking at me with an expression that's akin to shock and maybe disappointment. I think I've just made a dreadful, dreadful mistake.

SIXTEEN

EMILY

I sit in the busy pub garden listening to the swish of the trees and the burble of the river, overlaid by the rise and fall of relaxed conversation. As I wait for my godmother to let me down gently, my mind is already racing ahead to alternative options of where Aidan and I might flee to, other than a tent in the woods. Maybe some kind of house-sitting service. I think those kinds of jobs are advertised in specialist magazines, but maybe I could find something online. And yet, surely we'd need references. Unless we could somehow fake them.

Bianca's expression softens from one of shock, to one of pity. 'Of course, my darling. Of course you can stay in one of my houses. It would be my pleasure.'

I exhale, hardly daring to believe that she's agreed. I was so convinced she would say there were no properties available. 'Are you absolutely sure? I mean, I know you rent them out and get income from them and, the thing is, like I said, we don't have any money so we wouldn't be able to pay rent—'

'Don't give it a second thought. As it happens, I have a three-bed property coming up for rent soon. I've a feeling the existing tenants might have been a little careless, as they've been there for years. But if you don't mind redecorating and carrying out some light maintenance, then you're welcome to stay as long as you need it. Shall we say... a year's lease? No rent required, just cover the bills, yes?'

I'm lost for words. My heart is so full. The relief is so great that I can barely breathe. 'I... I honestly don't know what to say.'

'Then say nothing and give me a hug, you daft girl. Of course I was going to help you. You're my goddaughter, not to mention my favourite person in the world.'

'Oh, Bianca. You've saved our lives. Literally.'

'Well, don't thank me just yet. You haven't even seen the place.'

'I don't need to see it to know it's a lifeline for us. Where is it?' I'm hoping it might be a gorgeous townhouse in a bustling city somewhere. Bianca's taste is impeccable, so I'm sure her properties are all fantastic.

'Not too far away, but probably far enough for your requirements. North Dorset.'

'So, in the countryside?'

'You could say that. It's slap bang in the middle of nowhere and comes with five acres of fields and forest land. Not your cup of tea, I know, darling. But all my others are tenanted for the foreseeable.'

'Right now, it's exactly my cup of tea.' I must admit it sounds a little challenging, but Aidan and I will make it work.

'Well, good. There's plenty of opportunity to be self-sufficient, you know. You can sell logs, keep chickens, work the land, that type of thing.' She shifts back into her seat opposite me and makes a start on her salad.

This rural lifestyle sounds so far out of my comfort zone that it may as well be another planet, but desperate times call for desperate measures and Bianca is being more than generous.

Aidan and I will definitely make it work. 'Thank you so, so much. I don't know how I'm ever going to thank you. Yesterday everything felt so terrifying and hopeless.'

'I'm glad to help. More than glad. Honoured.'

'You won't say anything to Mum and Dad, will you?'

'You should tell them. Give them the opportunity to help.'

'You know they won't.'

Bianca dips her head in acknowledgement. 'Silly people. I love them to bits, but they were never cut out to be parents. A bit like me.'

'You're a way better parent to me than they've ever been!'

Bianca raises an eyebrow. 'That's because you're not my child. I don't *have* to be involved or responsible. But I choose to be. Emily, you know you're the daughter I never had. Are you sure you won't just let me pay off the debt for you? Then you can simply get on with your lives. It would take me a few months to free up the cash, but if these people would wait...'

My heart begins to beat faster at the possibility of getting our lives back in one swift go. But there are too many reasons why it would be a bad idea to accept cold, hard cash. What if Aidan started gambling again and lost it all, racking up more debt? Who would I be able to turn to for help then? And accepting over eighty thousand pounds of someone else's money would feel really wrong, even from my godmother. If it were from my parents, I would accept it as money owed for a shitty, neglected childhood. But from Bianca? No way. I couldn't risk ruining our relationship. Plus, there's the time issue – we don't have the luxury of waiting a few months. Maybe if she had instant access to the money, that would be a different matter.

I've surprised myself at my reaction to her supremely generous offer. Maybe I'm not as materialistic as I thought. Or maybe the baby hormones are playing havoc with my brain and I'll eventually come to regret my decision.

'Thanks, Bianca, but we can't take your money. The offer of a place to live is unbelievable though.'

She nods and I can't tell whether she expected this reply or if she's surprised by it. Either way, my godmother has saved our little family and I can't wait to tell Aidan the news.

SEVENTEEN

DANI

As I prepare my morning smoothie, Marcus sits at the kitchen island sipping his pomegranate juice and eating his breakfast of full-fat yoghurt sprinkled with blueberries and sunflower seeds and two slices of wholegrain toast with honey. To give him credit, he's been true to his word and has been following his fertility-boosting diet all week. At least he has been while he's at home. I can't check on what he eats while he's at work, but one step at a time. After Marcus agreed to eat more healthily, I asked Selena to draw him up a diet schedule. She said it would be better if he came for an appointment, but there was no way Marcus would agree to that, so she reluctantly agreed to email over a generic plan.

Even though we're both looking after ourselves, I'm really hoping I'm already pregnant. I have this feeling that it might have happened last week after the barbecue when we argued and then had make-up sex.

Marcus has almost finished his bowl of yoghurt and has started on the toast. He takes a huge bite and starts chewing. 'This actually isn't too bad.'

'Don't sound so surprised. Just because it's healthy, doesn't mean it doesn't taste good.'

'Yeah, well, it's not quite bacon and eggs, but it'll do. Can we skip the ginger tea though?'

'It helps with absorption.'

'With what?'

'Absorbing vitamins and minerals.' I place a tall glass of tea in front of him. 'Just drink half.'

'Fine.' He winces as he takes a sip. 'That is bloody vile.'

'Maybe try some honey in it,' I suggest.

'Never mind *honey*, it needs half a bottle of tequila.' Marcus gives an exaggerated shudder.

I giggle at the face he's pulling. 'Oh and don't forget, I won't be home until late tonight.'

'Yeah, don't worry, I remember.' He puts the tea back down and pushes it away.

'I've left your dinner in the fridge with instructions.'

'Don't I get a night off too?' He gives me his pleading face and puts his palms together, begging me.

I roll my eyes. 'Go on then. Just don't go mad on greasy stuff and alcohol, will you?'

'Scout's honour.' He does the little three-finger salute.

'You weren't a scout,' I scoff with a half grin.

'Almost. Me and Alex were thrown out of cubs.'

'You weren't?'

'God's honest truth. You can ask Al. Our Akela was a right bastard – Steve Duffy. Didn't like me and Alex. He went to school with our old man and let's just say Dad and Steve didn't get on.'

'That's terrible. I can picture you in your uniforms, all little and cute. So why did he throw you out?'

'Me and Al had a scuffle with another boy. Nothing bad, just normal kids' stuff. But it was exactly the excuse Steve needed. Sent us home with a note saying we were antisocial.'

I come around the island and gently squeeze my husband's cheek, feeling a sudden rush of love for him. 'Poor baby. We won't let anyone pick on *our* kids.'

'No way.' Marcus's face darkens. 'Anyone messes with the Baines kids and I'll knock their blocks off.' He leans forward and kisses me, pulling me in close to his body. He tastes of honey and ginger. I wonder if I can tempt him to come to bed for a quickie, but he pulls away and strokes my hair distractedly. 'Right, I better be off. Don't want to be late.'

I step back regretfully. *Never mind.* I'm pretty convinced I'm already pregnant anyway.

He's left the majority of his ginger tea, but I don't push him to drink it. Right now, I'm picking my battles. Marcus stands and scoops his keys and phone off the counter, then gives me a quick peck on the lips. 'Say happy birthday to Vicks from me.'

'I will.'

'Where are you girls going?'

'Harbour View for afternoon tea and drinks.' Although I'll be sticking to Perrier.

'Nice. Okay, well, have a good time, babe.'

'Thanks. See you later, Marc.'

Our goodbyes are interrupted by the whirr of the gate buzzer.

Marcus frowns. 'Bit early for the postman. You expecting anyone?'

'No. Maybe it's a parcel to sign for.'

Marcus takes his phone out of his pocket and swipes at it a few times. 'It's your brother on that knackered old bike of his. Bit early in the day for a visit, isn't it?' He holds out his phone to show me the video entry screen.

'Buzz him in then.' I always love catching up with my older brother, Jay.

Marcus rolls his eyes and does as I say. There's not much love lost between those two, but I'm not sure why.

I go into the hall and open the front door, watching as my brother cycles up the driveway in cycling shorts, a shiny cycling top and wraparound glasses. Marcus gives me another kiss and walks out of the door.

'Morning, Jay.' Marcus gives him a nod as he heads over to the garage.

'Marcus.' Jay nods back without a smile.

It bugs me that my two favourite people in the world don't get on, but I've given up trying to turn them into best friends. It's never going to happen. I'm not sure why Jay isn't keen on my husband; every time I ask, he denies it. And Marcus has taken offence to my brother's unwillingness to succumb to his charms, so he now doesn't bother trying to be friendly either.

I wave goodbye to Marcus, who drives his Porsche out of the garage and roars off down the drive. I turn to kiss my brother's cheek. Jay's been out for an early-morning cycle along the harbour before his shift starts and thought he'd stop in for a chat. He leaves his bike in the drive leaned up against a huge planter of lavender and follows me through to the kitchen.

'I'd forgotten how amazing that view is.' Jay stares out across the water as he loosens the strap of his cycle helmet and lays it on the counter. He smooths his sweaty blond hair.

'Do you want a cold drink?'

'I'd kill for a diet coke.'

I pull a can out of the chiller cabinet and reach up to the cupboard.

'Don't bother with a glass.' Jay reaches out to take the can, pops the tab and downs half of it in one go followed by a barely suppressed belch.

'Jay!' I throw a tea towel at him and he grins.

My brother is five years older than me, tall, wiry and charismatic. He's also divorced and broke, working as a Tesco delivery driver. His ex-wife Rochelle got the house in the divorce settlement and so Jay now rents a tiny bedsit in Parkstone. I've offered to help him out with a deposit on a flat, but he'd rather die than accept our help. He almost revels in his lack of money and wears his unmaterialistic soul with pride. In short, Jay and I are complete opposites, but we love one another to bits.

We grew up with just our mum. Dad left when I was too young to remember and didn't keep in touch with either of us while we were kids. Since becoming an adult, I've caught up with him occasionally, but Jay won't have anything to do with him. He's fiercely loyal towards Mum and I can't even mention our dad without him getting mad. Mum doesn't even know I've met up with him.

Jay and Mum are really close and see one another every week; basically, he can do no wrong. But I have a more compli-cated relationship with her. We love one another, but we clash a lot. She's quite critical of me and the choices I've made. According to her, I'm never satisfied. Which is why I never confide in her. Even when Marcus and I bought her the bungalow she was renting as a birthday present, she never really acknowledged it. She just said that she was perfectly fine rent-ing, but she supposed the bungalow would come to me eventu-ally anyway. As though I'd bought it as an investment for myself, rather than to help her out. I told her she could leave it to a cats' charity if she preferred. Anyway, that's mine and Mum's relationship in a nutshell – tricky.

My screwed-up childhood is part of the reason I want to start my own family so badly. I didn't get to have a regular, happy family life, so I want to create one of my own.

'Shall we sit outside?' I start walking.

Jay follows me onto the terrace. 'So how's things with you, Dani? I called you a couple of times.'

'Yeah, I'm sorry. I kept meaning to call you back, but I've been a bit grumpy these past few weeks and didn't want to spread the misery.'

'You know you can always talk to me. I don't mind if you

want to have a moan.' Jay stretches out on one of the sun loungers and closes his eyes just as a grey cloud passes across the sun and a chilly gust of wind blows off the water.

I sit on the lounger next to him and wrap my arms around my body, staring up at the sky. 'Looks like it might rain.'

He eventually opens his eyes and sits up. 'So, what's been getting you down, sis? Is Marcus treating you okay?'

'Marcus?' I frown. 'Yeah, why wouldn't he be?'

'Just asking.'

'It's nothing to do with Marcus. It's just... the usual. Trying to get pregnant and failing.'

Jay gives me a sympathetic look. 'That must suck. It's been a while now.'

'*Years*. I'm doing everything I can to boost my chances – keeping fit, eating well, taking all the right vitamins and minerals. But none of it's working. The doctors haven't found anything medically wrong with me or Marcus, so there's no actual reason why we can't. I'm thirty-one, so I'm not super-old or anything.' I slump my shoulders before mentally reminding myself that there's a chance I might be pregnant right now, so I shouldn't be miserable. But it does feel good to offload on my brother. Marcus is sick of hearing it and I don't like whining to my girlfriends as they all have children and I couldn't bear their pity.

Jay pushes his sunglasses onto his head and fixes me with a stare. 'Don't take this the wrong way, Dan, but I think you might be trying a bit too hard.'

I bristle. 'What do you mean?'

'Just that your body's probably stressed with all the strict diets and exercise and obses... I mean—'

'You were going to say *obsession*, weren't you? You think I'm obsessed with having a baby.'

'Not obsessed, just a bit too focused on it, that's all. I think you'd have a better chance of conceiving if you relaxed a bit. Thought about something else for a while.'

I tense up and grit my teeth. 'Thanks, Doctor Hewitt. Why didn't I think of that? I'll just magically turn my biological clock off and think about something else.'

'Oh, I knew I shouldn't have opened my mouth. I'm not having a go. I just want you to be happy.' He looks genuinely upset.

'Sorry, Jay. I know you do. Just ignore me.'

My brother comes over and gives me a hug.

'Urgh, you're all sweaty from cycling, get off.' He hugs me even tighter, making me laugh and shove him away. 'Are you hungry? Want some breakfast?'

'Thought you'd never ask.'

Jay follows me back indoors just as the first few fat spots of rain begin to fall. I slide the glass doors closed and give a shiver, thinking that Vicky won't be happy the weather's turned. She was hoping we could sit outside this afternoon. The Harbour View hotel isn't the same when the weather's bad.

I make Jay some scrambled eggs on toast and we sit at the table talking about less emotive things, steering clear of family topics. He tells me a few funny anecdotes from work and I remind him of some silly stuff we did as kids. While we chat, rain streams down the sliding doors and turns the harbour to grey and white chop.

'This is really good, Dan. Can I have some more toast? I need to keep up my energy for the cycle home.'

'You're not cycling home in this?' I give him an incredulous look as I slot two more slices into the toaster.

'It's just a shower. I'll be fine.'

'Let me give you a lift. Or better yet, why don't you let me buy you a car? You know Marcus can get you a decent runaround for peanuts.'

Jay scowls. 'Thanks, but I don't need a lift and I definitely don't want a car from...' He trails off. 'I like my life simple and streamlined. Minimal.'

'What about a simple, streamlined car?' I smile.

'Yeah, it's all simple until it breaks down, or fails its MOT, or the insurance premium goes up. No thank you. I'll stick to my racer. She doesn't let me down. And, anyway, driving reminds me of my day job.'

'Fair enough, bro.'

He finishes his breakfast and I make us a cup of tea, deciding to have a relaxed day at home instead of going to the gym like I'd planned. Maybe Jay was right about not obsessing about things too much. And anyway, if it turns out I *am* pregnant, then a rest won't do me any harm. My main goal today will be trying to resist doing a pregnancy test. I've got half a dozen of them in the bathroom cabinet, but it's too early to do one yet.

The rain is already easing as I wave my brother off down the drive and open the gates with the remote. Although I wish he'd let me spoil him, I also love him even more for being so unmaterialistic and self-sufficient. His ex-wife really messed up when she cheated on him. He might not be rich, but he has a heart of pure gold.

Back in the kitchen, I potter around, clearing away the breakfast things. Then I make myself a cup of raspberry-leaf tea, deciding to take it upstairs and relax for a few hours before getting ready to go out. As I settle on the bed with this month's copy of *Grazia*, I open it up to see the photo of a celebrity mum with her beautiful baby twins. I've always dreamed of having a big family, but I'd settle for just one – a beautiful mixture of me and Marcus. I don't care what gender. I just want a child to love and nurture. To guide through all their milestones. I just want to be called 'Mum'.

I close *Grazia* and place my hands on my washboard stomach, wishing it were rounded with the presence of a new life. I don't think I can face reading about some celebrity's perfect family, so I set aside the magazine and pick up my phone instead, scrolling through social media. Eventually, I do what I always do and trawl a few websites for tips on how to stay healthy during pregnancy. And, lastly, I indulge in my twin guilty pleasures of browsing children's clothes sites, finding cute outfits for babies and toddlers and looking on Pinterest for ideas on kids' bedroom and playroom décor. Usually, I scroll through these sites with longing and even bitterness, but today I can't help feeling a few ripples of hope in my chest. I place a hand on my stomach once more, picturing a little seed growing in there. *Just imagine.*

And that's when I feel it. The trickle that signals the end of this month's hope. I stay very still, hoping I'm wrong. But I know that when I reach the bathroom and check, I'll find a red stain in my underwear. I'll realise, once more, that nothing I do seems to make a blind bit of difference. The money, the diets, the healthy living, the nutritionist, the sex. None of it works. *None of it.* Not for me, anyway.

EIGHTEEN

Most people would think this was boring. Sitting in a warm car for hours. Just waiting and watching. But I don't think it's boring at all. It's all about perspective. The way I see it, this is the exciting part. The build-up. The tease. Waiting to get a glimpse. Waiting for them to do something out of the ordinary.

Waiting for them to fuck up.

NINETEEN

EMILY

Aidan arrives home early from work to find me in the kitchen surrounded by cardboard boxes. Before we even get the chance to say hello, Josh rushes in from the garden and barrels into Aidan's legs.

'Hey, Joshy.'

'Daddy!'

Aidan bends down to kiss his son's head.

'Hi, Em. What are you doing?'

'What's it look like I'm doing? Packing.' I don't mean to snap, but everything is suddenly hitting home. The fact that we're leaving. That we may never be able to return. That my husband has gambled away our future. But I also know that's not the only reason I'm being so snappy. It's mainly to do with the text message I received today. The one that makes it clear that there's another reason I need to get away from here. A reason that's in no way my husband's fault.

Aidan shakes his head like he's annoyed at himself. Our son is talking to him about his day at preschool, but Aidan is too preoccupied to pay him any attention. He's too focused on me.

'How did it go at work? Did you manage to hand in your notice?'

I lay a hand on my bump and take a breath. Try to make my voice softer, less confrontational. 'Yes, all done.' Aidan and I worked out that if I gave a month's notice today, it would still give us enough time to skip town with a week to spare before Aidan's debt is due. It would have been safer for us to leave earlier, but every penny is going to count. Aidan will get his outstanding commission from work in two weeks' time, so that will be a little more cash to add to the kitty.

'And? Did they take it okay?'

I waggle my head from side to side. 'Doreen was annoyed, I think.' Doreen is the practice manager at the GP surgery where I work. She was the one who hired me in the first place and I'd told her at the time that I was hoping to stay for the long term. I've been there four years already and feel very settled and part of the team. I know I'll be missed just as I'll miss them. But I can't allow myself to dwell on that. I have to think of the positives – like having more time to spend with Josh and the new baby when it arrives.

'Did you tell Doreen to keep it on the down low?'

'I did, but she said she'll have to advertise for a new receptionist, so she's not sure how quiet she can be.'

Aidan nods.

We've decided not to tell anyone that we're leaving. This includes our friends – which will be really hard for me – and our family, which will be awful for Aidan. We're telling them that we're taking time out to travel around Europe for a few months before the baby's born. I hope it sounds plausible enough. I can't believe I might never get to talk to Luanne again. What will she think about me leaving? I hope she won't ask too many questions, but I know that's wishful thinking. She'll want to give me the third degree. Which is why I'll have to tell her at the very last minute, so I don't end up breaking down and telling her the truth.

'Daddy, you're not listening. I want you to play with me in the garden.' Josh tugs at Aidan's arm.

'Not right now, mate. Daddy's busy, okay?'

'No! Now!' Josh starts hitting Aidan's legs.

Aidan steps back from his son. 'Stop that, Josh. You don't hit!'

'No! You need to play with me, Daddy!' This time, Josh kicks him in the shin.

'Josh! That's very naughty!'

I sigh inwardly. Josh is obviously picking up on our stress. 'Josh, say sorry to Daddy.'

He scowls at me and I debate whether or not to put him in time out. But I don't think I have the energy for a tantrum.

'If you say a nice big sorry, then you can have two of these big boxes to play with in the garden. You can make them into a car or a boat.'

He looks at the boxes in question, weighing up my deal. After a moment he turns to Aidan. 'Sorry, Daddy.' He bows his head.

Aidan crouches down. 'That's okay. You mustn't do that again though, okay? You hurt my leg.'

Josh's eyes fill with tears. 'Sorry, Daddy. Shall I kiss it better?'

Aidan tousles his son's hair. 'That would be very kind. I'm sorry, too, Josh. Tell you what, why don't you get started with these boxes outside and then when me and Mummy have had a talk, I'll come and play with you, okay?'

Our son nods, his face as pale and stunned as his father's. Ever since I got back from seeing Bianca on Sunday, Aidan has had the same permanently stunned expression on his face. I think now that we have a definite plan, it's all becoming far too real.

He helps Josh carry the boxes into the garden and comes back inside, taking off his suit jacket and hanging it on the back of one of the dining chairs. 'Shall I give you a hand? What are you packing?'

'Just ornaments and things we don't use every day. Thought I may as well get stuck in.'

Aidan rolls up his shirt sleeves and looks around, unsure where to start.

'You can empty the dresser.' I point to a pile of newspaper. 'Just wrap everything carefully.'

He nods and makes a start.

'I also gave notice to Izzy on the house,' I say.

'How did that go?'

'She said she was really upset to lose such good tenants.'

Aidan stops what he's doing, grips the sides of his head and pulls at his short dark hair. 'I'm so sorry, Emily. You must really hate me.'

I shake my head. 'No, I don't hate you. I'm just shell-shocked by everything. It's a lot to take in.'

'I know, I know. I can't believe Bianca came through for us. She really is your fairy godmother. I mean, she's literally saving our lives.'

When I got back from Bath on Saturday, I told Aidan all about Bianca's North Dorset cottage and he almost cried with relief. He asked why I hadn't told him what I was planning and I replied that I hadn't wanted to get his hopes up. But after our initial euphoria at having this miraculous escape route presented to us, the fear began to kick in. We can both feel it surrounding us, pressing in. It's here in the house and outside in the street. It's at our places of work and at Josh's preschool. Until we leave Ashley Cross, we won't feel even remotely safe.

When I asked Aidan what these people would actually do to us if we couldn't pay, he couldn't or wouldn't elaborate. All

Aidan would tell me is that it wouldn't be anything good and that he didn't want us to stick around to find out.

Every creak in the house and car door slamming outside makes us jumpy. But we can't act in any way out of the ordinary because we don't know who might be watching. We have to continue as normal right up until the moment we leave.

As Aidan starts emptying the dresser and placing our possessions into one of the boxes, I sit down at the table for a short rest. 'I wonder what the actual house will be like.'

'I should think it will be really nice, knowing your godmother. I've never met anyone with such good taste.'

'She warned me it might not be in great condition. The last tenants were in there for years.'

'I'm sure it'll be fine. We can always make it nice.'

'You'd better get a DIY transplant.'

'Very funny. I'm not that bad.'

'Aidan, you put Josh's shelving unit together upside down.'

'At least I gave it a go.' He manages a half smile.

'We'd better get used to being more practical. From the sounds of it, we might end up living off the land.'

'We'll end up starving.' Standing there in his suit trousers and shirtsleeves and his immaculate French crop, Aidan looks genuinely terrified.

'Bianca said we can sell logs and keep chickens, grow stuff. I'm sure we can find a way to make some extra cash. The house sits on five acres. We should buy some books on farming. On... what's it called when you have a small farm? There's a name for it...'

'A smallholding?' Aidan offers.

'Yeah, that could be it. We'll buy a couple of books on small-holdings. Or maybe we should save money and take them out of the library.'

'Do you think we can do it? Live there out in the sticks with no proper jobs or friends?'

'Why not? I can bake and cook stuff from scratch like Nigella. We can have a kitchen garden. I could start a country-living account on Instagram and be a domestic goddess.'

'You can't go on social media, Em. The whole point is we're going off-grid.'

'I could use a fake name.'

'No. It's too risky.'

'Hmm.' I pout, disappointed. It would have been nice to have something to focus on and help me feel connected to the real world.

'There's something else we'll need to do.' Aidan puts down the plate he's wrapping and comes over to sit with me.

'What?'

'I think we'll need to change our names.'

'What?! That sounds a bit drastic.'

Aidan picks at his fingernails. 'It *is* drastic. But necessary, I think.'

'How will that even work? What about our bank accounts and cash cards? And I'm having a baby, in case you hadn't noticed.' I put a hand on my bump for emphasis. 'How am I supposed to get medical care if I can't use my real name?' I get to my feet and pace around the conservatory, really thinking hard about how this is going to work practically. 'What about Josh? How can we enrol him in a new preschool without registering him in the system?'

'Let's sort that out later. It's not vital for him to be in preschool. It's more important to get us settled first.'

My mind is racing with all the changes we're going to have to make. Whole new identities for all of us. It's so extreme. But at the same time I'm complaining about it, I also know it's very necessary. I think back to that last text message and my stomach lurches. 'I'll have to tell Bianca about our name change, just in case.'

'I suppose that'll be okay. I mean, she lives in Gloucestershire and doesn't know any of the same people, so it shouldn't matter. But make sure she knows to keep it all to herself.'

I nod, trying to think of any glaring errors we might be making. Any holes that need plugging, any loose ends that might be exploited in order to find us. 'Are you sure there isn't some other way to stop this from happening? Another loan from somewhere else to pay these guys off?' I think about calling Bianca and taking her up on her offer. But even if her offer were still on the table, she already said it would take months to free up the cash. Months we don't have.

'I'm sorry, Em. This is the only way to guarantee our safety.'

I nod, knowing he's right. I also realise that even without Aidan's debt, we have to get away. My husband's screw-up has ensured that I won't have to tell him my own troubles. At least I hope not.

TWENTY

DANI

I lie on my bed, morose and puffy-eyed. My normally flat stomach feels suddenly bloated and heavy. I'm being betrayed by my own body and I also feel so, so stupid for imagining that this month might have been any different to all the other heart-breaking months. That I might have actually been pregnant. I mean how arrogant and deluded was I to think that just because I believed it, it was true? I turn onto my side and bring my knees up to my chest, allowing more tears to slide down my cheeks. Maybe Jay was right when he said that I was trying too hard. That the stress of trying was having the opposite effect on my body and making it tense up and rebel. But what's the alterna-tive? Stop exercising? Eat any old junk food I feel like? Stop tracking my ovulation cycle? I don't think I can do any of those things.

I know my brother meant well, but he hasn't done the research that I have. He hasn't read all the articles and heard about all the success stories. I've spent years reading up on all the proven ways to improve chances of conception and one of those ways is to ensure you have a healthy body. I try not to think about the millions of pregnant women around the world who are ill and overweight or underweight or smokers or drinkers. Instead, I close my eyes and visualise my body as a welcoming place for a baby. A healthy, nurturing sanctuary.

I snap open my eyes and sit up, ignoring the familiar cramping period pains. I know that the best thing for me right now is to focus on positive energy and get rid of all this negativity. I'm going to go to Porter's and do a yoga class. Concentrate on being calm and Zen.

I change into my exercise gear, grab my gym bag and head out the front door where the clouds have cleared and the sun is making a reappearance. Where the traffic allows, I drive recklessly fast. My emotions are still all over the place – one minute I'm angry, the next I feel tears pricking at my eyes. But the mantra I keep repeating is that I need to stay calm, I need to breathe.

When I get to Porter's, I only have a minute to spare before the next class, so I race up the steps, then down to the changing room, stuff my bag in a locker and head straight to studio four. The sixty-minute class is exactly what I need and I come out feeling a little more relaxed. I'm still devastated, but at least my mind is calmer.

I make my way downstairs to the locker room to get my bag, making the decision to text Vicky that I can't come for birthday drinks. Then I'll go home and do some meditation on the terrace before Marcus gets back from work. But it looks like I don't need to text her, as I'm jolted from my thoughts by Vicky saying my name. She's walking up the staircase towards me, looking immaculate as always in her gym gear.

I manage a smile. 'Hi, Vicky. Happy birthday!'

'Thanks, hon.' We hug and she accompanies me down to the locker room. 'You ready for an afternoon of alcohol and cake? It's my yearly splurge and I cannot wait.'

'Sounds so good.' I pause. 'Look, don't hate me, Vicks, but

I've got the most vile period pains. I think I need to go home, take some paracetamol and crawl into bed.'

'Oh, no, poor you.' She stares at me. 'You do look a bit rough. Did you do a class?'

'Hatha yoga. I was hoping it might make me feel better, but if anything, I feel worse.'

She gives me a sympathetic look.

'Sorry, you don't need to hear me moaning on your birthday. You go and have an amazing time and we'll catch up next week, okay?'

She pouts. 'Me and Lou will miss you. It won't be the same without your beautiful face there.'

I try to summon some energy to see if there's any way I could drag myself out this evening. But aside from my cramping belly and mild headache, my whole body is suffused with an unbearable heaviness. I think I'm just very, very sad. 'I'm so sorry, Vicky. You know I'd go if I felt up to it. I'm not one for missing out on a good time with my mates.'

'I know.' She squeezes my arm. 'All right. Well, you get better and call me when you're up and about again. Maybe I can have a second birthday celebration next week.'

'Sounds like a plan.'

We hug goodbye and I retrieve my bag from the locker. I'm relieved that Vicky didn't guilt-trip me for not going this evening. She's actually quite a good friend. Not a super-close friend that I can confide my hopes and fears to, but then I don't really have anyone like that. Apart from my brother and Marcus of course.

I've never been a girly girl. I didn't really fit in at school. I was too quiet and insecure to hang out with the popular girls, too soft for the hard girls and too pretty to be accepted by the geeks. So I hovered between groups, taking whatever friendship crumbs were offered. Boyfriends were a different matter – I never had any problems there. But that didn't exactly endear me to the girls. They usually think I'm snooty. Like I think I'm better than them or something. But I don't think that at all.

I guess I'm wary of female friendships. I like having them, but I can never fully be myself. Not like I am with Marcus. I guess that's another reason why I'm so desperate to start a family. I want to create my own tribe where it doesn't matter what happens in the wider world, as long as we have our little family. It's a physical ache, a longing I don't think I'll ever be able to let go of.

The drive home is less hectic. I cruise along, enjoying the view of the harbour. The rain clouds have completely disappeared, the sky rinsed clean. It's a beautiful afternoon. Vicky will be able to sit out on the terrace at the Harbour View hotel after all. And I'll be able to meditate on my own terrace.

I'm looking forward to the peace and quiet of home, so when I make my way down the drive to be confronted by half a dozen cars and a heavy bassline from our outdoor sound system, I stiffen and feel my pulse start to race. What the hell is going on? Has Marcus invited his mates round again? I just can't deal with this right now.

There's no space to park on the drive and they've even blocked the entrance to the garage, so I'm forced to pull up onto the grass verge. Perry, our gardener, won't be happy about that. I exit the car and stand for a moment, listening to the sounds of raucous laughter and splashing above the dance music. The smell of burning charcoal wafting over the house. Marcus's friends are obviously in the pool, having fired up the grill. My meditation plans have gone down the toilet.

I really don't want to be the kind of wife who kicks off about stuff like this. After all, I was supposed to be going out, so why shouldn't Marcus have his friends round – or work colleagues, or whoever they are? It's just unfortunate that I'm feeling so rough. The last thing I want to do is socialise with strangers in my own home. This is supposed to be my sanctuary.

I decide that I'll just let Marcus know I'm back, ask him to turn the music down a notch and then I'll retreat upstairs to our room and watch some TV.

I know I don't look my best, but I don't care about checking my appearance right now. If Marcus can see I'm feeling rough, hopefully his guests won't stay too late. I let myself in and peer through to the kitchen to see if I can get a glimpse of my husband. The pool is situated off to the right in an enclosed section, so I can't see it from here. There's no one out on the terrace either. I text Marcus:

Hey, I'm home, can you come into the hall?

I wait for him to reply, trying to keep my agitation at bay. This is so not what I had in mind for this afternoon and evening. Two minutes have gone by and there's no reply. Maybe he's in the pool or chatting. He might not look at his phone for ages. I sigh, realising I'm going to have to go out there. I suppose I could just slink off to our room, but I'd rather he knew I was home. I catch sight of myself in the mirror. My hair is scraped back in a ponytail, my face – although fully made up – is pale and I have dark circles under my eyes. I look like a stranger to myself.

This is ridiculous. What am I doing skulking about in my own house? I march through the kitchen, gritting my teeth at the empty food packets, bottles and cans strewn across the work surfaces and also on my beautiful kitchen dining table. There are crumbs and wet marks on its pale wooden surface. The white marble floor is slippery with water and I realise that Marcus's guests must have been coming into the house while dripping wet from the pool, which is pretty disrespectful if you ask me. We've got a pool house – why couldn't they use that for the food and drink?

'Hey.' A twenty-something girl with long, black, dripping-wet hair, wearing a gold string bikini, comes into the kitchen and sits on one of my dining chairs with her wet arse.

'Hello, I'm Dani.' I'm trying to keep my temper at her proprietary attitude to my kitchen, but I can't help the acid in my voice. What the hell is this stunning woman doing in my house while I've been out?

'Oh, right, I'm Bluebell,' she drawls in a posh accent.

Bluebell? What the hell kind of name is that? Actually, in other circumstances, I'd think it was a beautiful name, but right now it's the stupidest name in the universe. 'Well, I'm *Dani*, as in Marcus's wife. This is my house.'

She instantly loses her nonchalant attitude, flushes and gets to her feet. 'Oh, right, you're Marcus's wife. I thought you were the maid or something.' She wipes the chair's seat pad ineffectively, realising it's now soaking wet.

I ignore the maid jibe. 'Is my husband out by the pool?' I don't wait for her to answer, but march outside past two men who are smoking and drinking beer by the barbecue. They give me a nod and look me up and down, but I don't acknowledge them. Instead, I walk through the gate across the pale-grey porcelain tiles to our stunning infinity pool that faces the harbour. Alongside it is the long, low, glass-fronted pool house that contains a sauna, two changing rooms and a state-of-the-art gym. There must be a dozen or so people out here on the patio – both men and women in swimming trunks and bikinis – sprawling on the sun loungers, knocking back champagne and cheering two couples who are playing chicken in the pool, the women on the men's shoulders trying to knock each other off, laughing and squealing.

Bluebell has followed me out and is saying something, but I can't hear her over the music and laughter. I can't spot Marcus anywhere.

'He's not here,' she says a little louder this time.

I turn back to her. 'What do you mean, he's not here? How can you all be here without my husband?'

'Oh, it's fine,' she replies airily. 'We ran out of champagne and Marc was the only one sober, so he went to pick up some more.'

'Right.' Aside from the fact that she's called him 'Marc', my stress levels are rocketing as I realise my husband has basically left a bunch of strangers alone on our property with access to all our belongings. He might not have been drinking, but he's certainly not behaving like a sober person, or even a sane person. *What the hell is going on?*

TWENTY-ONE

EMILY

Luanne holds the door open for me as I walk into the lobby of the Harbour View hotel. She's been on at me all week to come out for afternoon tea with her today. I've told her, *I'm sorry I can't make it*, at least a dozen times – because I've got too much going on at the moment and also because of the exorbitant prices – but she was insistent. Telling me she needs to discuss something important. Even Aidan said I should go. *It might be the last time you get to spend time with her.* The thought of that made me cry.

I hope Luanne hasn't got wind that we're leaving town. I'm not sure I could lie if she asked me outright, face to face. But how would she know about that? We haven't told anyone. I relax and tell myself to stop worrying, give myself permission to enjoy myself. Lu already said she's putting today's lunch on her expense account. I know she only said that to save me any embarrassment and is really paying for it out of her own pocket. But I can't afford to be proud, so I pretended to believe her.

It'll be lovely to have a few hours where I'm not stressing about everything that's going on with Aidan, or worrying about his gambling, or having to flee. And I really made an effort with my appearance today, as who knows when I'll next have the opportunity to go anywhere fancy. I've put my hair in a half-up and spent ages on my make-up. I'm wearing a blue-and-white empire-line dress and a pair of strappy sandals, which were probably a mistake as they're already digging into my swollen feet. But I'm determined to make the most of every second. I'm happy to suffer for fashion today.

Luanne gives her name to one of the staff, a young Eastern European girl with excellent English. 'Follow me. Your table is over by the window. We gave you the best view like you asked for.'

The restaurant is almost full and there's a nice chatty buzz as the sun streams in from the open glass doors that span the length of the vast room. Beyond the doors, a wide, stepped terrace is dotted with shady trees, verdant planters and seating areas. And beyond that, way down in the distance, is the deep-blue sparkling ocean, studded with green islands and tiny boats.

I spot a group of glamorous women I vaguely recognise sitting out on the terrace. I think a couple of them are from Luanne's health club. I can't see Dani among them. I lock eyes with a heavily made-up blonde woman and give a brief smile. I swear she saw, but she chooses to look away without acknowledging me. Oh well, if she wants to be like that, let her. I'm not going to let anything dampen my mood today.

'Surprise!' Luanne has come to a stop next to an occupied rectangular table that's decorated with flowers and clusters of helium balloons in pink, blue and white. I'm confused for a moment, not too sure what I'm looking at and then I realise that I actually know everyone at the table.

'Luanne!' I grin, suddenly wise to her ruse.

'It's your baby shower. Did you think we'd forget to throw you one?'

Quite honestly, I hadn't given it a moment's thought. Although I acknowledge that the old me would have been worried about exactly that. 'Oh, Lu! You didn't have to do all this!'

She smiles at my obvious pleasure and I throw my arms around my best friend in the whole world, inhaling clouds of Jo Malone perfume and trying not to bawl my eyes out.

'Bianca!' I spy my godmother, happy to see her and yet aware of a thud of fear in my chest.

As I hug her, she whispers in my ear, 'Don't worry, I haven't said anything to anyone. Let's just enjoy today.'

'Thank you,' I whisper back, praying I don't let anything slip.

One by one I greet my friends and family. Aidan's younger sister, Michelle, and my mother-in-law, Marion, stand and give me a hug. I'm surprised but pleased they came. Maybe they're finally warming to me after all these years, just as I'm on the brink of leaving their lives forever.

'Sarah! It's so lovely to see you again.' I wave to my friend Sarah Parr, who's seated across the table.

'Hey, Emily. Luanne invited me to your shower when we met last week at Aidan's birthday.'

I turn to Lu. 'You've been planning it since last week?'

'Of course. Didn't think I'd left it till the last minute, did you? What kind of best friend do you think I am?'

Everyone laughs.

I say hi to Caroline and Tamara, my work friends. Caroline works on reception with me and Tamara's one of the nurses. 'You two scrub up pretty well, outside of work.'

'Cheeky,' Tamara replies and blows me a kiss across the table.

I squeal as I spot Talia, my good friend from school who now lives in Southampton. I haven't seen her in person for years, although we often like and comment on each other's posts on social media and keep meaning to catch up in person. I try not to think about the fact that this could be the final time I see any of these people again.

'Okay, ladies, here we go,' says one of the waiting staff as they come over with trays of tiered cake stands stacked with mini sandwiches and petit fours. There's tea and coffee in vintage floral teacups, as well as cocktails and mocktails – I opt for a virgin mojito, which is to die for.

The whole afternoon is a blissful escape from reality. A day I know I'll never forget as long as I live. We laugh and cry and laugh some more. I eat until I'm stuffed and drink so many mocktails that I have to go up and down to the loo like a yoyo. Sarah joins me on my many trips to the ladies, being the only other pregnant guest.

After a couple of hours of wonderful conversation, Luanne stands and dings her glass. I look up at her and wonder if she's about to make an emotional speech that will make me sob.

'Bet you thought I was going to make a boring speech.' She laughs. 'Would I do that to you? No, I would not. Instead, let's do presents!'

'Yay, presents!' Tamara cries a bit too loudly. I think she's quite drunk.

Luanne gestures to a side table behind me that's stacked high with shiny wrapped gifts.

'You guys didn't have to do that.' I put a hand to my heart.

'Of course we did.' Lu rolls her eyes. 'Presents are the best bit. Apart from the cake and alcohol.'

I spend the next half hour opening everyone's gifts while we all ooh and ahh over baby toys, cute onesies and various luxurious pampering creams for mother and baby. Bianca has thoughtfully included an incredible gift bag of toys for Josh so he doesn't feel left out.

'There's one left.' My sister-in-law, Michelle, hands me the final gift – a silver box tied with a gold bow.

'Is this one from you?' I ask.

'No.' She shakes her head and we glance around the table looking for any takers.

'Who's it from?' Talia asks.

'I don't know. I think I've had a present from each of you already.' I look around at everyone again, but nobody claims it.

Marion points. 'There's a gift tag.'

I turn the gold label over and read it aloud. It's handwritten in neat but quite childish-looking script.

> *Dear Emily,*
> *Congratulations.*
> *Lots of love.*

I frown. 'There's no name.'

'Open it,' Lu urges.

I undo the bow. The silky gold ribbon slithers onto the table and then to the floor. I lift the lid and see lots of white tissue paper. I pull it out.

'What is it?' Sarah cranes forward.

Everyone is trying to get a better look.

It's an ornament of some kind. I pull it out of the box and everyone sighs. It's a cute ceramic cottage about the size of a coffee mug, maybe a little bigger. There's a cord attached with a plug on the end.

'It's a nightlight,' Marion says. 'How sweet.'

One side is open to reveal the scene within. I turn it around to get a better look.

'It's the Three Bears, from the fairy tale!' Sarah points. 'Look – Baby Bear, Mummy Bear and Daddy Bear. Oops, looks like Daddy Bear's broken. His head's come off.'

I see that she's right, the head is lying on its side in the base of the lamp. I reach in to pick it up but, as I do so, the rest of Daddy Bear crumbles into tiny pieces. No one seems concerned that the gift isn't from anybody here. At least, no one's owning up to it. Everyone agrees that it's such a shame it got broken and what an unfortunate accident it is.

But as I stare at the ruined family scene, I suddenly understand, with a chill, that it's no accident that the father figure has been broken.

I catch Bianca's eye and immediately look away, worried that we'll call attention to ourselves. I wonder if she's thinking what I'm thinking – that this gift has been left here as a warning.

It's doubly threatening that it's been given so soon after Bianca offered us the cottage. Does whoever's behind it know what we're up to? *No*, that's impossible. No one could know what I talked to Bianca about. It was just the two of us there. The fact that it's a ceramic cottage must be a coincidence. I think the warning here is to do with the family inside.

My family.

TWENTY-TWO

DANI

I've returned to the house and locked the sliders so that none of Marcus's friends can come inside. I don't care if they think I'm an antisocial bitch, there's no way I want any of them coming and going as they please while I'm in here on my own.

I make my way upstairs into our bedroom and close the door. The house is well soundproofed, but I can still make out the thump of music and the odd shriek of laughter from the pool. I plunk myself down on the end of the bed and stab at my phone. It rings twice and cuts to voicemail.

'Marcus, I've just come home to a house full of strangers. What's going on? Can you come back, please?' I've toned down my language and volume, but in my head I'm swearing and screaming. I walk over to the front window and look out over the drive, clenching my fists at the sight of all those cars – a couple of Range Rover Sports, a Jaguar XF, a Bentley Continental, some Peugeot sports thing and a couple of Audis. Still no sign of Marcus returning.

Those men by the pool looked pretty dodgy to me. Too much swagger. Too little respect. And the women didn't seem like wives or girlfriends. Too young and beautiful, like accessories rather than partners. What is Marcus playing at? I wonder if something has happened... whether he's being forced to entertain these people... if they're threatening him in some way. Or am I being overly suspicious?

How did my day go so wrong so quickly? It started out with so much hope, thinking I might be pregnant, followed by a visit from Jay and the prospect of a lovely afternoon and evening spent in the company of my girlfriends. Then I got my period and the whole day descended into shit. And, to top it all off, there's a bunch of freeloaders in my garden.

I really want to go out there and tell them all to piss off. But that would not go down well with Marcus. He seems to have a blind spot when it comes to his new 'buddies'. I don't know who they are and how they're connected to my husband, but I'm determined to find out. I have a sneaking suspicion that they're using him, taking advantage of his good nature. It's a pity I don't feel up to going out there and confronting them, only once I start, I know I'll end up saying something I regret.

I try calling Marcus again, but there's still no answer. Still no sign of his car in the driveway. Maybe I should leave them all to it. Go back to Porter's to work out my stress. My stomach still feels heavy and uncomfortable, but that's never stopped me doing a class before. The only thing stopping me is the thought of someone seeing me there and word getting back to Vicky. She'd be really hurt that I felt well enough to go to the gym, but not to go to her birthday bash. She might be so hurt that she and Louise cut me off. I don't want that. They're the only real friends I have.

I suppose I could tell Vicky I feel better. Spend the evening at the Harbour View with my friends. But the thought of that makes me feel even more exhausted. Besides, I really don't have it in me to get glammed up. Whatever I do, I don't think I can stay here right now. Even up here in my room, I feel under siege. Trapped. And when Marcus finally does come home, he'll want me to dress up and be sociable with his friends. Or maybe he won't. Maybe he'll be annoyed that I'm not out with Vicky and be relieved I want to stay in my room so that he can socialise without me passing judgement. That would be even worse.

I realise I have to go out. Maybe a run along the harbour will clear my head. Part of me rebels against going out while these strangers are in our garden, but Marcus thought it was fine to leave them here with full access to our property – at least I've locked the back doors.

Now that I've made the decision to leave, I feel so much better. I'm still in my gym kit, so all I need is my phone and water bottle. We have a drinks station built into the wall on the upstairs landing, so I don't need to go back into the kitchen, thank goodness. I don't want any of them gawping at me or asking why I've locked the doors. I fill up my water bottle with filtered tap water, jog down the stairs and leave the house via the front door, praying none of Marcus's guests come out to their cars while I'm leaving. Eventually, I'm through the gate and out onto the road where I do a few warm-up stretches before setting off.

The afternoon is sunny, but not too warm. There's a welcome freshness in the air that helps to clear my head and drain some of my toxic thoughts. This is actually really nice. I think I'll stay out for a few hours. I can run and then find a quiet spot on the beach to meditate.

The steady thud of my footsteps is soothing. Normally, I'd have my ear buds in and music playing, but right now I'm enjoying listening to the sounds around me. The clink of boats, the squawk of the gulls and even the hiss and drone of the traffic going by. I tell myself that I wouldn't be feeling so irritable if I hadn't just got my period today. It's just made everything else seem worse, that's all.

Before long, my thoughts start to fade away and I zone out,

reaching that wonderful stage of running where the endorphins kick in and everything else is secondary. My breathing is steady and my body feels as though it's gliding along the footpath. Nothing else matters right now.

An insanely loud car horn yanks me from my blissful state. I flinch but carry on running despite another couple of shorter toots up ahead. Then I realise there's a car cruising towards me. I alter my position so I'm further away from the kerb and glance up to see that it's my husband in his Porsche, a puzzled grin on his face. I slow down, jog on the spot, take a swig of water and wait for him to pull up alongside me.

Marcus buzzes down his window and leans over. 'Hey, Dan, I thought that was you. What are you doing? Thought you were out with Vicky and Louise tonight.'

'Obviously,' I reply, thinking of the pool party back home.

He frowns. 'Oh shit. Did you go home?'

'Uh, yeah. Is that okay, for me to go home to our house? Only when I got there, I found a twenty-year-old in a bikini sitting in our kitchen and a load of strangers having the time of their lives in our pool.'

'Oh bollocks. Sorry, Dani.' He turns off the engine. 'It was a last-minute thing. I knew you were out, so I invited a couple of the lads over and they asked if they could bring their girlfriends and it kind of escalated from there. I wouldn't have invited them if I knew you'd be home. I know you don't like me inviting people over to the house.'

'*What?*' I stop jogging on the spot and cross my arms over my chest. 'Who says I don't like you doing that?'

'You do.'

'It's not that I don't like you inviting people over, it's just I don't know them and they seem really...' I pause, not wanting to offend my husband, but then think, *screw it.* 'Dodgy.'

'They're fine, Dan, just a bit rough round the edges. You

should come back and meet them. What happened to your night out?'

'I didn't feel up to it.'

'Why not?'

I bite my lip and try not to let my voice break. 'I got my period.'

Marcus gets out of the car and comes round onto the pavement. He gives me a hug. 'I'm sorry, Dan. I know how difficult it is for you each month.'

I sniff back tears, not wanting to break down in the middle of a public footpath. I step out of his embrace. 'I really thought I might have been pregnant this month. I was so hopeful. I'm so stupid.'

'Nothing wrong with being hopeful.'

'There is if you're always disappointed. It feels like I'm taking a beating every time I find out it's not happening.'

'Get in the car a sec.'

'I haven't finished my run.'

'Just for a minute. I want to talk to you about something.'

I do as he asks and we sit in the Porsche's cool interior. 'Look, Dani, I'm working on something at the moment and if it comes off, all your prayers will be answered, okay?'

I stare at my husband. At his glittering blue eyes. 'Working on what?'

'I can't tell you.'

'Is it a business deal with those guys at the house? It's not something illegal, is it?'

He rolls his eyes and give me a look that says, *as if.*

'Look, I'm not being funny, but I'm not actually bothered about being richer. Right now, I'd be happy to live in a council flat if it meant we could have a family.'

Marcus takes my hand. 'Just stay positive, okay? Like I said, I'm working on something.'

'Fine. But all I really wanted to do this evening was relax at home.'

'Would it make you happier if I asked them to leave?'

It would make me ecstatically happy, but I won't ask Marcus to do that. I want him to figure it out for himself.

'Because if you want me to, I will.'

I shrug.

He sighs. 'Look, you carry on with your run and by the time you get back in' – he glances at his Patek Philippe watch – 'say half an hour, they'll all be gone and we can have a chilled-out evening, okay?'

I feel my stress instantly draining away. 'Are you sure?'

'Positive.'

I lean over and give him a kiss. 'Why don't you at least have a burger and a drink with them first. Let's make it an hour's time.'

'Perfect. I promise they'll be gone by the time you get back.'

'Thanks.' I get out of the car and start stretching again. 'Love you, Marcus.'

'Love you, too, babe.' Marcus starts the engine, waits for a gap in traffic and then roars off towards home. I watch him go, feeling infinitely better.

The rest of my run is blissful and I end it by doing some cool-down stretches and sitting cross-legged near the shoreline, attempting to empty my mind. After half an hour's meditation, I walk in the direction of home, ambling along the narrow strip of beach.

By the time I finally arrive at the gates to the house it's been almost two hours since my husband drove home. I frown at the sound of music still blaring, but maybe Marcus decided to leave it on. Our neighbours won't be too happy about the noise levels. I'll have to take over a bottle of wine later as an apology.

Marcus's friends should be long gone by now, so when I walk through the gates and down the drive to be faced with the sight of all their cars, my heart rate goes into overdrive. Then I remember that they were all drinking. Maybe they ordered taxis and left their vehicles here until tomorrow. But if that's the case, why can I still hear music... and laughter?

I let myself in and walk through to the kitchen. Through the open doors I can see that they're all still here, gathered around the grill or sitting on the deck furniture. The men with their hands all over the girls. Marcus catches my eye, smiles and beckons me over, but I'm not in the mood to be introduced to everyone. I feel like such a party pooper, but this is my home and I don't want it filled with a load of strangers when I'm feeling so low.

I guess I'll have to hide out in my room again. Marcus catches up to me in the hall. 'Hey, babe.'

I mumble a short hello.

'Come out and meet the guys.'

'I'm tired, Marc. Gonna go up to bed.'

'Come on,' he wheedles. 'Half an hour to say hello.'

'Not right now.'

'Christ's sake, Dani, stop acting like I've done something wrong.'

I whip around and glare at him. 'You said they'd be gone by the time I got home. You offered. It was your suggestion.'

'Yeah, but I couldn't kick them out after I invited them in the first place. That would've been rude.'

'So why did you offer to...? Oh, do you know what? Forget it.' I start stomping up the stairs.

'They won't stay too late, okay?' he calls after me.

I can tell he's had a fair amount to drink and isn't in the least bit sorry. He's not normally like this. He usually puts me first and doesn't care what others think about that. What's happening to our marriage? Who are these people that he's putting their enjoyment above my well-being? Is he trying to impress them? Whatever his reasons, I'm not happy and I'm going to get to the bottom of it.

TWENTY-THREE

EMILY

Our road is quiet and dark, the air cooler than it has been for a while. The orange streetlamps throw shadows across our narrow drive, adding to the unreal quality of the night.

Bianca messaged a couple of days ago to say that her property in North Dorset is now vacant. That our new house is waiting for us. Although I've never even seen pictures of it, I imagine the place as some cosy bolt-hole waiting to offer us sanctuary. A dream house set in the middle of a fairy-tale forest. And yet the thought of living out in the middle of nowhere is still quite daunting. I just have to hope there are no wicked witches or hungry wolves waiting to gobble us up. The image of that broken nightlight comes to mind. I ended up throwing it away and not mentioning it to Aidan. What would have been the point? He's already so stressed about everything.

I still have a couple more weeks of my notice left to work, so Aidan and I have decided to shift our belongings over to the new place. We can't afford a removals firm and, anyway, we wouldn't want to draw attention to the move by having a huge great van show up outside our house, so we'll just do it ourselves in stages.

To be on the safe side, Aidan has suggested we transport our stuff in the early hours of the morning to cut down on the possibility of neighbours asking questions. Or, more worryingly, anyone following us out there and discovering our plan to run away. Consequently, we went to bed at seven last night in the hope of getting a decent amount of sleep before our one a.m. alarm went off. Needless to say, neither Aidan nor I got a minute's rest as our brains were in overdrive. We gave up the pretence by nine and spent the rest of the evening packing more boxes.

'We can't stay awake like that every night,' I whisper to my husband as he settles a grizzling Josh into the back seat of the Audi.

'I know. We're both going to be shattered tomorrow.'

'Hopefully, it'll be easier once we've actually seen the place. I'm so nervous about where we're going to be living for the next twelve months.' I slide into the passenger seat and wait for Aidan to get in, wincing as he slams the door far too loudly, setting Josh off crying once again. I turn to soothe our son, stretching to take one of his warm, pudgy hands in mine and stroking his palm with my thumb.

As Aidan pulls out of the driveway, I cast my eyes over the neighbours' windows and the parked cars in the road, checking for signs that anyone might be watching us. Before we even stepped outside, I scanned the street from our window and only when I was satisfied that no one was out there, did I let Aidan start loading up the car.

Thanks to the darkness and the motion of the car, Josh settles back to sleep quickly enough. Aidan and I are quiet during the journey. On the couple of occasions where a vehicle pulls in behind us, I feel my anxiety shoot into overdrive, but once they turn off, I let myself relax a little.

Now we've left Poole behind and are deeper into the Dorset countryside, the narrow, hedgerow-lined roads have become completely deserted. Several times, Aidan's had to brake quite suddenly to allow small creatures to dart across the road or, in one case, a couple of black-and-white badgers who were shuffling along without any regard for their safety. It feels as though we're headed to a foreign land rather than to the borders of the same county.

I turn to check on Josh, who's still sound asleep. Poor little man, being dragged from his cosy bed in the middle of the night. I hope we can make things up to him. Hopefully, once we've relocated in a couple of weeks, he'll be able to enjoy the outdoor life. I don't know how he'll adapt to having no preschool. I'm worried how much he'll miss his friends, especially Ivy. I try not to dwell on that. It's just not helpful. I need to focus on the positives.

Rather than having the car's satnav disturbing Josh, I'm using the map on my phone to direct Aidan. 'Slow down when you pass the next turn on the left. The lane we want is straight after it.'

Aidan does as I say. Coming out here in the early hours is so strange. Everything feels surreal and dreamlike. It would all have felt far more normal if we could have visited during the day. But we just wouldn't have felt safe leaving home in broad daylight with a car stuffed full of boxes.

The lane is so rough and pitted that I'm glad we didn't bring my Mini. Aidan slows the Audi to a crawl and inhales sharply through his teeth as we jolt over a pothole. 'This isn't great for the suspension. We're going to have to get a four-wheel drive.'

I glance at Google Maps, which is telling me we've arrived at our destination. 'I think we're here. The property should be somewhere on the right.'

The headlights illuminate a wooden sign and I can just about make out the words *Briar Hill Farm*. 'There!' I point to the sign and Aidan pulls a sharp right. We turn onto another road, which I'm guessing is part of the property. Thankfully, this surface is smooth and well maintained and it feels luxurious not to be bounced around any longer.

Up ahead, under the glare of the headlights, I can make out a cluster of buildings. To the left are a collection of outbuildings including a large barn and to the right is a charming stone cottage that looks as though it was drawn by a child. Perfectly symmetrical, there's a door in the centre with a sash window either side and three upstairs windows. As we get closer, I give a start as security lights flash on, bathing us in a bright white glow. I then notice an alarm box set beneath the eaves, its red light flashing intermittently. Bianca told me she was going to upgrade the security for us and I can see she really meant it.

'Wow!' Aidan brings the car to a stop and switches off the engine. 'Your godmother rocks. I mean seriously.'

I nod. 'She really does.'

'And we can genuinely stay here for a year rent-free?'

'That's what she said.'

'I'm scared we'll never want to leave.'

We sit for a moment taking it all in: the house, the barns, the towering trees looming behind the buildings like a natural protective screen. The absolute seclusion of the place.

'Let's hope the inside is as nice as the outside,' I murmur. Although at this stage, I'm so in love with the exterior that it could be a hovel in there and we'd make do.

'What shall we do about Josh?' Aidan turns around to check on our son, who's asleep, clutching his blanket to his flushed face, his mouth wide open. 'Seems a shame to wake him.'

'Let's leave him in the car. He'll be fine – we'll be coming in and out unloading boxes and there's no one else here.'

'Okay.' Aidan turns to me with a nervous smile. 'So, shall we have a look inside?'

I think this is the first time since Aidan dropped his bomb-shell that I've felt hopeful about things. If we can get away from Ashley Cross safely and make things work here, then I really feel like we might have a chance at happiness. Maybe we'll love it so much that we'll stay here permanently. Find work and pay rent. But I'm getting ahead of myself. I'm basing all my optimism on a first viewing in the dead of night. We haven't even looked inside yet.

We step out of the car and walk towards the front door. Even the air smells sweeter here. Fresh and summery. I take the key from my bag along with the sheet of instructions that Bianca sent in the post. It fits in the lock easily and I open the door to a dark, musty-smelling hallway. Once inside, I turn on the light and enter the alarm code into the panel situated on the wall to the right of the door. Once the beeping stops, I relax a little and glance around. Aidan follows me inside.

The hall is narrow and a little grubby, but nothing that a coat of paint won't fix. Both the floor and staircase have stripped wooden floorboards. There's a door on either side of the hall. A quick peek reveals equal-sized reception rooms with the same gorgeous floor – one room contains a couple of retro brown sofas and a bamboo and glass coffee table, the other has a dark wooden six-seater dining table and chairs and a carved mahogany sideboard. Unbelievably, both rooms have white shutters, which I've always dreamed of having but never thought we'd be able to afford.

The staircase sits straight ahead at the end of the hallway. There's a downstairs cloakroom set under the stairs with a loo, sink and a rack of coat pegs. Next to the staircase is another door that leads down a couple of steps into a good-size rectangular kitchen with white painted units and oak worktops. There's a huge blue complicated-looking range that I'll have to teach myself how to use and a small circular pine table with four farmhouse chairs. The floor has what looks like the original flagstones, grey and pitted with age.

Back out in the hall, Aidan and I stare at one another, our eyes wide. Aside from the fear of what we're running from, it feels like we've won the lottery. I'm still a city girl at heart. I still love the hustle and bustle. But if I were ever to be seduced by country living, then this property is a pretty good place to start.

'Shall we look upstairs?' Aidan puts his foot on the first stair.

'Let me just quickly check on Josh.' I nip outside and the lights flash on once again, illuminating our son, who's still fast asleep in the back seat of the car. I smile to myself and gaze out at the vast expanse of overgrown front garden, cleaved in two by the long driveway. I can only see as far as the pool of light allows. Beyond that, all lies in darkness. Above, the stars are as bright as I've ever seen them. I look back at the house. The upstairs lights wink on one by one and I see my husband's silhouette outlined in the central window through the open shutters. I wave and he beckons me upstairs.

I smile and make my way back inside. Upstairs has a similar warm but somewhat neglected vibe – probably because no one's living here at the moment. There are three large double bedrooms – one with a contemporary en-suite shower room – and a separate family bathroom that's also quite modern, thank goodness. We head back into the largest bedroom, which sits at the back of the house. I peer through the large window into the darkness, but all I can make out are a few swishing trees. Everything else is black. The room is square with dark wooden furniture comprising a small double bed, two double wardrobes set either side of a wide chimney breast and a dressing table and mirror in front of the window. There's a worn Persian-style carpet covering most of the floorboards.

'Can you believe this place?' Aidan asks, taking both my hands in his.

'I feel like I'm dreaming.'

'I know. It's perfect. And we haven't even explored the barns and the land yet.'

'The amount of land makes me nervous. We've got no experience of farming. The only thing I've ever grown in my life is a strawberry plant. And even then the slugs managed to eat all the fruit before we could.'

'We'll learn. It'll be fine.'

'Okay, if you say so.'

'I do.' Aidan fixes me with a steady gaze. 'Let's take this opportunity and really make it work for us. It can be a new start.'

I nod. 'Will you promise to stop gambling?'

Aidan blanches in response to my blunt question. 'I think... that once we close our bank accounts and move in here, you should take my laptop and my phone. I'll get a cheap phone that doesn't have internet access. That way I won't be tempted.'

'I think that's a good idea. Because, Aidan, I don't want to go through anything like this again. This house is amazing, but I'd still rather none of this had ever happened. That we were back living our normal, boring life.'

'I know. I do too. I'm really sorry about all of it.'

'I know you are.' I put my arms around my husband and we hug. 'Now we're here, I wish we were moving in already. The thought of spending two more weeks in Ashley Cross where we're in danger feels crazy to me. Can you not quit your job straight away?'

'We can't afford to miss out on your wages and my commission. We're gonna need the money for food and bills.'

'You're right, I know you're right.' I sit on the bed on the brand-new mattress that's still covered in plastic. *Bianca*. She must have bought it. She's so thoughtful and generous. I don't know how I'll ever be able to thank her.

Aidan glances at his watch. 'It's almost three thirty. Shall we get these boxes unloaded and start making our way back? I'd like to be home before people start leaving for work.'

My body rebels at the thought of leaving. I realise I'm

looking forward to making this place our own. To painting and decorating and unpacking all our stuff.

We turn off the upstairs lights and head down the stairs. Aidan reaches the bottom and waits for me to catch up. 'You know we still haven't thought about what our new names will be.'

I stop on the bottom stair. I don't want to lose my name. I like the name Emily. But Aidan's right. If we want to stay off the radar, we can't be Emily and Aidan any longer. 'The only other name I quite like is Annie. It also sounds a tiny bit similar to Emily, so if you slip up, hopefully no one will notice.'

Aidan tilts his head and presses his lips together. 'Hmm, *Annie*. I think I like it.'

'Yeah?'

'Yeah.' He nods and leans over to kiss me. A proper long, deep kiss. It's unexpected and, along with our hug earlier, it's the first time we've been even remotely intimate for weeks.

We finally pull apart and smile sheepishly, then make our way out to the car where our son is still sleeping. We each lift out a box from the boot. 'I don't really feel like an Annie, but I guess it will grow on me. I hope so. What about you?' I follow him inside and we walk through to the kitchen. 'Have you thought about a name yet?'

'I have no idea. What about my middle name, James?'

'I really like it, but I think it's too obvious. They might realise we've changed our names, so then they might assume we're using our middle names – not that I would ever in a million years use my middle name.' I dump my box on one of the kitchen counters.

'Oh yeah – Enid.' Aidan smirks and I punch him in the arm.

'My parents' idea of a sick joke.'

'You're right about the middle-name thing though. Okay, what are names that sound like Aidan?'

'I dunno, *Baden*?'

My husband gives me a look and we both snort with laughter. 'Is that even a real name?' he asks.

'Who knows. But you're so not a Baden.'

'What about David?' he suggests.

I think for a moment. 'Yes. I like that, it's a classic kind of name. *David*. David and Annie.'

'Annie and David.' Aidan sets his box next to mine.

We then decide that Josh will become George and my heart gives a pang. I love the name Josh. It suits our son so well. But his safety is more important than sentimentality.

By the time we've unloaded all the boxes into the house, we've decided that our family will change from Emily, Aidan and Joshua Graham to Annie, David and George Mortimer.

As we lock up the house and get back into the car, I feel like I'm caught in a shadow world. A kind of limbo where I'm waiting for my real life to begin again. But is my real life back in Ashley Cross, or will it start here in this picture-perfect cottage in the middle of nowhere?

TWENTY-FOUR

DANI

The house is silent and still. After another hot day, the marble floor is blissfully cool against the soles of my feet, so jamming them into running shoes isn't the nicest sensation. I'm still not sure I should be doing this, but my husband has left me little choice.

After the pool incident a few weeks ago, my relationship with Marcus hasn't been the same. He's distant, as though my being around him is an annoyance. He's not rude or horrible, just distracted, and I can't seem to draw him back. His so-called colleagues have visited the house on a few more occasions. I guess they're here on average a couple of times per week, thankfully without their girlfriends, or whoever they were. The word *escort* keeps popping into my head, but maybe I'm being unfair. Marcus is always edgy before they arrive and he acts differently around me after they've left, flipping between being irritated and then overly affectionate to make up for his moods. I've tried to talk to him about it, but he keeps brushing me off. I know it sounds ridiculous, but sometimes I wonder if he might be scared of them.

The thing is, I've had enough. I need to find out who these

associates of my husband really are and what's going on. My marriage means everything to me and I'm not prepared to let it slip away. However, getting information out of Marcus these days is almost impossible. When I ask him who his friends really are, he's vague. He said something about them importing cars. But on a previous occasion, he told me he was training one of them up to work in the showroom. So which is it? Something isn't right here and it worries me that Marcus is keeping secrets. We used to tell one another everything, sharing our hopes, dreams and problems. These days I'm lucky if he tells me what he wants for dinner.

He's gone out for a drink with his brother this evening and won't be home until late, so I'll have plenty of time to do what I need to do. I lock up the house and click the remote to the garage, my stomach doing nervous swoops at the thought of what I have planned. It's not quite twilight as I get in the car, leave the property and head towards Ashley Cross.

I'm not proud of it, but last week I did some snooping around my husband's study to see if I could find a clue as to what's going on. He hasn't expressly told me not to go in there, but it's an unwritten rule that the study is Marcus's private space. He never invites me in and he always closes the door behind him, unlike the other rooms in the house whose doors are always left ajar.

His office is a masculine space – a combination of contemporary and traditional with a glass desk, bookshelves for display only (Marcus isn't much of a reader), black-and-chrome filing cabinets, a modern leather sofa and an enormous flatscreen TV. I started my search in the filing cabinets and desk drawers, but there was nothing of any interest. I even took out some of the books and flipped through the pages in case something fell out. I don't know what I was expecting to find – a piece of paper with a cryptic clue or a receipt for something illicit. I found nothing, which was both a relief and also frustrating.

That fruitless search has led me to tonight.

Marcus's car showroom is located at Ashley Cross on a busy main road. I park out of sight in a residential side street. Dusk is falling and the streetlamps wink on one by one. It's always quite buzzy here in the evenings, especially during the summer months, with crowded bars and restaurants and people strolling along the pavements and relaxing on The Green.

Dressed down in my gym gear and a baseball cap and sunglasses, no one gives me a second glance as I duck into the nondescript covered doorway, the staff entrance to the showroom. Of course, it's closed at this hour, the metal shutters pulled down over the huge plate-glass windows. But I have a spare set of keys, so I hurriedly let myself in, switch on the corridor light, shut the door firmly behind me and punch in the alarm code.

I'm not confident that the code is still the same as it was a few weeks ago when Marcus was out with a client and needed me to fetch him some paperwork. I'm sweating slightly as I tap in the final digit, unsure if all hell is about to rain down on me in the form of sirens and lights. But after a short chirp, the alarm is silent.

I exhale and open the door to the dark and silent showroom. Reluctant to switch on the overhead lights, I use the torch on my phone to light my way. In the eerie gloom, I weave through Maseratis, Ferraris, Daimlers and other luxury vehicles until I reach Marcus's office on the other side of the room.

I locate the key to unlock the door and enter the office. Closing the door behind me, I feel as if I've just completed an assault course, my heart thumping so loudly I have to stop where I am for a moment to calm down. It's almost completely dark in here. There's an opaque window at the back that opens onto an alleyway and a large window at the front, both shuttered like the showroom. Again, I don't want to risk switching on the light in case it somehow seeps through the shutters. My phone light will have to be enough.

Now that I'm in here, I have to work out how to go about this. But how do I find something when I don't know what it is that I'm looking for?

Marcus's office is large and square with white marble floors the same as at home. There is plenty of modern artwork on the walls, a chiller cabinet stocked with drinks, a black lacquered shelving unit, a glass desk with drawers and two filing cabinets underneath and two inviting leather armchairs for his clients.

After a thorough search, I find nothing in any of the drawers, shelves or filing cabinets and I finally come to the conclusion that I'm looking for something that doesn't actually exist. A reason to justify my husband's uncharacteristic behaviour. When it could simply be the fact that he's growing tired of spending time with me. Maybe he's finding more pleasure in the company of his new friends. After all, it can't be much fun being with a wife who's obsessed with getting pregnant to the exclusion of everything else. Am I driving him away?

I glance around my husband's office. A place reserved for important clients only. Even *I* rarely come in here. I sit in his black leather office chair, thinking about him sitting in this spot, working, talking to customers, making deals, thinking, planning. I gaze at the artwork straight ahead of me, at the broad, dark brushstrokes against the white canvas. Something clicks in my mind.

At home we have a safe in our dressing room. It contains cash, jewellery and important documents like our passports. The safe has been built into the wall and is hidden behind a painting. I angle my phone on the desk so that the torch shines at the artwork and I walk over to the wall. I lift the first canvas off its hook and feel a jolt of anticipation when a small safe is revealed. It's the exact same model as the one back at the house.

After setting the canvas on the floor, I turn the dial, hoping that the combination is also the same.

The safe door swings open and my breath hitches. I wipe my palms on my leggings and lick my lips. If Marcus is hiding anything, surely this is where I'll find it. A distant thud startles me. It sounded like a door being pulled shut. I cock my head for a moment and listen, but all is quiet, so I get back to focusing on the safe.

Inside are stacks of cash, all used twenties in thick bundles. That doesn't surprise me; I've always half suspected that Marcus does cash deals from time to time. We've never talked about it, but he has the same bundles of money in the safe at home and Marcus is happy for me to help myself.

Inside the safe, next to the cash, I notice a slim hardback notebook. I take it out and open it up, my curiosity piqued. I start reading the dated entries, which are in my husband's hand-writing. I frown and have to reread several notes to make sure I'm understanding this correctly. When it's clear that I'm not mistaken, my skin turns cold and my heart begins to thud.

I hold the notebook with shaking fingers now, staring at the lines of handwriting and wondering what to do. I can't remove the notebook without alerting my husband. I snatch my phone off the desk and take photos of each page, trying to ensure the pictures don't blur. Once I'm done, I replace the notebook back in the safe, trying to recall its exact position. I should have paid more attention before I removed it. I take a photo of the cash and notebook inside the safe, just for good measure, and then I close it up and replace the painting.

I actually feel sick. Shaken. I thought Marcus was keeping secrets, but I never in a million years suspected *this*. I'm so shocked by my discovery that I almost don't register the sound of footsteps beyond the closed office door. Footsteps that are getting closer.

TWENTY-FIVE

Apparently it's not just him who's been naughty. She's got her secrets too. I think it might be fun to pay him a visit and let him know what his wife's been up to. I think I'll enjoy watching his face as he learns that juicy piece of information. Poor bastard. He better enjoy himself while he can. Because his time is running out.

TWENTY-SIX

DANI

The blood swims faster in my veins. My breath catches in my throat. There's someone outside the door to Marcus's office and chances are they're about to come in. I've already returned Marcus's notebook to the safe and rehung the painting, so at least I won't get caught red-handed. I also prepared an excuse for why I'm here, but now that I have to use it, it seems so flimsy and patently untrue. If there were somewhere to hide, I would take that option, but there isn't. It must be Marcus out there. Maybe he won't come into the office. Maybe he's just checking on the cars. He might even be here with his brother. That would be really embarrassing for me. My heart is clattering like a freight train. I switch on the light so it doesn't look as though I'm skulking in the shadows.

The door handle goes down. I wince and prepare to brazen things out, my eyes on the opening door.

A man walks in. Not Marcus. He's brandishing a length of metal pipe. I give a squeak of alarm and take a step back. We lock eyes and he relaxes his shoulders, lowers the pipe and loses the aggressive expression.

'Dani. Good thing you're standing over there. I could have

clobbered you with this.' As soon as he speaks, I recognise him. It's Marcus's employee Jonesy. I'm half relieved it isn't Marcus or some random intruder, but there's something shifty about this man. Something I don't like. I wonder if he really is an employee or if he's something else. Something worse. His eyes sweep the room. Thank goodness I replaced the painting so he can't see the safe. His gaze finally travels back to me. 'What are you doing in here?'

I'm annoyed by his question. 'What am *I* doing in here? This is my husband's business. What are *you* doing in here?' I put a hand on my hip.

He gives me a lazy smile. 'This is my place of work, why wouldn't I be here?'

'Um, maybe because it's nine o'clock at night and the place is locked up.'

'Yeah, well, your old man's a bit of a slave driver, if you must know. I've come in to catch up on some work.'

'What, in his office? I know for a fact he doesn't like people coming in here.'

Jonesy stares at me without replying. He runs his thumb along the pipe.

I give an inward shudder. 'Yeah, well, I'll leave you to it.' Suddenly I'm desperate to get away from this man. I don't feel safe being alone with him here, especially as no one knows where I am. I head towards the door, but he doesn't move out of the way. I can't seem to swallow and my heart is pounding.

'So...' He leans the pipe against the wall.

'Can you move please?'

'He doesn't know you're here, does he?' Jonesy smirks.

'*What?*' The absolute cheek of this guy.

'Marcus doesn't know you're here. But you can tell me what you're doing; I can keep a secret.'

I weigh up my options. If Jonesy tells my husband I was snooping in his office, I'll be forced to have a really difficult conversation with him. Marcus might even realise that I've seen his notebook. I make a snap decision and soften my body language. 'If you must know, I was looking for the keys to the Lamborghini. The girls and I wanted to have a cruise round town while Marcus is out. He doesn't like me driving the merch – not since I had a little scrape in the Aston. But it's fun, you know?' I give him a conspiratorial smile.

'Yeah, I do know. Fast cars are a bit of a turn on for me too.'

'So, you won't say anything?'

'Your secret's safe with me.' He taps the side of his nose.

'Okay, great, thanks.' I try to sidle past him.

He stops me, placing his hands on my shoulders and giving me a lazy smile. I realise with a shock that he's wearing the same aftershave as my husband. 'Hey, where do you think you're going?'

My stomach drops. I do not like this man touching me, but I need to keep him sweet.

'You want the keys, right?' Jonesy cocks his head.

'What?'

'To the Lamborghini. For you and your friends?' He raises his eyebrows and, in that instant, I understand he knows I'm lying about the car. But I continue with the pretence anyway.

'Oh, yeah, I *did* want the keys. But I'm actually... I'm uh... a bit too shaken up to drive it now.' I curse my stumbling words. I sound like such a liar. I decide to take an indignant approach instead. 'You scared the shit out of me, coming in here with that metal pipe.'

He raises his hands and I use the opportunity to take a step back. 'Self-defence. Thought you were an intruder. Have to admit, it was a nice surprise to find my boss's hot wife here instead.'

I don't want to prolong this conversation, so I back out into the showroom. 'Thanks for not saying anything!' I call back over my shoulder.

'Hey, Dani!' he calls after me. 'You do know the Lamborghini's a two-seater, right? Not enough room for you and your "friends".' He makes air quotes.

I flush, realising my error. 'Just as well I didn't find the keys then.'

'Yeah, just as well. You realise you owe me now. For keeping your secret.'

I give a small fake laugh, but I'm more than a little worried. Being in debt to this man doesn't feel like a good position to be in. It makes me incredibly uncomfortable to know that creep has got something over me. But then I realise that if it comes to it, I'll simply tell Marcus what I told Jonesy – that I wanted to borrow one of the cars. Whether he would believe me or not is another matter. But then I realise that I'm stressing about the wrong thing. My thoughts are drawn back to the notebook and the huge secret that Marcus is keeping from me. That's the thing I should really be worrying about.

TWENTY-SEVEN

EMILY

Josh is asleep upstairs while Aidan and I pick over the unappetising leftovers from the fridge – a hunk of cheese, a piece of cucumber, half a tomato and some hummus. We've added some crackers and the end of a loaf of bread and are eating off squares of kitchen roll because all the plates are packed. But I'm so keyed up that I have no appetite anyway. We're sitting at my lovely, brightly coloured dining table, which we've decided to leave behind because there's no room for it at the new place. I run my hands over its surface, feeling ridiculously sentimental at the thought of leaving it. Especially as the table in the new house isn't at all to my taste.

After two weeks of stealthily moving the rest of our belongings, tonight is finally the night of the big move. Aidan returned his Audi to the leasing company today and I've sold my beloved Mini – another hard goodbye. Earlier this week we paid cash for a second-hand Isuzu four-wheel-drive pickup truck, which is currently parked down the road instead of in our driveway, as we don't want to arouse any suspicions.

We've informed everyone we needed to inform that we're going travelling for a few months before the baby's born. I told

Luanne about it this week and she was shocked but excited for me and a little jealous that Aidan and I were going to have all these amazing experiences. I felt dreadful that I couldn't tell her the truth about what's really going on, and even worse when she said how much she's looking forward to getting cuddles with the new baby when we get back. I don't even know if or when I'll ever be able to see her again. The thought of that is shocking to me.

While Bianca's property is gorgeous, I'm still very apprehensive about being cut off from my friends and colleagues. Will Aidan and I be enough for one another, or will we grow bored? We're not used to spending every single day together. What if we become irritable or annoyed with one another? I'm hoping there'll be enough to keep us occupied, what with all the redecorating, maintenance and trying to grow our own food. We haven't discussed whether we're going to allow ourselves to make friends with the locals. Or whether we need to stay isolated for our safety. I guess there'll be plenty of time to work that out when we get there.

Aidan and I were given quite a hard time by his parents when we told them we were going travelling. His mum said we were crazy for leaving when I'm six months pregnant. 'What if you need medical help? What about your blood pressure? What if the baby comes early and you're on the road somewhere?' I can't really blame her for being anxious and it actually felt nice to have her worry. She's not normally so warm towards me. Michelle was more jealous than anything. She grumbled that she didn't realise we were so well off to be able to stop working and go jetting off around Europe. If only she knew the half of it.

When we returned from their house, Aidan was really down. I think that lying to his parents really brought home what we're actually doing. He doesn't know when he'll be able to see them again, if ever. That must be a huge burden. This is probably the only time I've been grateful for having disinterested parents.

I can't let myself believe that we'll have to stay in hiding for the rest of our lives. Surely something will happen to get us out of this situation and give us back our freedom. I guess I'm praying for a miracle.

Aidan wolfs down the last of the crackers and takes the empty packets out to the wheelie bin. When he returns, we finish up cleaning the kitchen. I've made sure every room is sparkling. Aside from wanting to ensure we get our full deposit back, I don't want Izzy to be faced with a mess. I remember her mentioning how the previous tenants left the place in a right state and she spent a fortune getting it habitable again. I'm certain she won't be disappointed. She's also agreed to buy the white goods, dining table, beds and sofa from us as she's going to let it furnished next time.

As I do a last sweep of the kitchen, checking inside the oven and cupboards, I wonder who will be moving in here next. Will it be a young family like ours? Or maybe a couple or a single person? I hope they enjoy living here as much as we have.

'How you doing?' Aidan comes back into the kitchen. 'I've checked the list and it looks like we're pretty much done here.'

'Did you take a photo of the gas and electric meters?'

'Yep.' Aidan waves his phone at me. 'And all the remaining cases and boxes are down in the lounge waiting until I can load them into the truck.'

Now that we've finally finished packing and cleaning and are ready to go, my anxiety levels are ramping up again. I sit for a moment and start my deep-breathing exercises to keep my blood pressure down. The last thing we need is for me to be admitted to hospital for pre-eclampsia. That will ruin everything. Although, if the worst happens and I do have to go into hospital, I've told Aidan to inform the staff that I'm in danger from a stalker and that they mustn't give out my details to anyone who might call. I'm not sure if this is even possible, but I'm hoping so.

The next couple of hours tick by slowly. The TV has already been packed away, so we sit in the conservatory making small talk, willing the time to go faster. We've decided to start loading up the truck at around one a.m., once most people are in bed. That way, we should be able to leave by one thirty. My stomach hasn't stopped churning. I'm trying to send soothing vibes to my baby. I wonder how much of my anxiety they can pick up.

I'm just about to ask Aidan how much commission he's due from the showroom when I'm startled by the loud buzz of the doorbell. Aidan and I immediately look up and then stare at one another.

'Who's that?' he whispers.

I shake my head and shrug.

'Stay there.' He holds up his hand.

'You're not going to answer it!' I get to my feet.

'No. I'm just going to look out the lounge window. See who it is.'

'What if they see you looking? They'll know we're here.'

'Okay, uh...'

The doorbell buzzes again followed by a loud rapping. Whoever it is, they're insistent.

'Let's go upstairs.' I start tiptoeing across the kitchen.

Aidan grabs my arm. 'Wait! What if they look through the letterbox?'

'The hall light's off. They won't be able to see us.'

'Okay.'

As we creep along the hallway to the staircase, I try not to think about who could be standing on the other side of our front door at eleven thirty at night. My heart is racing like crazy. I'm imagining a group of thugs ready to break the door down. What if they succeed? I knew we should have left town sooner. Aidan talked about needing an extra month's wages and commission, but what good is money if we're dead? Alternatively, it could be someone else. The person who's been texting me. Who won't leave me alone. The person who's given me another reason to get out of town, fast. With a deep shudder, I think about the latest threatening message.

I need you to agree. Last chance.

I try to put it out of my head, but I can barely breathe. Aidan follows me up the stairs. I begin my ascent treading slowly and carefully, but as I near the top, panic takes over and I almost fall face-first onto the landing in my haste not to be seen. The doorbell goes again – a harsh buzz that vibrates through my whole body. I'm seriously scared. And I'm worried the noise will wake Josh and they'll hear him call out, realising we're home.

'Are you okay?' Aidan hisses as I stumble and right myself.

'Fine.' I hurry to Josh's room and glance at his sleeping form before crossing to the window.

'Don't open the curtains,' Aidan warns.

'I'm not stupid.' I position myself at the side of the window as my husband stands behind me. Slowly I inch back the edge of the curtain and peer down to the doorstep, praying whoever's down there doesn't look up.

TWENTY-EIGHT

EMILY

I open my eyes, but it's still so dark that I close them again and try to get back to sleep. It feels so different here. So quiet. Like we're in a tiny boat alone at sea with no land around for miles. We finally left our home at one thirty a.m. after we were completely sure that the stranger ringing our doorbell had left. We watched him from the corner of Josh's bedroom window. He waited on our doorstep for a couple of minutes, ringing the doorbell and knocking so loud I thought he'd bring the neighbours out. Finally, thankfully, he gave up and walked back down the path and onto the pavement. His bike was leaning against our wall and, after a last glance up at our house, he cycled away. From that quick glance up, he looked to be in his twenties or early thirties, but neither Aidan nor I recognised his face.

I try to dismiss my uneasiness about who he might have been and try to focus on the here and now. The air in our new bedroom is stuffy and I can't tell if it's because it's such a warm night, or because the house hasn't been lived in for a while, or if this is what the air is always going to be like in here. I'm sure I can smell the previous occupants – their unfamiliar scents and perfumes lingering like redundant territory markers. Their smell makes me unsettled and, inexplicably, angry. I can see why some people buy incense and crystals to cleanse the aura of their new homes. I think I might try something similar tomorrow by opening all the windows wide and wafting one of my precious scented candles throughout the house.

We arrived here at around three a.m. and decided to go straight to bed rather than start unloading the truck. We were absolutely shattered from night after night of broken sleep. But although I'm still exhausted, I've only managed the shallowest of sleeps, waking every forty minutes or so. It doesn't help that the baby presses on my bladder every time I lie down and then as soon as I stand up to go to the loo, the feeling passes.

Anyway, I daren't look at the time on my phone again as it only depresses me. I'll just wait until it's light and then I'll get up. Hopefully, things will feel better in the daylight. In fact, I realise we haven't even seen this place during daylight hours. Which is very strange indeed.

I must have fallen asleep again because I wake, but it's still pitch-dark. I dreamed I was living in a treehouse, but there was a storm and the tree was swaying so much I thought I was going to fall out. I turn over onto my other side.

'You awake?' Aidan whispers.

'Yeah. I'm having a rough night's sleep. You?'

'Same. I'm wide awake. I wish it were morning already.'

'What's the time?' I suddenly feel much better now that Aidan's awake too. An ally for my insomnia.

'That's weird.' Aidan sits up next to me, the glow from his phone giving him a ghostly appearance.

'What?'

'It says the time's ten fifteen.'

'That can't be right, it's still dark.'

Aidan gets out of bed and goes over to the window. Suddenly a million shafts of light flood the room.

I wince and blink. 'What's going on?'

'The shutters.' Aidan gives a short laugh. 'They blocked out all the light, so we thought it was the middle of the night. No wonder we felt so wide awake.'

'Oh no.' I sit up suddenly. 'What about Josh?!'

'You mean George.'

'Ugh, yes, I'm not going to get used to that.'

Aidan and I rush out of our bedroom to check on our son in the room next door. I'm filled with relief to see him crouched down on the floor, rummaging through one of the packing boxes containing his toys. It was his birthday last week and we had a beach party where he received lots of lovely gifts which have been keeping him happy and occupied for days. I can't believe our first child is four already.

'Do you like your new room?'

Josh nods. 'I'm going to make a zoo with my animals.' He pulls a wooden tiger and elephant from the box.

I bend to give him a kiss. 'That's a great idea. Maybe we can collect some leaves and make a jungle for them.'

'Yeah!'

'Shall we have some breakfast first?'

We all head downstairs to the kitchen. The first thing I notice is the light filtering through the windows and half-glazed back door. And the view. There's an overgrown garden with fruit trees, a large greenhouse and beyond that a meadow bordered by hedgerows and lofty trees that look like they've been around for decades. It all looks so tranquil and beautiful. But at the same time, it's quite terrifying because I have no idea about how to look after land or trees or any of it.

'Mummy, there's a swing! Can I go on it?'

I bring my gaze back to where Josh is pointing and see a

homemade wooden swing tied to the lower branch of an apple tree. 'That looks fun.'

'Let me check that it's safe first,' Aidan says.

'After breakfast,' I add.

We potter about in the kitchen trying to locate food, crockery and cutlery, finally settling Josh at the table with a bowl of honey loops. Aidan finds the key to the back door and opens it, letting in the summer breeze and birdsong. *It's an adventure*, I tell myself. *I'm lucky to be in such a magical place.* If I say it enough times, maybe I'll actually start to believe it.

'Do you know how that works?' I point to the range.

Aidan thumbs through a pile of papers on the countertop. He pulls out a manual with a photo of the range on the front. 'No, but we can work it out.' He flicks through the first few pages. 'Says it's multifuel.' He shrugs and puts the manual back down, then catches my eye. He must see my stricken expression because he smiles. 'Honestly, don't worry. I'll work it out and then show you, okay?'

'I think I'm just tired.'

'Of course. It's been a stressful few weeks and last night was mad with that bloke ringing on our doorbell.'

'Do you think he was one of the' – I lower my voice – 'loan sharks?'

'Possibly. I don't know.'

'They won't find us here, will they, Aidy?'

'No. Not a chance.'

'Because if they do, well, it's so remote. There are no immediate neighbours to help us.'

'Don't think like that. How will they find us? We have no family ties to this area. All our friends and family think we've gone travelling abroad. We've changed our names. No one has our forwarding address. We've even closed our bank accounts.'

I exhale and lean against the counter. 'I know. You're right.

I guess it will just take time to settle. To not feel like we have to look over our shoulders.'

'And don't forget, the loan's not due for another week and a half, so no one will be looking yet anyway. By which time it will be too late. We've already left.'

'That's true. I just hope no one followed us here.'

'We were so careful, only coming over here in the early hours, staying in our jobs so no one became suspicious.'

'What's *aspishus* mean?' Josh asks through a mouthful of cereal.

I shoot Aidan a worried glance. We really shouldn't talk about this stuff in front of our son. When he was younger, all this would have gone right over his head, but now that he's four, he's becoming more aware of what's going on and curious to know more.

I come and sit opposite Josh. 'Suspicious means when you think someone might have done something. So I might be suspicious that Daddy has stolen some of your honey loops.'

'Daddy! You can't do that!'

'Wasn't me.' Aidan raises his hands in the air and then makes himself look super guilty by glancing around the room.

Josh giggles and we spend the next twenty minutes talking about trivial, fun things.

After breakfast, we go outside and Aidan tests out the swing before letting Josh have a go. There's a strange animal-type sound coming from behind the greenhouse. Aidan hears it too and he goes to investigate while I push Josh on the swing as he urges me to push him higher.

'Guys, you have to come and see this!' Aidan sounds excited rather than worried.

I stop the swing. 'Come on, let's see what Daddy's found.' I take my son's hand and we run across the grass and around the greenhouse where we're greeted with the sight of an enormous chicken coop and several clucking chickens. Around the coop is a large white bow and attached to the bow is a card. I come closer and read what's written.

Welcome to your new home, love Bianca.

'Can you believe this?' Aidan's eyes are wide with excitement. 'Chickens! That means fresh eggs.'

Josh is crouching by the side of the coop, sticking his fingers through the wire. 'I like chickens. Are these ours now?'

'Don't poke your fingers in. Do chickens bite?' I ask my husband.

He laughs. 'I don't think so. They haven't got any teeth. They might peck though.'

'We're so not prepared for any of this. I mean, it was lovely of Bianca, but I don't think I can cope.' Panic is rising in my gut. This place is somebody's dream property. But it's not mine. I feel totally out of my depth. Ill-prepared for all of it. I'm trying not to think about our little house in Ashley Cross. It's not my home any more. It will soon be someone else's and I will have to get stuck in and make this work, only it's so overwhelming right now.

Aidan sees my face and turns to our son. 'Tell you what, Joshy, let's play with the chickens later. Right now, why don't we go back inside and make that zoo we were talking about?'

I don't correct him about calling our son his old name. We haven't even explained to him that his name is going to be George now. I mean how do you tell a four-year-old that we're changing his name? We'll have to come up with a way of selling it to him. But I can't even think about that now because my brain is spinning out with everything. My mouth is dry and my head is throbbing. 'I think I need to sit down.' I sink to the ground cross-legged and bow my head into my lap.

'Em, are you okay?'

'Annie,' I mumble back. 'I'm Annie now.'

'Don't worry about that now. Are you dizzy? Shall I call an ambulance?'

'No, no, I'm fine. Things just went blurry for a minute.' I close my eyes, trying to block out the noise of the chickens. I take a few deep breaths, but rather than calm me it only reminds me that the air smells so different here. That this isn't home.

TWENTY-NINE

DANI

I walk quickly along the narrow dusty pavement with my head down, hoping I don't bump into anyone I know. I'm in Parkstone, not too far from home and only a few streets away from Jay's bedsit and Mum's bungalow, but I'm not here to see either of them today.

It's been a stressful and horrible two weeks and I feel like I've been living a double life. Ever since I discovered Marcus's notebook, I've been looking at my husband in a completely new light. I must be a really good actress, because he hasn't suspected a thing. Jonesy has been as good as his word and kept my fake secret about why I was in Marcus's office.

A few months ago, if I'd been this distant, Marcus would have been all over me, asking what was wrong and trying to fix things, but these days he's so preoccupied he barely notices anything's wrong. I guess that's a relief. But I wish I could confront him about it. I'm worried about him. Worried about the sort of trouble he might be in. Those colleagues of his... I really don't think they're good people, but I think Marcus must be in so deep that he can't get out. No wonder he's so remote; he must be under an incredible amount of stress.

I've been toying with making him aware that I know he's in trouble, but every time I'm on the verge of bringing it up, I wimp out. Marcus has never kept me in the loop when it comes to his business and I really have no idea how he would react if I told him what I discovered.

I check the house numbers as I trudge up the steep road past rows of squashed-together terraced and semi-detached houses in varying states of repair. Everything I do these days has felt forced and heavy, like I'm dragging my anxiety and fear around with me wherever I go.

Eventually I reach my destination, a semi-detached red-brick house with a neat front garden and a smart iron gate. That's a good sign, I think to myself, the fact that the place is cared for.

I open the gate, noting that it doesn't squeak and walk along the path to the UPVC double-glazed front door. There are two bells. I press the one that says 32A. A few moments later I hear the sound of someone hurrying down a set of stairs. The door opens and a man stands before me in jeans and a plain navy T-shirt. He's in his thirties, average height, average build, with mid-brown wavy hair.

'Rob?'

'Hi, yeah. You must be Dani.' He holds out his hand and I shake it. His grip is firm and his palm is cool and dry. 'Come in.'

I step into a dim hallway and follow him up stairs and through a door into his flat. It's clean and fresh smelling, but everything is fairly nondescript and neutral – plain walls, cheap carpet, thin doors. When I spoke to Rob on the phone, he gave me the address of his office in Poole, but I didn't want to risk being seen going in there, so I asked if we could meet somewhere out of the public eye. He suggested his flat, so here I am.

A beautiful grey cat walks past me in the hallway, brushing up against my legs. I reach down to stroke its head.

Rob stops and turns. 'That's Harvey. He belongs to the

family next door, but he keeps following me in here. I think he likes the peace and quiet.'

'He's gorgeous.'

We enter a bright living room with magnolia walls and bland furniture. Rob gestures to a beige sofa. 'Please have a seat.'

'Thanks.' I perch on the edge of the sofa while Rob takes his phone from his pocket and places it on the pine coffee table. 'Do you mind if I record our meeting?'

'Um, no, that's fine.' Although in truth it makes me a bit uncomfortable. 'You won't play it to anyone, will you?'

'No, absolutely not. This is just for me, so I don't forget any important details.'

'Oh, okay. I've never done anything like this before. I don't really know how it works.'

He gives me a warm smile and his face transforms from average to almost handsome, his soft grey eyes crinkling at the edges. 'Honestly, don't worry. I'll just ask you a few questions and you can tell me what brought you here, okay?'

I nod, my mouth suddenly dry. I found Rob McAvoy online and gave him a call before I could change my mind. His website had the best testimonials in the area. I realise that for most situations, it's better if you can get a personal recommendation, but a private investigator isn't exactly the sort of service you can ask your friends and family about. Not if you want discretion. Which I very much do.

I wish I could seek help from someone other than a complete stranger, but my friends are too gossipy and I wouldn't trust my brother not to confront Marcus or do something equally rash. Ironically, the only person I would want to talk to about a problem like this, is Marcus.

Rob presses the record button on his phone and says the date and time along with my name. 'So, on the phone you said you need my services as a private financial investigator to look into your husband's business affairs, is that correct?'

I nod.

'It would help if you could answer out loud.' Rob gestures to the recorder.

I clear my throat. 'Sorry, yes, that's correct.'

'Could you outline what exactly it is you suspect? And what information you need from me.'

I inhale deeply and blow out a breath, wondering if I'm making a terrible mistake by telling this stranger what I've discovered. But at this point I don't feel as though I have a choice. At least as an ex-policeman he has some proper training and knows his way around the law. I swallow my doubts and launch into a retelling of the night I found the notebook in my husband's office. And what it contained.

THIRTY

EMILY

Despite being almost eight months pregnant, I've never felt so fit and healthy in my life. My sickness has disappeared, my headaches have vanished, my body – aside from my bump – is lean and toned. Every day, we've been waking early with a list of tasks that need our attention. We've already repainted the interior of the house using the large pots of white emulsion we found in the tool shed. We've unpacked our belongings and it really is starting to feel more like home.

Our biggest challenge has been looking after the land. Surprisingly, Aidan has really stepped up. He's thrown himself into the forestry side of things while Josh and I have been tending the chickens and also the incredible kitchen garden we discovered behind the fruit trees, in the form of twelve large, raised beds. There's so much there – potatoes, carrots, lettuces, radishes, tomatoes, soft fruit and more. I'd been hoping to find some blogs to help me get started, but unfortunately we can't afford a landline or internet. The only form of communication we own is a couple of burner phones with brand-new numbers, but there are only a few random spots in the house where you can get good reception.

I did stumble across a couple of helpful gardening and cookery books in the kitchen, which must have belonged to the previous tenants. They made some really useful notes in the margins which have been more helpful than the actual content of the books. I'm planning to find our nearest library and see if I can join without any ID. If not, I'll just have to read in the library rather than bring any books home. But that's a task for another day. Probably after the baby's born.

Josh has flourished. He's loving everything about our new lifestyle. He's either out with me in the garden or sitting on the ride-on mower with his dad. He's growing like a weed, his little body becoming strong and tanned. We're not letting ourselves think about schools yet, but if it comes to it, I'm considering homeschooling. Although I think that will be even more of a challenge, especially with the added responsibility of a newborn to care for.

Aidan keeps talking about getting some goats and sheep, but we can't afford to do that yet. He's also started advertising some of the seasoned timber from the barn using a handmade sign, that he's stuck out on the main road, that simply says: *Eggs and Logs*. We've had a few customers, but not nearly enough to keep us going. And the seasoned wood won't last forever which means he's having to teach himself how to fell trees to ensure we'll have logs to sell next year.

So, the upshot is we're creating a life for ourselves, but we're not quite self-sufficient yet, which is worrying. Especially as it's the height of summer now and things are likely to get a whole lot harder over the winter. Despite having solar panels and a septic tank, which have eliminated many of our bills, there have been a lot of unforeseen costs along with a hefty council-tax demand, food costs and other random expenses that have mounted up.

As far as our new names go, we're getting the hang of speaking them aloud, although I'm still finding it hard to think

David, Annie and George in my head. I have to force myself to make the change each time.

It's a warm evening and we're sitting on a rug in the garden eating a homegrown omelette, chips, tomatoes and beans. We eat our meals all together as a family these days, rather than on our laps at separate times. It feels idyllic with the mellow sun warming our skin, the warble of birdsong and the swish of a summer breeze through the trees. But I know this relaxed lifestyle will end if we don't find a solution to our money worries.

'Mummy, I've finished, can I go and play?'

'Yes, but no going into the woods on your own, okay, George? Stay where we can see you.' I'm still not comfortable with letting our son run loose here. Even though it's technically our land, there are too many accidents waiting to happen to a four-year-old with no fear. Not to mention the threat of violent debt collectors.

Josh runs off into the meadow beyond the trees and I squint after him, making sure he's in my line of sight.

Aidan pops the last chip into his mouth and gives a contented sigh, stretching his legs out in front of him. He's looking better than he's looked in years, his body growing leaner and more muscular by the day, his brown eyes clear and sparkling, his naturally curly hair longer and blonder, bleached by the sun. Outdoor living suits us all. 'That was delicious. Thank you.'

'No problem.' I shift positions to try to get comfortable on the rug. My bump is feeling particularly heavy today.

'You've been quiet this evening. Everything okay?'

I almost don't want to bring up my worries and tarnish this beautiful day, but it can't be put off any longer. Not if we don't want everything we've worked for these past few weeks to come to a grinding halt. 'I'm worried about money.'

'Oh.' He frowns. 'Well, we're doing okay, aren't we? We've

got the garden and the chickens and the logs and kindling. We don't need much – just enough to eat, really.'

Aidan and I decided that *I* would look after the money as he still doesn't trust himself not to gamble. I haven't even told him where I've stashed it because it might prove too much of a temptation for him. He's asked for cash a couple of times, supposedly for supplies, but I've offered to pick up the items myself, which we both know means that I don't trust him with the money. It sucks having to be the bad guy. I feel awful, treating him like a kid, but he says he understands. I wish we could share the burden, but it just wouldn't be helpful for Aidan's addiction.

I need him to understand that the money situation isn't great, but I don't then want him to think he can solve it by kidding himself that he could win more – that's what got us into this mess in the first place. 'We're doing okay. But we're down to our last two hundred pounds. And when you factor in council tax and water rates, diesel and toiletries, we're not going to last much longer. If we get hit with an unforeseen cost, like the truck breaks down or we need more stuff for the baby...'

'We've still got all George's old baby things, so we should be fine.'

'Yes, but there's so much more we'll need, like nappies for a start.'

'We can get reusable ones.'

'They're still really expensive.'

Aidan chews his bottom lip. 'Yeah, you're right. I suppose I just don't want to think about that side of things. Not when everything else feels so good.'

'I know. It's shit. We're working so hard and doing really well, but it's just not enough. And that's without paying rent.' I don't tell him that these are the worries that have been keeping me up at night since we got here. He could do without that kind of guilt trip.

We sit in silence for a while. Josh looks like a little wood sprite in the distance, jumping around the meadow waving a fallen branch above his head, his blond curls glinting in the sunlight. I think about going over to tell him to be careful the branch doesn't poke him in the eye. I'll head over there in a minute.

'So?' Aidan looks at me.

I'm not sure when I became the one with all the answers. 'There is one thing I thought of, but I don't think you're going to like it.' We stare at one another for a few moments.

'Not the lodger thing.' He gets to his feet and stretches his arms above his head before sitting back down. 'You already mentioned that and I think it's a really bad idea. We're trying to keep a low profile.'

'Okay.' I feel my temper rising, but I know it's just anxiousness over our financial situation. 'So what do *you* think we should do?'

'It's a pity we can't get broadband, because then we could try to get some kind of online job.'

I'm wary of us going back online because I don't quite trust my husband not to start gambling again. He says he's over it. But before we moved, I checked out some self-help sites which said that gambling addiction is really hard to kick. That it takes work and willpower and lots of help. And stress and money worries aren't exactly the best route to overcoming addiction; they can trigger it. 'We can't get online here, so do you have any other suggestions?'

He runs a hand over his head and starts picking at blades of grass. 'No.'

'I mean, I don't want a stranger coming into our home either, but what choice do we have? Think about the monthly rent we could charge. It would be amazing to have regular money coming in each month. To not have to worry. And then, maybe in a year or so we'll have built up the business and can be more self-sufficient. Then we can go back to living on our own again.'

Aidan nods slowly. I think he might be gradually coming around to the idea. 'You don't think it might put us in danger?'

'I don't see how. We could advertise locally. We're using different names anyway...'

'Let me think about it.'

I knew I should have mentioned my worries earlier. I'd been scared of rocking the boat, of making him anxious about money, of making him think about gambling again. But it's got to the stage where we can't put it off any longer. I'll give him a couple of days to come around to the idea or think of an alternative. But after that, I think I'll have to push for us to do it.

At least we haven't seen anything suspicious regarding the people who are after us. I'm even daring to hope they might forget about us altogether and realise we've gone for good. But eighty-three thousand pounds is possibly too much to let go without a fight. I'm not stupid. We're not safe yet. Not by a long way.

THIRTY-ONE

*So things have taken a backward step. But I'm not giving up. I
pride myself on seeing things through and I'm pretty confident
that something will come to light eventually. There's no time
limit on this thing. Well, not for me anyway. For them it's
another matter altogether.*

THIRTY-TWO

EMILY

As I pin our advert to the corkboard at the entrance to the local convenience store and post office, I'm struck once again by how much this place feels like it's in a time warp. Like I've gone back in time to the fifties or something. Not that that's a bad thing. It's just not at all what I'm used to.

The first time I came in here for the weekly shop, I'd thought I could simply duck in, load up my basket, pay and leave without engaging. But as soon as I approached the overly friendly grey-haired lady behind the counter, she launched into an animated conversation about how gorgeous Josh is and wasn't it hot out and she hadn't seen us before, were we visiting? I tried to think of something vague to say in response, but I was caught off guard and ended up telling her we'd just moved to the area. That precipitated a whole raft of new questions including asking us where we lived and where we'd moved from.

I couldn't think quickly enough and so told her we'd moved into Briar Hill Farm. Thankfully, she didn't press me on where we were from. Instead, she went on to give me the lowdown on the previous tenants, a family of five who'd lived there for a few years but had to move back up north as one of the grandparents had dementia, adding that she was sure the eldest girl had shoplifted from them on a couple of occasions.

She introduced herself as Sheila, the owner of the store. All this local gossip has made me more determined to keep Sheila at arm's length. So I've managed to always appear to be in a terrible hurry whenever I see her, to deter her from asking her questions. Unfortunately, her husband Bob is equally garrulous. They're like a gossip tag team. Although today I'm quite grateful for their nosiness as I'm hoping it will work to our advantage and she might put the word out that we're looking for a lodger. I finally managed to convince Aidan that it was the only way for us to stay afloat, but we've agreed to re-evaluate our situation in six months' time.

It's a shame we couldn't put an ad in the local paper, but we have no bank cards or bank account to pay for it. We're still working out how we might get fake identities so we can start living normally with our new names. Top of my list would be to get a bank account and register with a doctor, but we're not having any luck whatsoever with IDs. We don't know anyone in those kinds of circles and we can't even go online to search. And even if we could find someone, I'm sure the cost would be astronomical. Our baby's due in four weeks, so it's looking increasingly likely that I'll have to use my real name and risk exposing our whereabouts. We've decided that when I do go into labour, we'll go to a hospital over the county border and give our old names and address. I haven't had any check-ups at all since we left Ashley Cross, but I feel perfectly healthy, so I'm hoping that stays the same throughout this final month.

Sheila has started restocking the biscuits near to where I'm standing at the noticeboard.

'So you'll spread the word for us, Sheila, about wanting a lodger? It's a lovely room, freshly decorated and they'd have their own bathroom.'

'Of course I will, Annie. Only you'll want to warn them about that single-lane track. It can get pretty treacherous along there in the winter. You won't have experienced that for yourselves yet.'

'Well, yes, but it's probably better not to mention that straightaway. Let them come and see the place for themselves first.'

Sheila straightens up and gives me a stern look. 'I think it's better to warn them up front – that way you'll weed out timewasters.'

I glance away for a moment and roll my eyes. 'Okay, Sheila, whatever you think best.'

She nods and gets back to her biscuits. Maybe Sheila isn't the best person to spread the word after all. She might end up putting people off rather than encouraging them. Oh well, too late now.

'Emily?'

I turn towards the open door at the sound of my name while simultaneously realising that whoever it is out there has used the *wrong* name. My blood freezes in my veins. Sheila looks up, her eyes narrowing. Before she can say anything, I head outside into the bright sunshine, squinting at a couple of familiar faces. *Shit*, it's Sarah and Dom, our friends from Ringwood. I haven't seen them both since Aidan's disastrous party a few months ago and then Sarah came to my baby shower the week after. I hope Sheila didn't notice that Sarah called me Emily. I tell myself that it's okay, I can deny it.

'I thought it was you!' Sarah beams and we hug awkwardly. 'We've come out for a walk with my parents. Just stopped off to get some drinks and snacks.'

Dom kisses my cheek and I say hello to her young-looking parents. Her mum's hands are resting on the handle of an expensive-looking black-and-red pram.

'Is that...?'

'Yes!' Dom replies with a huge beaming grin. 'We had a little girl last month – Maisie.'

'Congratulations! Such a cute name,' I gush, all the while panicking on the inside. I tell myself it'll be fine. They don't live in Ashley Cross; they don't know any of our friends. 'Can I have a peek?' I walk over to the pram and glance down at the tiny sleeping baby swaddled in a pale-yellow blanket. 'She's absolutely adorable.'

'We're besotted,' Sarah's mum replies. 'You look like you're due soon.'

'Four weeks,' I reply.

'I thought you'd gone travelling around Europe?' Sarah frowns. 'Or maybe I got that wrong.'

Shit, how did she hear about that? I turn back to my friend. 'Yes, we're supposed to be in Italy right now, but I had to fly back as my aunt hasn't been very well. She's fine now though.'

'Oh, I'm sorry to hear that.' Sarah's eyes drop to my bump. 'But you'd have had to come back before now anyway, wouldn't you? I mean, you wouldn't be allowed to fly this near to your due date.'

What is this, a police interrogation? 'That's right. We've decided we're going to spend our last couple of weeks in East Anglia and the Fens.'

'Oh, lovely.'

I can tell she thinks I'm crazy, travelling around the country while I'm about to pop. God knows why I said East Anglia and the Fens – I think I remember learning about the area in a geography lesson at school. I just don't want her to think we live around here in case she lets it drop in conversation with the wrong person. 'How did you hear we were travelling?'

'Luanne told me.'

'Oh, right. I didn't realise you two were friends.'

'We weren't, not until you introduced us to her and Troy at Aidan's party. The four of us really clicked that night. And then of course there was the baby shower. We've actually met up a few times.'

'Lovely!' *Fuck*. Now she'll tell Lu that she's seen me here. 'Well, I'd better let you get on with your walk. It was so nice to see you. Tell Lu I'll call her when we get back from our travels.' My mouth hurts from the effort of smiling.

'Will do. And good luck with the birth if I don't see you before!' Sarah and Dom head into the shop while her parents wait outside with the baby. I give them a wave goodbye and somehow I manage to climb into the Isuzu and drive away without crashing. But my heart is going like a jackhammer and my hands are shaking.

Why didn't we move further away from Ashley Cross? I should have known we'd bump into someone we knew. You can't live in an area all your life, move thirty miles up the road and not expect to run into a familiar face. But Briar Hill Farm was our only option. It was either that or a tent. I hope Sheila doesn't say anything to Sarah. I can just imagine her saying something like, *Are you a friend of Annie?* And then Sarah will look at her blankly and Sheila will say, *You know, that lady you were talking to.* And then they'll realise I've changed my name and Sheila will start gossiping and Sarah will tell Luanne.

A car horn beeps from behind and I focus on my surroundings only to realise I've veered onto the wrong side of the road. I turn the wheel to straighten up and take a breath, raising a hand to thank the car behind for the warning. Thank goodness it wasn't a police car. That would have been a serious complication. I wonder if I should go back to the store and speak to Sheila, see if I can find out if she actually *has* spoken to Sarah, or if my imagination is going into overdrive unnecessarily. But I can't face going back in there right now. All I want to do is go home and try to calm down. If that's even possible.

THIRTY-THREE

DANI

Marcus is in an unusually good mood when he gets in from work, which is rare these days, but a very welcome change. We've been leading such separate lives these past few weeks that it's strange and unexpected when he comes into the lounge, sits next to me on the sofa, brushes my hair aside and kisses my neck.

'You smell really good, Dani.' He looks up at the TV screen. 'What you watching?'

'Just catching up on a drama that Vicky recommended.' I press pause on the remote and throw my arms around him, enjoying this rare closeness.

'Oh yeah? Any good?'

'It's okay. Are you hungry? Shall I make you something? I could fry you a steak if you like?'

'What have I done to deserve that? Sounds good, but I already ate – I had a pad thai at work earlier.' Marcus's fertility diet went out of the window weeks ago, but I haven't given him any grief about it. If the contents of that notebook are anything to go by, then I think he's under enough stress without me adding to it. I wish there were something I could do to help him, but then I'd have to admit that I went behind his back. Maybe I should just ask him outright. The question is on the tip of my tongue as Marcus leans into the sofa and stretches his arms above his head. 'How was your day, babe?'

I lose my nerve. 'Not bad. Went for a run, had lunch with Jay. How about you?' I feel as though I'm reading off a script, paranoid that Marcus can sense my anxiety. Everything I do or say these days is laced with a tight worry that I can't shake and I know I won't be able to relax until this thing is resolved one way or another.

'Yeah, I had a pretty good day actually. Made a couple of great contacts.' He sucks air in through his teeth and drums his legs with his fingers. 'Do you want to do something this evening? Go out for drinks? We haven't been out in ages.' His left leg is jiggling, a sure sign that he's restless.

'If you like. Where were you thinking?'

'I don't mind. You choose. I'm going up to have a shower and get changed.' He glances at his watch. 'Won't be long.' He leaves the room, whistling a tune. He really is in a very good mood. I wonder what that means. Could all this worry finally be over? Could we finally be free of his so-called colleagues? That would be amazing. I can hardly let myself hope that things might go back to normal. Back to when it was me and Marcus against the world in our exclusive little unit, without all his hangers-on and creepy new employees.

'Okay, Marc, I'll come up and get changed in a minute. Love you.'

'Love you, too, babe.'

Once Marcus has left the room, I switch off the TV. Sometimes I wish I'd never snooped around his office in the first place. They say that ignorance is bliss, but I don't really believe that. Whatever's going on, I need to know. Need to see if there's anything I can do to help. If he's got financial problems, then we need to work through them together. And if he's somehow in danger, then that surely involves me too.

If I told Marcus my concerns, he'd brush my worry aside, tell me not to be so daft, that *everything is fine, babe*. So I have to do this secretly, my way. I may be blonde and pretty and without a college education, but I'm not an idiot. I have a brain and I can use it just as well as my husband. Maybe better. I want him to take me seriously. So I'm going to discover what's going on and I'm going to fix it. Although, if his good mood is anything to go by, maybe he's fixed it on his own.

I'm about to get up from the sofa when my phone pings with a message. My stomach clenches when I see who it's from. *Talk of the devil.* I open up the text.

I've found everything you asked for.

My skin prickles and my heart begins to pound. I tap out a reply.

Sounds serious.

It is. Do you want to meet?

I tense up at his confirmation that it's not good news. My mind races, trying to think of a believable excuse to give Marcus for why I suddenly can't come out this evening. I text back:

Yes please. Shall I come over to yours?

Okay. 8ish?

Perfect.

Gripping my phone tightly, I take a breath before getting up off the sofa. I jog up the stairs and head into our dressing room to pick out something nice to wear. I hear the faint hiss of the shower from the en suite. Marcus always takes ages, so I should have a good few minutes to compose myself.

Shucking off my capri pants and cami top, I select a more form-fitting number for drinks with my husband. I slip on a minidress with a ruffled hem and pale-pink stiletto sandals. I re-apply my make-up, brush my hair and sit on the chaise, clutching my phone, waiting for Marcus to emerge from the bathroom, which he eventually does in a cloud of steam.

'Wow, you look good, Dan. Won't be a minute.' He starts to dry himself with an oversized dark-grey towel.

'Mum just called. She needs my help with her pension forms. She's in a state about it.'

Marcus throws me a glance and rolls his eyes. 'She only ever contacts you when she needs something.'

'I know, but I'm going to have to go over there. Apparently the forms have to be in by tomorrow. She's panicking.' This isn't a total lie, my mum did ask for my help with the forms, we just haven't arranged a time and date yet.

'Why hasn't she asked Jay to help her like she always does?'

I hate lying like this, but I have to do it. There's no way I'll be able to relax until I discover what it is that Rob has found. 'Jay's on a shift this evening, so Mum's got to make do with me.'

'Want me to come with you?' Marcus sits at the dressing table and starts blow-drying his hair.

I raise my voice to be heard over the dryer. 'No, that's okay. I'll do it – no point in both of us having a boring evening. Why don't you go for a drink and I'll meet you there – as long as Mum doesn't keep me too long.'

'I suppose so. Why the hell did she leave it until the last minute? Honestly. And you'd think she could have at least called you earlier in the day, rather than seven thirty in the evening. I sometimes think she does these things on purpose to wind you up.'

'Yeah, well, that's my mother for you. Never straightforward.' I silently ask her to forgive me for badmouthing her. 'Anyway, the quicker I go, the quicker I can get out of there and meet up with you.'

'Okay, how about we meet at the Silver Sail? Steve and Ted will probably be down there, so I can have a few beers with them until you get there.'

'Sounds good.'

Marcus turns off the hairdryer and works some product through his hair. He catches my eye in the mirror. 'You really do look beautiful tonight, Dan.'

'Thanks, you're not bad yourself.' I wink.

'Still got it.' He does that annoying thing where he tenses his pecs so they move up and down.

I laugh and once again wish I didn't have to lie. But at least I can justify it because I'm doing it for us. For our family. Marcus will thank me in the end.

THIRTY-FOUR

EMILY

Josh yawns and takes a bite of his sandwich, his eyes growing heavier with every chew.

'I think you can have a nap after lunch.' I pour us each a glass of water. Aidan's still out working in the forest and said to eat lunch without him, but I spy him out of the kitchen window heading back.

'I'm not tired,' Josh insists, letting out another massive yawn that makes us both laugh. He follows this up with a scowl. 'I'm not tired.'

'I'll read you a story, okay?'

'The one about the unicorn?'

'Yes. And then this afternoon, you can help me and Daddy move the things out of our bedroom.'

'Because the new person's coming?'

'That's right. They're moving in next week.'

Who knew that rooms for rent would be so in demand in such a remote area? We had five phone calls in the first few days of the advert going up. One guy was really young and sounded like he might be a bit of a party animal, so we discounted him. Another call was from a couple, but we thought that it would be too much of a squeeze to have two extra people in the house. But the other three all sounded promising on the phone, so we invited them to come and view the room, which also gave us the chance to see if we thought they'd be suitable. We have to get along with whoever we choose, as we're going to be opening up our house to them.

'Why are they sleeping in your bedroom?' Josh asks. 'Because that's not fair.'

I smile. 'It's fine. Our old bedroom has its own bathroom, so they'll use that one and then you, me and Daddy will share the big bathroom.'

'Oh, okay.'

All three interviews were interesting in their own way. The first one was a woman in her forties. She saw that I was pregnant and made no attempt to disguise her feelings. Before setting foot inside, she looked from my bump to Josh and said, 'No offence, but I can't be doing with a young child and a screaming baby. I need peace and quiet.' Neither Aidan nor I attempted to change her mind. As she was leaving, she gave us a rueful look and told us she was quite disappointed. She said she'd liked the sound of the place from the advert as she wanted somewhere quiet in the countryside where she could have some peace and tranquillity. As though we'd somehow misled her by not stating the ages of our children in the advert.

The second visit was a man in his late twenties who didn't say an awful lot. When asked, he told us he was a mechanic at a local garage. He, at least, came upstairs and had a glance around the room. He nodded and said he had a couple of other places to view. I got the feeling our place was a bit remote and quiet for him.

We ended up being third time lucky, offering the room to a woman called Lindsey Jones, who's in her thirties and has just gone through a divorce. She works at a gift shop in Blandford and doesn't have enough money for a month's deposit, but said she could give us a week's deposit if that would be okay. She said she could drop it round in a couple of days. She seemed so nice that Aidan and I agreed even though we could really have done with that month's deposit up front.

'Hey, you two.' Aidan comes in through the back door, bringing the scent of pine, earth and sunscreen with him. He leans down to kiss us both before washing his hands at the worn butler sink. He sits with us, eating a doorstop sandwich that he can barely get his jaws around. Josh and I have already finished our lunch, so I beckon our son onto my lap where I stroke his hair until his eyes close and he's leaning into me, fast asleep.

'I'll take him up to his room,' I whisper. 'He could do with a half-hour nap.'

Aidan nods. 'Want some tea?'

'Please.' I carry our son upstairs and lay him on his bed. We've been up since six working in the garden, so it's no wonder he's tired out. I walk over to the window to close the shutters, but my eye is caught by movement in the distance. A car. It's coming down the driveway. I'm frozen at the window, watching the vehicle's steady progress, sunlight glinting off its blue metal roof. I don't recall the make of Lindsey's car, but it was silver, not blue. So who is this? I need to tell Aidan.

I close Josh's shutters and then close his bedroom door before hurrying downstairs into the kitchen.

'David, there's someone here. Someone in a blue car coming up the driveway.'

My husband's eyes widen. He drops the rest of his sandwich back onto the plate and gets to his feet. He follows me into the dining room where we peek through the wooden slats just in time to see the car pull up outside the house. We immediately step back away from the window into the gloom.

'Who do you think it is?' I hiss.

'No idea.' Aidan's face is pale.

We watch as a man gets out of the car, a navy Ford Mondeo

Estate. He looks our age, or maybe a little younger, fair-haired with a stocky build. He looks up at the house and closes the car door. There's no one else with him.

'I don't recognise him. Do you?'

Aidan shakes his head.

'What should we do?'

He rubs his forehead. 'It's probably fine. It could be anyone. A neighbour, someone trying to sell something...'

Although expected, the doorbell makes both of us jump. We stare at one another wide-eyed. 'I hope that didn't wake Josh.'

'That's the least of our worries,' Aidan replies.

'I'll answer it,' I say decisively. 'Best thing is for us to act normally. We're David and Annie Mortimer, we live here, it's fine.' But even as I say those words I wonder if we really are fine.

I decided not to tell Aidan about bumping into Sarah and Dom at the post office last week, as I didn't want him to worry or overreact. The last thing we need is to uproot and move again. I don't think I could face it. And, besides, where else would we go? But the truth is, I know Sarah will tell Luanne about seeing me here and I worry that the news will start flying around our friendship circle. Once it gets out, everyone will start speculating and it could get back to the people who are after us. Aside from that, there's someone else who I'd rather didn't know where I am.

I realise that I need to take that advert down from the noticeboard at the post office. If anyone starts snooping around the area, they might see it. I need to calm down. My imagination is running away from me just because of a random visitor at our door.

'Don't answer it,' Aidan says, clutching at my arm.

I dither for a moment before shaking him off. 'It's just one person and they didn't look exactly threatening.'

The doorbell chimes again.

'I'll go,' he offers.

'No. They'll know your face. I look different to how I used to. My hair's curlier. I'm more tanned and freckly now. Plus I'm about to pop.' I point at my belly. 'He's not going to do anything to a pregnant woman.'

'No.' Aidan snaps. 'I'm going.'

'Let's go together.'

He nods. Aidan marches out into the hallway first and pulls open the door. I stand in the shadows behind him. 'Hello,' he barks a little too aggressively.

'Uh...' The man reddens. 'Oh, sorry, I uh... I was sent over here by Sheila and Bob from the post office. They said you had a room to rent.' He has a soft Dorset accent and the poor guy looks like he wants to run away.

Aidan clears his throat. 'I'm sorry, but we've already let the room.'

His face falls and I feel bad for him. 'It's just that I'm not having much luck finding anywhere and your house looks amazing. I'm just about to start a new job as a chef at the Cross Keys – do you know it? It's a great little hotel. But I don't want to live on site because it's nice to have separation from the job. Are you sure you haven't got another spare room? Looks like quite a big place.' He grins endearingly.

'Sorry, we offered the room to someone else yesterday and it's not as big as it looks from the outside.'

'So have they moved in yet?' he pushes.

'No, but—'

'Have they paid their deposit?'

'Look, I'm sorry you've had a wasted journey.' Aidan makes to close the door, but the man makes a last attempt to win us over.

'Look, if I like the room, I can pay you a month's deposit plus two months' rent up front, if that makes a difference? No worries if not.' His shoulders sag and he looks like he's about to leave.

I tap Aidan on the shoulder and he turns to me. I give him a pointed stare that conveys how much we could do with that amount of money.

'I also have really good references from my last place in Bridport,' he adds.

'Just wait there a minute.' Aidan closes the door and heads back into the dining room. I follow him and wait while he taps his lips with his fingers.

'Well?' I prompt.

'You want to give him the room, don't you?' Aidan shakes his head. 'What about Lindsey?'

'Lindsey's lovely, but the reason we're letting the room is because we have no money. Lindsey can only give us one week's deposit and I get the feeling she's not going to be too reliable with the rent.'

'Yeah, but who is this guy?'

'He said Sheila and Bob sent him over, so he must have seen our advert, or maybe they know him.'

'Hmm.'

I rub my belly and try to think about what to do for the best. 'Let's just show him the room and take his details. We can check his references and make a decision later. If he's dodgy, then his references won't check out and that will be that.'

We return to the hall and Aidan opens the front door once again. The man is standing a little way away with his back to us, his hands in his jeans' pockets. He turns at the sound of the door opening. 'Gorgeous spot you got here.'

Aidan nods. 'Thanks. I guess you can come and see the room if you'd like.'

'Brilliant.' His face lights up and he suddenly looks a lot younger than I initially thought. He walks back over, steps inside and gives me a shy smile. 'When are you due?'

'Three weeks.'

'Blimey.'

'I know.'

'You'll have to keep your voice down,' Aidan says. 'Our son's having a lunchtime nap upstairs.'

'No worries. Engaging stealth mode.'

Aidan gives a begrudging laugh. 'I'm David Mortimer, by the way, and this is my wife, Annie.'

'Nice to meet you both. I'm Jonathan Dean.'

THIRTY-FIVE

EMILY

It was a no-brainer to let the room to Jonathan rather than Lindsey, especially as his references turned out to be glowing. I felt terrible calling her up to give her the bad news, but she said she understood. Which made me feel even worse. But there was no way Aidan and I could turn down three months' rent up front. Cash like that will really take the pressure off and will also mean we can put some money aside for emergencies and unforeseen expenses.

'You haven't got much stuff,' Aidan says, bringing a holdall and small case into the hall. He's helping Jonathan bring his gear in from the car as it's now started to rain quite heavily. I'm actually pleased the weather's turned. It's been quite a dry summer so far and the garden could do with a proper soaking. I smile to myself at how much I've changed. Rain used to be an inconvenience – something that would spoil social engagements or ruin my straightened hair. Now it's a blessed relief that gives me an evening off from watering the garden.

Jonathan follows my husband into the hallway. He's carrying a large plastic box with a lid. 'Do you mind if I put this in the kitchen somewhere? It's got my personal cooking equipment – a few pans, knives and cookbooks. I don't want to take them to work in case they go walkabout.'

'Yes, sure, follow me.' I point out a couple of empty cupboards that we've cleared for his food. 'You're welcome to use these, but let me know if you need any more space.'

'That looks perfect. Thanks. I'll just stick my equipment up here for now.' He hoists the box up and slides it onto the top of the cupboard.

'So is that it?' Aidan asks. 'Just your cooking stuff and a couple of cases?'

'Yep. That's the lot. After I split from my wife, I let her keep everything apart from my clothes and a few sentimental photos. She and the kids need that stuff more than me.'

'You're separated?' I ask.

'Divorced now, but it's all amicable. I miss my little ones though.'

'How old are they?' I can't imagine how hard that must be, to be separated from your kids.

'Maya's four and Zac's seven.'

'Do you see much of them?' Aidan sets the cases down on the flagstones.

'I get to have them every fortnight. But I won't bring them here. I'll go back to Bridport a couple of times a month and have them to stay at my parents' house.'

'Is that where you're from, Bridport?' I ask.

'Born and bred.'

'How come you've moved up this way?'

'I got a job as head chef. Too good an opportunity to turn down.'

'I'll take these up for you.' Aidan lifts the cases again.

'No, that's fine. I'll take them and make a start on my unpacking. Don't suppose you've got an iron, have you?'

I show him where we keep the iron and ironing board and he says he'll do it in his room and bring them back down afterwards. I ask if he wants to eat with us this evening, but he says he's got a shift at the restaurant, so he'll be going out at five and won't be back until late. Aidan gives him keys to the front and back doors and he disappears upstairs to his room.

'It's weird, isn't it?' Aidan sits at the kitchen table. 'Having someone else in the house.'

'I know, but he seems really nice. I'm sure we'll get used to it and, if we don't, we'll ask him to leave. Anyway, think of the financial security we'll have for the next few months.'

'You're right.' But my husband doesn't look too happy.

I feel equally unsettled, especially as this was all my idea. But I can't let Aidan see that I'm worried too. 'How about a slap-up meal tonight to celebrate not being skint? Anything you fancy?'

Aidan and I spend the next ten minutes writing out a dream shopping list of all the extravagant food we've been missing over the past weeks. Of course, we know we won't be able to splash out like this all the time, but it's exciting to treat ourselves like this as a one-off. I wish I could go to a proper supermarket, but Aidan and I agreed that we'd stay local and stick to the closest store for our supplies. The further afield we go, the more chance there is of being spotted by someone we know. I try not to think about my encounter with Dom and Sarah.

Once we've finished the list, I get to my feet. 'I'll take Josh with me to the store.'

'Okay, drive carefully. It's pouring out there.'

Josh has spent most of the day watching DVDs, a rare occurrence due to the bad weather, but I manage to pry him away from the TV with the promise of sweets. With my phone and shopping list in my bag, we set out in the truck along the bumpy track to the store.

We take our time with the shopping. Sheila and Bob have taken the day off and their part-timer, Colleen, is working today. She's friendly but not overly chatty, which suits me fine as I'm able to concentrate on the job in hand. Josh and I cruise the aisles, not really sticking to the list at all, but selecting what we fancy. My son is swept up in my excitement and is taking full advantage of my good mood by selecting various cakes and packets of biscuits I would never normally allow him to buy. As the trolley fills, I get an attack of the guilts and end up putting a lot of it back on the shelves, but it's still enjoyable not to be counting the pennies so strictly.

Finally we're done and I load the groceries into the three bags I brought with me, pay Colleen and take the bags out to the truck where I secure them under the tarp. I wonder if Aidan and Jonathan have had another chance to chat, or if our new lodger has stayed in his room. I'm sure, with time, we'll get used to him being around. Hopefully, he'll become a good friend. Being a chef, he may even bring home a few leftovers from the hotel, or cook for us – wouldn't that be a treat – although it might be too much of a busman's holiday. In any case, it will be great if this whole lodger situation works out.

I drive home well below the speed limit; the roads are slick and visibility is poor with the rain still lashing the windscreen. I'm already pretty wet from loading up the truck and I'm looking forward to getting into dry clothes and unpacking the shopping.

Despite the dark, bloated clouds, the hammering rain and this god-awful rattling truck, today is the first day I feel anything approaching happiness. I make the sharp turn down the lane that leads to our cottage and think contentedly of the three loaded shopping bags in the back under the tarp.

'Mummy, is the new man going to help make dinner?' Josh is strapped into his car seat next to me, kicking rhythmically at the glove box. I've given up asking him to 'please stop doing that' and, anyway, I can barely hear his kicks above the sound of the rain.

'No, George. Daddy and I are going to cook tonight.'

'Can I help make the dinner?'

I glance across at my little brown-eyed son, at his straw-coloured curls darkened by the rain. 'Yes please. That would be lovely. You can set the table if you like.'

The cottage comes into view at the end of the lane. Today, it's just a dark, drizzly shape with a few smudged outbuildings next to it. A cluster of leafy trees overhang the barn and garage, dripping and swaying in the late-summer storm.

'But, Mummy, I don't want to set the table. I want to do the cooking.'

My attention is taken by the sight of the grey cottage door swinging open. My first thought is that it's Aidan coming out to help unload the groceries. But then the door slams violently shut.

'Mummy, I want to do the cooking, not set the table!' My son tugs at my arm.

'Yes, yes, okay, Georgie. Course you can help Mummy with the cooking.'

'And Daddy can cook too.'

'Yes and Daddy.' But I'm not really listening any more. I pull up on the drive, as close as I can get to the path. The front door has swung open again but there's no one standing in the doorway. I realise the door has been left open and is banging in the wind. If it keeps swinging and banging like that, it's going to come off its hinges and that would be a hassle and expense we can do without.

Did I leave it open? No. I wouldn't have been so careless. Maybe it was the lodger. His car isn't out front. He must have left for work already. I'll have to remember to tell him that the front door needs a firm push in order to close it properly. If I can hear it banging from here inside the truck, then surely Aidan must be able to hear it from inside the house? Why hasn't he come along to close it?

The windows of the cottage are dark, streaked with rainwater. I shiver and suddenly get a bad feeling. 'George, can you stay here for a minute while Mummy goes to check something?' I tuck my damp brown curls behind my ears and take a breath.

'I need a wee.' He's wriggling in his seat.

I give a sigh and tell myself that I'm worrying over nothing. Aidan has no doubt gone out the back to check on the chickens, or maybe he's in the garage. Thinking about it, he's probably the one who left the front door open. 'Okay then, Georgie, come on. Let's go in. We're going to get very wet again. We'll have to run!'

I unclip my son from his car seat and we sprint for the house. I leave the shopping in the truck. I'll come back for it once the rain eases – or maybe Aidan will get it for me. George dashes to the loo as I stand in the hall and call out to my husband.

There's no reply.

Although it's only five thirty, the cottage is dark and shadowy. I switch on the hall light, but nothing happens. I switch it off and on again before accepting that the bulb has gone. I don't think we have any spares. So annoying that this has happened after my shopping trip – I could have bought a replacement if I'd known.

'David!' I call out again, remembering to use his new name just in case Jonathan's around. There's no sound or light coming from any of the downstairs rooms. My vision blurs. I blink the rain away from my lashes.

My son reappears from the cloakroom.

'Did you wash your hands?'

He nods and holds them out for me to inspect.

'Good boy. Let's go upstairs and get out of these wet things.' I click on the landing light. Again, nothing happens. Must be a fuse. Or maybe the storm has knocked out a power line.

'It's dark, Mummy.'

'I know. We'll have to be careful on the stairs. Hold my hand.'

We walk up together and go into his bedroom where the light doesn't work either. In the gloom, I help him change into dry clothes and I towel-dry his hair. He finally shrugs me off and digs his Batman torch out of his toybox. He starts flashing the bat signal onto his walls.

'Are you going to stay and play here for a minute while I get changed?'

He looks up at me. 'And then we'll do the cooking?'

'Yes, definitely.' I give him a wink. 'Stay in your room, I don't want you tripping down the stairs in the dark.'

'Okay, Mummy.'

I leave his room, closing the door firmly behind me. I push at the door to our bedroom, pressing the light switch out of habit, irritated when the darkness remains. The door won't open properly for some reason. There's something in the way. Maybe my dressing gown has fallen off the hook again and got caught under the door. But as I push once more, the door thuds against something. Something that feels large and heavy, like a piece of furniture.

I realise my heart has started to pound quite loudly and uncomfortably. I'm not sure why. There's a prickling sensation down my back as though someone is watching me. Sweat gathers at my armpits. I swallow and freeze before plucking up the courage to turn around. But the small landing is empty. I'm being silly.

I take a breath and squeeze myself through the gap in my bedroom door. Luckily, it's just about wide enough. I peer down at the dark shape that was blocking the door, but I can't quite make sense of it.

And then, all of a sudden, I can.

I scream his name and then I clamp my mouth shut. I don't want Josh coming in and seeing... this. I can barely look myself. Am I here? Is this real? This can't be happening.

My husband is lying face-up on the bedroom carpet. His

eyes are open, but he's not looking at me. He's staring up at the ceiling. But I don't think he can see the ceiling. I don't think he can see anything. Because there's an obscene dark line across his throat. His throat has been cut.

I think Aidan's dead.

THIRTY-SIX

EMILY

I sink down to my knees and pick up my husband's hand, press it to my face and kiss it over and over, willing the life to come back into it. It's still warm. Maybe I'm mistaken and he's still alive.

'Aidan? Aidan, can you hear me?' My voice is high and wavery, my ears feel like they're blocked. I say his name again even though I know it's hopeless. I look at my husband's face. His eyes are glassy and still, his mouth slack. I can't bring myself to look at his neck again, but I can smell a sweet metallic tang that catches in my throat and makes me gag.

No, no, no. This can't be real. How can this be real? Who did this? Oh my God, our new lodger. No. He's from Bridport, he's a chef. He's got two children. He would never... But then I realise it must all have been lies. All a big elaborate hoax to get into the house. It's too much of a coincidence. And his car isn't outside any more, so he must have gone already. I carefully lay Aidan's hand back down on the ground.

I knew we were in danger, but I never really believed it would come to this – finding Aidan's body on the floor. This isn't happening. This is not real. I'm in a nightmare and I'm going to wake up any second back in Ashley Cross. My alarm will go off and I'll open my eyes and be grumpy that I have to go to work today. I'll tell Aidan that I had the most horrific, outlandish dream, that he'll never believe what happened.

I blink as sharp tears sting my eyes. My whole body is trembling. Shivering violently. I place my hands on my bump, trying not to think about the fact that my child will never call Aidan *Daddy*.

I pull my phone from my bag, but there's no signal. There's never any bloody signal in this place! I stagger to my feet and wave the phone around, but whichever angle I hold the phone, there are still no bars. Why didn't we get a landline? I'm sure we could have afforded one. I could have found a cheap deal somewhere. I have to call the police. They'll be able to catch Jonathan or whatever his real name is. He drove a blue something or other. I can't remember what make it was. What *was* it?

Josh! I have to get my son. We need to get out of here. Drive to the police station. I don't want to leave my husband alone, but I have to get Josh to safety. I squeeze back through the bedroom door, swallowing down nausea and trying not to spiral into full-blown panic for the baby's sake and also for Josh. I can't let him see that anything's wrong. I don't want to scare him.

This is all my fault. If I hadn't insisted on a lodger... But how did they even find us? *Sarah*. It must have been her telling Luanne and then everybody found out and I'm so, so stupid. We should have left here the minute I knew our location had been compromised. But I thought it would be okay. *I* did this. This is my fault. How can Aidan be gone? It's just not right. It's *monstrous*.

Why did they kill him? Why didn't they at least try to get the money from us? If they'd just waited and spoken to me, I could have called Bianca. She offered and I turned her down! If I'd only said yes a few months ago, she could have possibly freed up the money by now. I must have been mad. Why did I put my pride ahead of the safety of my family? I should have taken the money and then we could have contacted the loan sharks and offered to pay them. We could have returned back home and continued with our lives. I could have got Aidan some help for his gambling. It would have been fine. What was I *thinking*?

I know exactly what I was thinking. I'd wanted to get away from town and here was my chance. Aidan owing all that money gave me the perfect opportunity to run away from my own mess. And now it's all messed up anyway. I've lost it all.

I stand in the shadowy hallway outside Josh's bedroom for a brief moment as the rain lashes the window and thunder rumbles across the fields. I don't have time to delay, but I can't let my son see me this upset. I wipe my eyes with my fingertips, take a shuddering breath and go into his room.

'Hey, Joshy. You've got to come with Mummy now. We're going out, okay?'

'Mummy! My name's George. Joshy was the old name, that's not a good one any more. George is the best one.' He's repeating back all the things we told him about his new name and it's breaking my heart.

'Okay, darling.' I pull him in close to me for a hug so he can't see the fresh tears that are falling down my cheeks and into my mouth, onto my neck.

'Oh, you're all wet, Mummy.' He pushes me away. 'You have to get into nice dry clothes like me.'

I realise my clothes and hair are still soaked from the rain. 'I'll get changed later, but right now we need to go back outside for a little drive.'

'With Daddy?'

An image of Aidan lying on the floor flashes into my mind. I swallow, but it feels like there are knives in my throat. 'Not Daddy. Just you, me and baby bump, okay?'

I take Josh's hand and we turn to leave. But before I make a move, I hear a creak from the room next door. *Jonathan's room.*

THIRTY-SEVEN

It's all going perfectly to plan. I enjoyed it all. Being welcomed into their home and given the guided tour, like they were doing me some huge fucking favour. They lapped up my story about the ex-wife and kids and I laid it on thick with their whiny son, so now they all think I'm Mr Children's Entertainer of the Year. They're convinced we'll all be really good friends now because I'll be so pathetically grateful for their shitty little bedroom with its creepy wooden furniture, out here in the middle of nowhere. Yeah, like that's what was ever going to happen.

THIRTY-EIGHT

EMILY

I stare at my son and put my finger to my lips. He copies my gesture, his eyes wide. Blessedly he doesn't appear to be scared. I'm hoping he thinks this is just some kind of silly game we're playing.

I take Josh's hand once more and we tiptoe over to his door. This is crazy. If Jonathan really is in the room next door, he must know we're up here too. And if that's the case, then there's no way he's going to let us leave the house. How will we get out? What's to stop him doing the same thing to us that he did to Aidan? Would he kill a pregnant woman and her child? Would he?

Please let him leave the house now and let that be an end to it. Maybe he's just gathering his belongings together and then he'll go. Maybe he's not even interested in me and Josh.

I wonder if instead of leaving and drawing attention to ourselves, we should hide? Curl up into a ball and wait for him to go? But there's nowhere to conceal ourselves in Josh's room apart from obvious places like under the bed or in the wardrobe. Places Jonathan will discover instantly if he decides to come looking. And, besides, I doubt I'll fit in either.

Perhaps I should make the first move. Call out to him and tell him I'll get him the money if he spares us. Surely he won't want to turn down that amount of cash. That is, if he even believes I can get it for him. I guess there's only one way to find out. I push the door slightly ajar and open my mouth. But nothing comes out. *I can't do it.* I can't call attention to us. The thought of confronting the man who did that to my husband sets me off shaking again.

'Are we going out?' Josh whispers.

I push my finger to my lips once more and nod. If I weren't so hugely pregnant, I'd carry my son down the stairs, but I'm unsteady enough on my feet as it is, without adding more weight. Especially on such steep stairs. We creep out onto the landing, my heart rising up my gullet, my pregnant belly suddenly heavy and clenching. I hope that wasn't a contraction. I pause and breathe, gesturing to Josh to tiptoe down the stairs and mouthing at him to go *carefully* and *quietly*. He nods and goes down with exaggerated care.

With the storm still raging outside, it's dark and shadowy on the stairs. I pray Josh doesn't lose his footing. I pray he gets to the bottom okay. Once my belly has stopped clenching, I follow behind, holding carefully onto the banisters. I daren't risk looking over my shoulder for fear of losing my footing, but I already imagine I can hear Jonathan's footsteps coming down behind me. The urge to let out a scream is so powerful I bite the inside of my cheek to keep myself silent.

Somehow, Josh and I both make it to the bottom in one piece. Josh turns and gives me an excited thumbs-up. His little face is so adorable that I can't wait to tell Aidan how brave and good our son is being. Until I remember that I'll never be able to tell Aidan anything ever again. I choke back a terrified, grief-stricken sob.

As I grab our still-wet coats from the banister, I realise Josh isn't wearing any shoes. I curse and get him to slip on his wet shoes from earlier. I can't bend down to help him, but he manages quite well himself, even though it feels like he's taking an age. My heart is pounding so loudly that I can barely hear myself think. Meanwhile, I fumble in my bag for the car keys and chance a quick glance up the stairs. No one there. The landing above is dark and silent. Maybe that creak I heard earlier was nothing. Perhaps Jonathan is long gone and I've scared myself over nothing. After all, his car isn't outside. And why would he stick around now he's had his revenge? The answer comes unbidden: *To clear up loose ends.*

Whether our lodger is here or not, Josh and I aren't hanging around to find out. We dash outside through the wind and rain to the truck. Our fun shopping trip earlier seems like it happened months ago. The bags of groceries are still sitting under the tarp like something from another lifetime.

I open the passenger side first and help Josh climb in. I'll buckle him into his car seat once I've got in on my side. 'Mind your fingers,' I warn, placing his hands in his lap. We're almost home free. Once we're both inside the truck with the doors locked, I'll finally be able to breathe again.

I close the passenger door and the breath leaves my body as my stomach clenches once again. There's no mistaking it. That was a contraction. Please let it be a Braxton Hicks contraction, a false labour pain. This baby is not due yet. I can't go into labour. Not now. *Please stay where you are, little one.* I exhale in short puffs, my hands on my belly, willing him or her to be patient.

Once the contraction subsides, I waddle around to the driver's side and yank open the door. But how will I be able to drive if another one of those pains hits me again? Right now, I don't have a choice. I need to get Josh and myself to safety.

The wind tugs the car door from my hand and blows it shut again. 'Shit.' As I reach for the handle once more, something cold touches the side of my head. I reach up to brush it off

before my brain clicks in and I realise what it is. My skin turns
to ice and I cry out in shock.

'Sorry, Emily. Can't let you leave just yet.'

It's Jonathan. And he has a gun pressed into my temple.

THIRTY-NINE

EMILY

Jonathan is holding a gun. *A gun.* But even more chilling is the fact that he's used my old name, confirming my fear that he must work for the loan shark. He fooled us so thoroughly with his nice-guy act.

I turn my head slowly to look at him. His mouth is curved into a smile, but his eyes are hard and glittering. It's not the open, friendly face from earlier. This is the face of someone very different.

'I had to go to the barn to make a phone call. Signal's better out there. But you already know that, right?'

I didn't know that. But right now, I have more pressing matters on my mind.

'I disabled your truck while you were in the house, so there's no point trying to make a break for it. You need to come back in the house with me.'

'Please don't scare my son. He's only four.'

Jonathan shrugs. 'You should have thought about that before you did a runner.' I open my mouth to protest, but he cuts me off. 'Of course I'm not going to scare little Josh. What kind of person do you think I am?' He grins at this and I shudder. Jonathan twitches the gun in the direction of the house. 'Come on, I'm getting soaked out here.'

I walk back to the passenger side and open the door.

'You're the new man,' Josh says. 'Is that a real gun?'

'No, of course not,' I answer. 'It's part of the game we were playing. I need you to be a good boy and come with me back into the house.' I'm trying and failing to keep my voice steady. I'm terrified that as soon as he gets us back into the house, Jonathan will put a bullet in each of our heads or, even worse, use a knife like he did with Aidan. My body starts shaking again.

Josh looks from me to Jonathan and decides to get out of the truck without a fuss. He slides out onto the ground. I take his hand and we all walk back over to the house. It takes me an age to unlock the front door as my hands are shaking so badly, but eventually the three of us enter the dark hall. My mind travels up the stairs into our bedroom where my husband lies. All alone. This can't have happened! Aidan can't be dead. It's just not possible. Why didn't I spot his gambling addiction earlier? If I'd known about it, I could have got him help. We could have avoided all this. Am I about to die too? *Is this it?* I place a hand over my bump, wanting to scream with helplessness. Surely there's something I can do to get us out of this nightmarish situation.

Jonathan directs us toward the front lounge and makes us take a seat on one of the sofas. The huge window lets in a damp light, but it's still pretty gloomy in here. Josh and I are dripping wet and shivering. 'Take off your coat, Joshy.'

Josh stands and does as I ask. 'I'm *George*.' He frowns as he hands me the coat. 'Joshy's a baby name.'

I drape his coat over the arm of the sofa. 'Sorry, you're right. It's George.' Poor boy. He's had so many changes to get used to.

I can't expect him to flip back to his real name again just like that.

'Are you going to do some cooking now?' Josh asks our captor without any fear.

'No,' Jonathan replies. He's staring out of the rain-soaked window and I wonder if he's waiting for someone else to arrive. The question is, who? The only ray of hope is that he hasn't harmed Josh or me yet. Surely if that were the plan, he would have done it already. There's no reason for him to have delayed. In fact, Jonathan is barely paying either of us any attention. Even so, he still holds the gun down by his side and I'm not sure whether or not he'll use it if we attempt to run.

'Mummy said you aren't cooking with me and Daddy tonight because you're going to work. Are you going in a minute?'

Jonathan doesn't answer. My son is looking up at him questioningly, but this stranger doesn't even glance his way. Why on earth did I think I could trust him? Why did I think it was safe to invite him into our home?

Josh's chin starts to quiver. 'Mummy, I'm hungry. It's too dark and I'm too cold. Can I have my sweets from the shop now?'

'Shh, be quiet, darling. Just be quiet for a minute.'

'No! I'm hungry!' Fat tears start to roll down his cheeks.

Jonathan's face darkens and he huffs out an irritated breath.

My body tenses with anxiety. I take my son's hand and kiss his wet cheek. 'Okay, if you sit nice and quietly, I'll get you something to eat in a minute, okay?'

Josh nods and hiccups.

I open my mouth to ask Jonathan for permission to get something from the kitchen for Josh, but he cuts me off.

'No. You're not going anywhere. I need you both to sit still and shut up.'

'Mummy, he told you to shut up!' Josh's mouth has fallen open.

My stress levels are rocketing and I'm also panicking that I'm about to have another contraction. I glare at our captor. 'I don't know how much you know about four-year-old children, but they don't follow the same rules as you and me. Unless you let me get him a snack and settle him down with some toys to keep him occupied, *this*' – I gesture wildly at my son's impending meltdown – 'is only going to get worse.'

'Oh, for Christ's sake,' Jonathan mutters under his breath. 'Fine.' He aims the gun at my head and directs us out of the room towards the kitchen. 'Get him something to eat and then you can leave him in there.'

I'm about to protest at leaving my son alone in the kitchen, but actually it might be better for him if he's away from this dangerous man, especially if someone else is about to show up at the house. I don't want Josh listening to any angry conversations or witnessing any violence. I couldn't bear to have him traumatised in any way – that is, if he isn't already.

Under the watchful eye of this man, I make my son a peanut-butter sandwich and find a packet of iced gems in the back of the cupboard that I was saving as a treat. I dig out some play dough, paper and coloured pens from a drawer and angle a large torch on the table so he can see a little better.

'Okay, let's go.' Jonathan inclines his head towards the door.

'One minute.' I give him a pleading look and he nods. As Josh starts to eat his sandwich, I crouch down next to him. 'Now, listen to me, Joshy, uh, George. You've got lots of lovely food and some nice things to play with. I need you to stay in the kitchen now, okay? Don't come out until I come back. If you can stay in the kitchen for a long, long time, then I'll get you the biggest surprise present you've ever seen, okay?'

My son's eyes widen at the thought of whatever wonderful thing he's imagining. 'A big present?'

I nod. 'But only if you stay in the kitchen. You can't even open the door, or we won't be able to get the present. Do you understand?'

He nods. 'I can stay. I can stay here and make animals with the play dough.'

'Good boy. And I'll be just next door in the lounge, okay? And then I'll come and get you.' I wrap him in my arms and kiss both his cheeks, followed by a kiss on his forehead and finally one on his wet curls. A tear drips down my face. I quickly swipe it away and stand up. I nod at Jonathan, letting him know I'm ready to go. I wish I had the strength and courage to snatch the gun from his hand. But I know I would never dare. I suck in one last greedy stare at my son before we leave the kitchen and head back to the living room.

Jonathan points to the sofa. I sit, my mind still with my son in the next room. It feels as though he's a million miles away rather than on the other side of the wall. After a few panicked moments, I realise that there's an upside to Josh not being here with me – now that he's out of earshot, I feel like I can finally ask some questions of my own.

I try to make my voice soft and friendly. 'Are you waiting for someone to show up?'

Jonathan doesn't reply. He's back to staring out the window again. It looks as though the storm is easing out there, the wind and rain less violent.

'Are you planning to hurt us?'

Still no reply, but his mouth tightens. I don't want to antagonise him, but I can't just sit here in silence. At least if I knew what he wanted from me, I could work out how much danger Josh and I are in.

'Look, the least you can do is tell me if you're going to hurt us. You killed Aidan. You killed my husband, so of course I'm worried that... well, that you might be about to do the same to me.'

He turns to me. 'What did you expect? You don't make a deal like Aidan did and expect them to forget about it when you don't hold up your end of the bargain.'

'*Them.*'

'What?' He glances back at me with a scowl.

'You said *them*. Which means you're not the one giving the orders. Maybe you're being forced to do this?'

'You don't know what you're talking about.'

'So tell me.'

He shakes his head dismissively and turns back to the window.

'Look, Jonathan, I don't know who you are or what your real name is. I don't know where you live. So if you just leave now, I can tell the police that it was a robbery gone wrong. I won't even mention the fact that Aidan owed money. No one else needs to get hurt. My son is only four and I have to get to a hospital. I think I'm going into labour.'

'No, you're not. You're not due until next month.'

'How do you know that?'

He turns around and sneers. 'I know everything about you. When Aidan made his deal, we made it our business to know.'

'I can give you money.'

He laughs at this. 'If that was the case, we wouldn't be here now.'

'You don't understand. I know someone who'll give me the money. I can probably get it for you now.' I'm not sure Bianca could get it for me that quickly, but if they knew the money was in the pipeline, surely they'd be interested.

'Forget the money. It's too late for that. Your husband made a deal he can't back out of.'

'He's dead though. You killed him. So how can he not "back out of" a deal?'

'You need to be quiet.'

'Please tell me what's going on.'

'Just shut up, or I'll have to shut you up.'

I clamp my teeth together and concentrate on trying not to cry. This man has no compassion. No thought for me or Josh. I'm not sure what he and his people want from me, but I'm sure it's not going to be anything good.

FORTY

DANI

I slide into the driver's seat of my hire car – a silver Ford Focus – close the door and attempt to pull my seatbelt on, but the damn thing keeps sticking. I realise I'm tugging at it too hard, so I let go, exhale through my teeth and try again. Finally it glides across my body and I snap it into place with a click.

I gaze at the rain-smeared windscreen, the view beyond obscured, and I realise I'm going to have to calm myself down quite a lot. I know there are other ways to do this. Safer ways. Ones that don't put me in any danger, but I've been so blind-sided that it's impossible to think straight. Being proactive is the only thing that makes any sense to me right now.

All other options and conversations will take too much time. I can't risk waiting around. And, anyway, I want to be there to see with my own eyes. As I turn on the engine, the wipers start up, clearing the screen so I can now see the blurry road and pavement, the bright shop signs and a few pedestrians hunched against wind and rain.

There's a sudden gap in traffic, so I pull away from the car-rental company forecourt and into the steady stream of vehicles. The interior of my hire car has that just-cleaned smell. I can also detect a faint sour odour of vomit that turns my stomach. I don't have time to take the car back and ask for a new one, so I crack the passenger window an inch, despite the driving rain that spatters onto the empty seat next to me and onto my hand every time I change gear.

The journey over to Marcus's showroom is slow. As I drive, my heartbeats thump throughout my whole body from the pads of my toes to the tips of my fingers, like a warning tattoo. But I accept my fear and I swallow it down like medicine.

When I met with Rob last week and he told me what he'd discovered over the past couple of months, I was shocked and yet not shocked. Because part of me was already anticipating it. And yet it sounded so outlandish that I almost didn't believe him. Not until he showed me proof in the form of records and photographs and the most convincing piece of evidence – a recorded phone conversation that gave details along with a date and place.

Rob said we had to call the police. But I convinced him to let me call them in my own time. To let me process it all first. A few days wouldn't make any difference. Rob was kind. He made me tea and let me cry all over him. He said he was used to giving difficult news, but that didn't make it any easier. I said there was no way I could face Marcus that night, so Rob let me crash on his sofa.

I was supposed to be meeting my husband for drinks at the Silver Sail that evening, but I called and told him I couldn't make it. I continued the lie that I had to stay and help my mum with her pension forms. I told him I was going to stay the night at her place. Marcus was disappointed but didn't push it, thank goodness. I'd never have been able to compose myself in time to act as though nothing had changed. I needed time on my own to come to terms with exactly what was going on. To work out what to do.

I've only known Rob a short while, but I already feel like I can properly trust him. Not something I've ever felt about anyone aside from my brother. Well, not since Marcus, anyway. But staying over at his place that night felt like I was taking advantage of his good nature. I didn't want to drag him into my situation beyond the job he was doing for me. Which is why I didn't tell him what I was planning next.

I paid Rob's fee and went back home the following morning, not letting Marcus know what I'd discovered. Because I want to see it for myself before confronting him. That way he won't be able to deny it. To sweet-talk his way out of it.

Eventually, I reach Ashley Cross. The traffic crawls past The Green and I turn left down a side street and then right into another. I cruise past the rear of Marcus's showroom, relieved to see the black curves of my husband's Porsche still in the car park. I keep going until I spy a parking space just a short way along the road. Then I pull in, turn off the engine and angle my rear-view mirror so that I have a clear view of the exit to the showroom car park.

After around half an hour, my stomach lurches as I spot Marcus's Porsche idling at the exit of the showroom's car park. With shaking fingers, I restart the car and try to prepare myself for what's to come.

I'm startled by my phone ringing. My first thought is to ignore it, as I don't want to miss my husband's departure. But I decide to at least see who it is. I slip it out of my bag and look at the screen. It's Marcus! I hope he hasn't spotted me lurking here. Surely not. That's why I rented this hire car in the first place – my cherry-red Range Rover is far too distinctive. I sink down in my seat a little, but I'm sure I'm parked too far away for him to see me, and the visibility out there is terrible.

I think about ignoring it but realise it could be helpful to hear what he has to say. I quickly slide my finger across the screen before I get cold feet. 'Hey.'

'Hey, Dani. You okay?'

'Fine. You?' I'm waiting for him to ask me what I'm doing parked down the street in a stranger's car. But he doesn't. He still presumes I'm in the dark about everything.

'Yeah, good. Look, I'm just calling to say I might be late home tonight. Like really late. I'm taking a car to a client for a test drive.'

'Oh, okay. Does it have to be *you* taking it?'

''Fraid so. It's a big deal – a music producer who could bring in a lot more business.'

'Okay, well, good luck then. Drive carefully. Looks pretty stormy out there.'

'I'll be fine, Dan. Love you.'

'You too.' I end the call and exhale, dropping my phone on the passenger seat.

I'm paranoid that he might have sensed something in my voice. But then I tell myself not to worry. It was a perfectly normal conversation. Just as I'm composing myself, Marcus's Porsche roars past, showering the Focus with an arc of muddy spray.

'So much for driving carefully,' I mutter.

I wait a few beats before pulling out behind a VW Golf. I can still see the squat shape of Marcus's black Porsche up ahead. I worry about losing him, but I breathe deeply and tell myself that I can do this. I already googled how to tail someone without being spotted and I had a few practice sessions earlier in the week where I picked a car at random and followed it for as long as I could, keeping my distance so that they were way ahead. The trick will be not to get so close that he spots me and not to get so far away that I lose him. I chose this colour and model of hire car specifically because it's so popular I'm hoping it will fade into the background. Thankfully, the weather is on my side today.

Time alternately speeds up and slows down on the journey. I leave the town behind and soon find myself in the stormy wilds of the countryside. I'm not at all keen on these narrow lanes and I cringe every time there's a blind corner, convinced I'm going to have a head-on collision. Now we're on these deserted roads, I've pulled back. Every time he drops out of sight, I worry that I've lost him. But then I'll catch a distant glimpse and relax once again.

My neck is stiff and my arms are sore from holding the wheel so rigidly. I take a few deep breaths to try to relax and move my jaw from side to side – I'm so tense it's locked up.

A tiny hopeful part of me had wondered whether Rob might have got things wrong. If Marcus might indeed be going to visit a music producer who wants a test drive. But – aside from the weather being in no way conducive to test-driving a performance car – the fact that my husband is driving his Porsche had already convinced me that the music producer is fictional.

Disappointment burns my throat as Marcus leads me directly to the destination I suspected.

FORTY-ONE

EMILY

After what feels like forever, I see lights through the window. Jonathan straightens as a dark car comes into view, blurred by the rain. As I watch the vehicle's progress, all I can think about is Josh in the next room. Please let him be okay. Let him be enjoying his sandwich and his iced gems. Let him be having fun making little animal figures out of play dough. I try not to think about the bad things that could happen, like, *What if an iced gem gets stuck in his throat and I'm not there to save him?* I should never have given him such a choking hazard. What was I thinking? But then I tell myself not to be so stupid. Anyway, I've thought of it now, so surely it won't happen.

At least I've had no more contractions. Those earlier ones must have been false labour. Thank goodness for small mercies. I realise I'm having all these crazy random thoughts to try to distract myself from the new visitor out there. I imagine it must be the big boss. The person who runs the money-lending outfit. Hopefully, I can persuade whoever it is to let us go in return for payment. Although they've already had more than their pound of flesh – Aidan has paid the ultimate price. Will these people even let Josh and I live after we've seen their faces? *Don't think about that. Stay positive. Stay focused. We're still alive. We're still here.*

The vehicle has pulled up out of view, so I can't see who's inside. A car door slams. I listen for another slam, but there's just the one, which is something at least. Jonathan must have left the front door on the latch because I hear it opening, bringing in a violent rush of cool damp air that makes me shiver.

'In here!' Jonathan calls out gruffly.

The door to the living room opens and I look up nervously, wondering what to expect. A hand reaches out for the light switch, flicking it on and off a few times. 'Bit bloody dark in here.' A man's voice.

'I cut the power,' Jonathan explains.

The man walks in, stocky, well dressed, shaking out a black umbrella and leaning it against the wall. I know him.

'*Marcus?*'

'All right, Emily?'

'*Marcus,*' I repeat. 'Do you two know each other?' I glance from one to the other. 'Do you know Jonathan? He said he wanted to rent a room. But he killed Aidan. He *killed* him! And he's keeping me and Josh here against our will.' But even as I blurt all this out like some naïve child, I know that I may as well be talking to myself, because Marcus is giving me an amused look and I understand that Marcus must have been the man my husband owed money to. This was Marcus's doing all along. Aidan didn't tell me. Suddenly it all makes sense. Why Aidan was so angry that I'd thrown the surprise party and invited his boss and his wife. And why he hadn't handed in his notice at work – because then Marcus would have guessed he was planning to leave town.

'What are you going to do?' I ask.

Marcus throws me a pitying smile and I place both hands on my stomach protectively.

'We'll get to that later. But first I've got a bone to pick with you, Emily.'

I stare at him uncomprehendingly.

His smile widens. 'You never thanked me for my present.'

I blink, still not understanding.

'The three bears.' He chuckles. 'Thought that was quite clever, myself. Good bit of symbolism, lopping off the Daddy Bear's head like that. Shame you didn't take the warning.'

I grit my teeth and shake my head in disgust. At the time, I'd thought the broken nightlight was a sick gift from the loan sharks, never realising that Aidan's creditors and Marcus were one and the same. Never truly thinking they would actually follow through with their threat.

I can't believe I ever thought I knew Marcus. I'd assumed he was this charismatic local businessman who enjoyed working hard and spending his money. Sure, he was a bit of a wide boy and a definite player. But aside from that, I saw him as an employer who was good to his staff and charming and kind to his friends.

I now realise it was all an act. That's not who he is at all.

FORTY-TWO

DANI

I pull over just before the turnoff and cut the engine, stretching out my arms and neck while the rain drums down onto the car. A rumble of thunder sounds off in the distance. My phone has fallen into the footwell, so I lean forward to retrieve it and open up a browser. I curse when I realise there's no signal out here. *I can't get internet access.* I should have realised that might be the case so far out into the countryside.

Luckily, I'd already downloaded a satellite image of the property. I didn't want to drive straight up to the front door, as they'd see me coming and get jumpy. So I decided to take another route in. I've already earmarked where I'm going, but it can't hurt to double-check the image.

I end up parking down a narrow lane adjacent to the property, locating a spot where the hedgerow ends and a section of wire fence begins. So far as I can tell, the lane is deserted, so I nip out and spend the next five minutes using my newly purchased wire cutters to make a gap in the fence large enough for me to squeeze through. It's harder than I thought it would be. I should have worn gloves. But eventually I snip a raggedy line from top to bottom, my hands now blistered and torn in several places.

It's not too late for me to jump back into the car, turn around and drive home. I think longingly of our luxurious living room with its cosy fire and sofas. There's nothing so nice as curling up indoors while a storm rages outside. *But then what?* Wait for Marcus to come home, knowing what I know? I can't keep pretending. And what about Aidan and his family? No. I have to do what I can to make this better.

I shove the wire cutters deep into the pocket of my parka, make my phone call with the two available bars of signal and squeeze through the gap in the fence. Walking cautiously towards the house, I approach from the side, cursing the heels on my leather boots as I sink into the long, wet grass, then stumble across gravel. At least I had the foresight to wear a rain-coat with a hood, but I can only see straight ahead – it's like wearing blinkers – and the hood is flapping about in the wind so that I have to hold it in place. I must look ridiculous. But that's the least of my worries.

Finally, I come up on the house – a pretty cottage-like farm-house. It's not dark out, but the weather is definitely gloomy enough to warrant having the lights on. And yet the house is in darkness – there's not one light showing anywhere. Perhaps they're in one of the back rooms. On the driveway I walk past Marcus's Porsche and a pickup truck that I don't recognise.

Now that I'm here, I'm desperate to get this over with. To get it done. I lift my hand to knock at the front door but stop just short of the knocker, instead deciding to see if it will open first. My instincts were correct, the door isn't locked. It's stiff but yields to a firm push. As the door opens, my pulse begins to pound and an anxious heat skims my body. I take a breath and follow the sound of voices into the room off the dark hallway to my right. I open the door and look inside.

'What the hell... *Dani?* What are you doing here?'

FORTY-THREE

DANI

Marcus is standing with his back to a large window, his face a mask of shock as I open the door to the living room. A man stands behind him, but I can't make out his features in the gloom. A woman sits on a sofa and I realise it's a very pregnant Emily Graham. I'm relieved to see her in one piece.

'What am *I* doing here? I was going to ask you the same thing.' My voice sounds cooler and calmer than I feel. My heart is clattering in my chest. As my eyes adjust to the gloom, I recognise the man standing next to my husband and I give an internal shudder.

'I told you, I've come to meet a client.' Marcus's face is a shade of red somewhere between discomfort and anger. 'Did you follow me here?'

'So, is Aidan's wife your client? I thought they lived in Ashley Cross. And why's Jonesy here too?' I'm playing dumb because I want him to admit to me what he's doing here. But when I notice what's in Jonesy's hand, I take an involuntary step back. 'He's got a gun!' I stare in shock at the weapon he's holding loosely by his side. I knew they'd have weapons with them, as Marcus told Jonesy to bring his shooter during the phone call Rob recorded. But to have one pointed at me is paralysing.

'Jesus, Dani, I can't believe you followed me here. *Why?*' Marcus turns to peer out the window. 'Where's your car? Where did you park?'

Still frozen in shock, I somehow manage to stammer out a few questions. 'What are you doing here with Emily? Where's Aidan? Haven't they got a little boy? Where is he?' I force myself to look at Jonesy. 'Why have you got a gun?'

Marcus strides over and gently takes both my hands, concern in his eyes. 'It's not what you think, Dan.'

'And what do I think?'

'Look, what I'm doing here is a good thing. I'm collecting on a deal. And it's a deal we've been waiting for, for a long time.'

I notice that Emily is very pale and quiet. She's clutching her stomach and breathing deeply. I give myself a shake, wrench my hands from my husband's grip and walk over to Emily. 'Are you okay?'

She shakes her head and a tear runs down her cheek as she starts to gasp and pant.

'Fuck's sake, Marcus, it looks like she's going into labour! What've you done? Where's her husband?'

'Aidan's dead,' Emily gasps through her contraction. 'They killed him.'

'No!' I cry.

'He owed them money. My son Josh… is in the kitchen.'

I grow cold at the knowledge of what they've done to her husband. That I'm too late to save him. I should have called the police last week when I found out. But I could never have imagined it would get this far. Could never have believed Marcus would be capable of murder. The room tilts and I taste bile. 'Aidan's *dead*? One of you killed him?' I turn to my husband. Marcus doesn't reply, just presses his lips together in a thin, angry line. His silence answers my question. Jonesy hasn't said a word this whole time.

Everything hits me at once. I stare at my husband, a stranger to me. Nothing like the man I thought he was. How did I not know any of this? I saw the notebook containing transaction details, loan repayments, extortionate rates of interest. I saw the evidence that proved who he was, what he did, but I still didn't put two and two together. Back then, I'd thought that it was *Marcus* in trouble with these people. That he'd been keeping a record of his own repayments. When all the time it was *him*. My husband is the one responsible for it all.

Rob discovered that Marcus had recently expanded his business into making loans for desperate people; that he was intimidating clients who didn't pay on time. He found proof that Marcus had no scruples when it came to making deals. Terrible, impossible deals with huge interest rates and worse. But to go this far... *murder*...?

To find out that he actually hurts people for a living. To see Marcus here like this with my own eyes is something else. I can barely process it. I've been naïve. Blind. But how could I believe the man I loved would be capable of such horror? Why couldn't he just have stayed content with his car business?

His new business associates are nothing to do with his car showroom. They're debt collectors, muscle men, thugs. No wonder I got a bad feeling about them.

I feel like yelling at Marcus, weeping that Rob's discovery was worse than I thought. But I do neither. I need to keep Marcus and Jonesy calm.

Instead, I go over to Emily and help her to her feet. 'Show me where Josh is.'

'Stay where you are,' Jonesy grunts.

I ignore his instruction, trying not to show how shocked and terrified I really am. Why the hell did I come here? What was I trying to prove? Everything I am is screaming at me to get out, to run and hide. But somehow, despite my racing pulse and queasy stomach, I manage to keep it together. 'This is ridiculous,' I snap at my husband. 'She's having a baby. We're getting Josh and we're going to the hospital.' My hands are trembling as I put my arm around Emily to help support her. I find myself making soothing sounds, telling her she's going to be okay, all the while trying to push out the knowledge that my husband has killed a man. Someone I knew. We try to edge past Jonesy even though he's pointing the gun at me now.

'I told you to stay put.' Jonesy's eyes are hard. There's no smirking or flirting today. I have no doubt he would shoot me if my husband told him to.

Marcus gives a low growl. 'Put the fucking thing down, Jonesy. That's my wife you're aiming at.'

Jonesy gives us both a disgusted look, but at least he lowers his gun.

I stare at my husband. 'Can you take that thing off him, Marcus? He doesn't need a gun. I don't think Emily's in any state to give you any trouble, do you?' I'm saying these words as though we're arguing over what to have for dinner tonight. But in my head, I'm screaming, *You're a fucking murderer!* Over and over again. The only reason I'm not screaming out loud is because I don't want to anger them. I need to keep things calm so they don't hurt Emily and her child.

Marcus nods. 'Put the gun away, Jonesy.'

He hesitates, but eventually does as my husband asks, tucking it into the back of his jeans.

'Let's get Josh.' I turn to Emily. 'You said he was in the kitchen?'

'I thought he'd be safer away from the gun,' she replies weakly. Her contractions seem to have passed for the moment and she's talking almost normally, although her face is pale and her hands are shaking worse than mine.

I stand and glare at my husband. 'Like I said, Emily, Josh

and I are going to the hospital now, okay?' I hold my breath, willing him to see sense and agree.

'No.'

'What do you mean, *no*?' I feign outrage, but my insides have turned to water. I know there's no way he's letting us walk out of here.

'Jonesy, take them upstairs and lock them in a room for now.'

'Marcus!' I stare at him, but he doesn't catch my eye.

'We'll talk later, Dani. Right now, I've got a few things to discuss with Jonesy.'

'No! Not upstairs!' Emily takes a step backwards as tears stream down her cheeks.

I'm shocked by her outburst. I would have thought she'd prefer to be away from her captors. '*What?* What's the matter?'

'Aidan's up there. In our bedroom.' She points at Jonesy. 'He... cut my husband's throat.'

'*Jesus.* That's just... that's...' I blow out a long breath and put a hand to my own throat. I try not to picture Aidan lying up there. Try to keep my voice steady when all the while I'm freaking out inside. 'I'm so sorry, Emily.'

Marcus nods at Jonesy and tilts his head in the direction of the hall. Emily continues to back away. Marcus fixes me with a stare. 'Dani, get her to co-operate, or Jonesy's gonna lose his temper.'

I weigh up my options and realise we have no choice. I decide it's probably for the best if we go upstairs. At least we'll be able to talk freely up there. 'Hey, Emily, I think we should go somewhere quiet if the baby's coming. How about Josh's room, can we go in there?'

She bites her lip and nods, tears still streaking her face. I can't imagine how hard it must be for her to think about going up there, knowing her poor husband is lying dead in one of the bedrooms. Maybe it's marginally better than facing the two thugs down here.

I throw Marcus a look of disgust and he gives a single nod of satisfaction. 'Good girl, Dan. Make sure she and the baby are all right. We'll talk about this later. You'll understand everything once I've explained it to you. I've got some business to discuss with Jonesy first.'

I know exactly what he wants to discuss with me and it's outrageous. I need to work out what I'm going to do about it and I also need to warn Emily. I only hope Marcus will abandon his plan once I've told him I want no part in it. For now, I can't even bear to look at him.

'Oh and leave your phone down here, Dan.'

'There's no signal in the house, boss,' Jonesy chips in.

'Doesn't matter. Leave it anyway.'

I take my phone from my bag and leave it on the coffee table. Jonesy chaperones us out of the living room at gunpoint and we fetch Emily's adorable son from the kitchen where he's making play-dough shapes by torchlight.

'Mummy!' He gets up and starts showing her his creations. 'I was good and stayed in here, so will I get a big present now?'

'Yes, sweetie, you will. But it will have to be a bit later because all the shops are shut right now.'

'It's dark.' I reach for the light switch.

'Doesn't work,' Emily says. 'Jonathan or Jonesy or whatever you're called' – she scowls at him – 'cut the power.'

I grab the torch from the kitchen table, not wanting to be trapped upstairs in the pitch-dark as night falls.

'Come on, let's go.' Jonesy moves the gun back and forth.

The four of us climb the stairs at a snail's pace, with Jonesy at the rear telling us to get a move on, prodding the gun into my back. I stop and tell him to lay off and thankfully he does. I'll be relieved when we get into the bedroom, away from this evil scumbag.

We finally reach the top of the staircase and I follow Emily into her son's room at the front of the house. Jonesy stands in the doorway. 'Don't even think about trying to leave this room. I'm wedging the door shut, so it's pointless anyway.' With that he closes the door and I hear fumbling and bashing against the door handle as he does whatever he needs to, to secure us inside the room.

I stride across to the window and glance down at the drive to check that my husband hasn't stepped outside. It appears to be all clear out there. I hold the torch up to the window and switch it on for five seconds followed by two short flashes, hoping my earlier phone call was taken seriously. I wait ten seconds and then flash the torch twice again.

'What are you doing?' Emily gasps and bends forward as another contraction kicks in.

I put my finger to my lips and wait for silence on the other side of the door. Once I hear Jonesy's footsteps retreating down the stairs, I keep my voice low and start to explain.

FORTY-FOUR

DANI

'I made a plan to get you all out of here. I'm sorry I was too late to save Aidan. I really am.'

'What plan?' Emily lets out a low moan and holds onto her lower back.

'Before I arrived, I called the police firearms unit, explaining what was going on here. I told them they needed to send a team to rescue you and then I hung up before they could ask questions. I also told them I'd call or text when I got here to let them know how many bad guys there were, but I didn't realise there'd be no signal inside the house. I'm hoping when they arrive, they'll see my torch at the window and realise that two torch flashes equals two bad guys.'

Emily is walking around the room, moaning and panting. I'm not sure if she's even listening to my explanation. And all the while I'm talking to her, I can't stop thinking about Marcus. *My husband.* About the marriage I thought we had. The fact that it's well and truly over. I can't even let myself think about what this means for my hopes of having children. Perhaps that's why fate didn't grant me a child with him. How did it even come to this?

Josh is pulling at Emily's hand. 'What's the matter, Mummy? Have you got a tummy ache?'

Deep in the middle of labour, Emily is in a world of her own, not even able to pay attention to her son.

I answer Josh instead. 'Hey, come here. You know the baby in Mummy's tummy?'

Josh lets go of his mother's hand and takes a step towards me.

'Well, that little one is getting ready to come out and meet you, so Mummy might make some funny noises to help the baby along, okay? It's nothing to be scared of.'

'I'm not scared!' He folds his arms across his chest. 'Is it like when the chickens lay their eggs and make funny chicken noises?'

I manage a weak smile. 'Yes, it's exactly like that.' I peer out the window once more, willing the police to arrive before Jonesy or Marcus comes back upstairs. If the police didn't believe my call, I'll have to find a way to convince Marcus that I'm no threat.

'Are they here yet?' Emily asks, palms flat against the wall, her head down.

'The police? Not yet. I hope Josh doesn't get freaked out when they arrive. It might get noisy down there.'

She's panting and sweating, gritting her teeth. 'He's got... Bob the Builder ear defenders.' Emily points to a basket in the corner. 'Not sure how good they are, but... better than nothing.' It's hard for her to talk through her labour pains. I'm praying I won't have to deliver the baby myself, because I seriously don't have the first clue what to do.

I rummage around in the basket and pull out a pair of bright-yellow defenders, which Josh puts on willingly. I flash the torch at the window once more and then we sit on the bed with her son between us. Waiting.

Emily's between contractions again. I squeeze her hand to try to offer some reassurance. 'How long until the baby comes?'

'I don't know. Not long.' Her voice wavers. 'I think the second one's usually a lot quicker than the first. I don't think I'll make it to a hospital in time.'

'Are you feeling okay? Do you need me to do anything?'

'I just want to get out of here. Can you talk to me about something, *anything*, just to distract me from thinking about the next contraction?'

'The thing is, Emily, I need to tell you about the real reason Marcus came here tonight.'

She shifts on the bed. 'What do you mean, the real reason?'

I clear my throat, not sure where to start. Not sure if I should even be telling her this right now. When Rob first told me what he'd discovered about Marcus last week, I was shocked, horrified, but also a little sceptical. This was my Marcus we were talking about. He wasn't like that. He would never do those things. But to be faced with the real version of him downstairs... I still can't comprehend it. It took all my willpower down there not to scream at him for ruining our lives, for resorting to intimidation and violence to get what he wanted. And now I have to explain to Emily just how bad a person Marcus really is.

'So what do you know about my husband?' I ask.

'Up until today, I thought he was Aidan's boss and that was it.' She wriggles backwards on the bed and leans back against the wall. Josh shifts back with her and leans his head against her shoulder. She swallows and pushes her hair back off her face. 'A few months ago, Aidan told me he had a gambling problem and owed a lot of money to some dangerous people. There was no way we could pay it back, so we left town, changed our names and came here.'

'That must have been scary for you.' I walk over to the window once more and flash the torch, growing increasingly more worried that no one is going to show up to help us. What if the police don't arrive?

Emily continues. 'It was terrifying. Luckily, we had this place to escape to. But a while ago I bumped into a couple of my old friends at the local convenience store. I think that's how Jonathan, or Jonesy, or whatever his name is, found us. Aidan never told me that it was his boss he owed money to. I couldn't believe it when he showed up here today.'

'And that's it? That's all you know about their deal?'

Emily frowns. 'Yes, why? What else is there?'

I sigh, dreading telling her the rest. 'You won't know this, but Marcus and I have been trying to have a baby for years. Without any success.' I shrug, trying to make light of it.

'Oh, I'm sorry.' Emily gives me a sympathetic look, but I can tell she's confused by my apparent change of subject.

'When Aidan told Marcus he couldn't pay off the loan, Marcus said there was another way to pay the debt in full.'

Emily's face grows pale and I wonder if she's guessed what I'm about to tell her.

'Marcus said that if Aidan agreed to give him your new baby for adoption, he'd waive the loan.'

'What the hell?'

'Aidan agreed.'

'Aidan did WHAT?'

'Shh, keep your voice down,' I hiss. 'We don't want them coming back upstairs.' I walk over to the bed and crouch down so we're at eye level. Josh is fast asleep now, curled up on the bed next to his mother. 'Aidan signed an adoption contract. I have a copy of it.'

'And you *knew* about this?' Emily closes her eyes as another contraction hits.

'No, I only found out last week. I hired a private investigator to look into my husband's business affairs and he discovered the contract, among other things. I had no idea about any of this stuff – not the money lending or intimidation or violence or *any of it*.' Tears sting my eyes as the horror of it hits me all over again. 'I think that must have been why Aidan wanted to get away. He probably only signed the contract to keep Marcus off his back. I'm sure he'd never have actually done it.'

'*Shit*.' Emily closes her eyes and starts panting through the pain. 'I can't believe he... signed that contract! How could he have even thought about doing something so... despicable? It's our child, for God's sake!' She gives a low moan and I can't tell if it's from distress at my revelation or from her labour pains.

'I know, I know. But he probably had no choice at the time. Yeah, he signed a contract, but how could something like that even be legal? And you both did a runner, so Aidan was obviously never going to go through with it.'

Emily shakes her head, her face contorting as the pains take hold. 'He'd better not have even *thought* about giving our baby up. Not for one second.' She exhales through clenched teeth. 'I suppose it now makes more sense... why he was so desperate for us to get away.'

I kneel on the bed and take Emily's hand while she tries to breathe through her contractions. I feel useless. I didn't want to have to tell her all this while she's in labour. But I had to warn her of what Marcus is planning once this baby is born. Surely he can't expect me to go along with such an insane plan.

Her eyes snap open. 'Marcus must have a screw loose if he thinks I'm giving up my child – there's no way he's taking my baby, contract or no contract.'

'Of course not,' I agree. 'But if the police don't show up, we may need to let Marcus think that we'll go along with it. Just until we can all get safely away from him, okay? We don't want to piss either of them off.'

Emily grits her teeth through the pain and nods. 'I don't know if I can. He's a psychopath. He knew it would be impossible for Aidan to pay back all the money. Getting the baby was probably his plan all along. You need to help me keep my baby, Dani. You won't let him take it, will you?'

'Of course I won't. But, like I said, we might have to pretend for a while.'

'If you knew what Marcus was up to, why did you come here alone?' Emily pants. 'Why put yourself in danger? You should have just told the police and let them deal with it.'

I shake my head. 'It's hard to explain. I needed to do this. To confront my husband at the scene of the crime. See what kind of man I was married to. Try to talk him out of his mad plan. Part of me didn't really believe it could be true. I wanted to get here and be proved wrong.'

'It was brave of you.' She looks me in the eye. 'I'm really glad you came. I mean it. Thank you, Dani.'

I reach out and give her hand a squeeze, glad that I can at least be here with her. She doesn't respond further as the labour pains take over.

'Where are these bloody cops?' I return to the window with my torch, flash it twice and stare out across the stormy meadow. Dusk is falling. It'll be fully dark soon. I really don't want to be here any more. I glance down at the drive and experience a flash of fear as I pick out several dark shapes creeping along the front of the house. With a sudden rush of relief, I realise it must be the police. I can hardly believe they're actually here. I feel as though I'm watching a movie. 'Hey, Emily. Good news. They're here.'

Emily and I lock eyes and hold our breath. It seems like her contractions have subsided for the time being. She gathers Josh close to her. He has his thumb in his mouth and opens his eyes, confused for a moment, before snuggling into his mother's side. 'Come away from the window,' she whispers to me.

I nod and hurry over to the bed, my heart clattering at the sound of raised voices and thumping footsteps downstairs as the police storm the property.

FORTY-FIVE

DANI

NINE MONTHS LATER

'She's just the sweetest thing.' Emily kisses Lydia on her button nose while I allow bubbles of happiness to float up from my belly and settle around my heart.

'She is, isn't she?' I smile at my friend, still unable to believe it. My little Lydia is only three weeks old and I have to pinch myself every day. Turns out that while I was rescuing Emily and Josh from my husband, I was actually two weeks pregnant with my own beautiful daughter. It was a total shock. Doubly so, as I didn't even realise the fact until I was three months into my pregnancy.

Today is the first properly warm day of the year and we're having a rare afternoon outside in the garden. 'Do you want another coffee?' I look enquiringly at Emily, but she's too besotted with Lydia to look up.

'No thanks, I haven't drunk this one yet.'

The two of us have become close since the day it happened. I suppose our relationship could have gone one of two ways. We could just as easily have never spoken again. But we definitely bonded through our shared trauma and I guess you could say we've become good friends.

Despite her fascination with my daughter, I'm worried about Emily today. She seems more distant and absentminded than usual. Not exactly unhappy, just a little vacant. Perhaps she's simply not getting enough sleep. Or maybe it's the stress of everything catching up with her. I'll try to have a proper talk with her one evening, once the kids are asleep. Get her to open up.

As for myself, despite the fact that Marcus is now doing time in Winchester Prison and I've filed for divorce, I've discovered a strange new happiness with the baby I've always yearned for. It's way more exhausting and scarier than I imagined and I don't know what on earth I'm supposed to be doing half the time, but I wouldn't change it for the world.

Of course, our big house by the harbour has gone, along with Marcus's car showroom and all the money. His assets were frozen and I've been told I'm unlikely to ever see a penny of it. But that's okay.

After that terrible day last year, I couldn't face going back to our house, so I stayed at Jay's for a couple of nights. My brother was understandably shocked and concerned. Although he never liked Marcus – had always had a bad feeling about him – he'd never imagined *this*. Jay desperately wanted to help, offering me his sofa for as long as I needed it. But his one-room bedsit was far too small for the two of us. He called Mum, who insisted I move into the bungalow with her. I was reluctant at first, but Jay made me see sense. Luckily, the bungalow is in her name, so it hasn't been caught up in the investigation.

It was actually quite nice reconnecting with my mother. I don't think she's half as bad as I thought she was. Or maybe it's simply that she's softened towards me after finding out what I went through. It seems near-death experiences can make you and your loved ones re-evaluate life and relationships. My mum enjoyed bossing me around during the pregnancy and she's in heaven at finally becoming a grandmother – taking great delight in telling me how I'm doing everything wrong. Jay assures me her criticisms are bathed in love. I treat him to my full repertoire of eye rolls.

Turns out, I wasn't destined to put up with Mum's house rules for the rest of my life. My solicitor discovered that Marcus owned a rental property that he'd registered in my name and, apparently, I'm allowed to keep it. At first, I didn't want to touch a penny of Marcus's tainted money, but my brother talked me around. It was either live there or carry on living with Mum. And much as I love my mother, we both agreed that having our own space is vital for our new-found relationship and our sanity.

I moved in after Christmas, once I'd given the tenants notice to leave and cleaned the place up a bit. It's a large house in Ashley Cross just off The Green. Nothing like our luxurious pad by the harbour. Instead of glass, marble and designer artwork, it's all worn wood, cracked plaster and character features. All in all, it's a bit battered and bruised, but I kind of like that about it. It suits me and Lydia just fine. I love living here and having my freedom. Running my own life rather than letting someone else run it for me.

I used to live this life of immense luxury and privilege and I never really questioned any of it. The finances were Marcus's domain. He was the one who provided for us. He was the one who worked. Who wheeled and dealed. Only I never knew exactly what he was doing. And that was my mistake. I'm determined to teach Lydia how to be independent. To never have to rely on anyone for an income or a life. To be informed. To keep her eyes wide open.

I scoop little Bianca up off the grass before she makes her second attempt to dive into the flower beds. She's been crawling around like a wind-up toy all afternoon, so Josh and I are making sure she doesn't get into mischief.

After that dreadful day when Aidan was murdered and I had to tell Emily about his contract with Marcus, I felt hugely guilty around little Bianca. After all, this was the child that my husband had been planning to take away from her true parents. This was supposed to be his gift to me. So I couldn't help blaming myself – my aching desire to have a child was the reason for all of it. If I hadn't been so obsessed, then perhaps none of it would ever have happened. But Emily reassured me that I had no need to feel responsible in any way. This was on Marcus. It was his warped sense of right and wrong that drove him to do what he did.

'I can take her.' Josh holds out his arms to take Bianca. 'She likes it when I sing nursery rhymes.'

'You're such a fantastic big brother.' I give him a grin and place a wriggling Bianca into his outstretched arms where she settles immediately and starts grabbing at her brother's face.

Josh bounced back from the ordeal last summer. I don't think he really understood what was happening. Of course, he misses his father terribly, but Emily says she talks about Aidan with him a lot. She's determined that he'll never forget his dad. Poor little Bianca will never even get the chance to meet him.

Now that the two of them are occupied for a few minutes, I wander back to Emily and sit on one of the faded wrought-iron seats next to her. 'You okay, Em?'

'I'm fine,' she replies absently, crooning softly over my little Lydia.

We sit in companionable silence for a while, listening to Josh's nursery rhymes and the sounds of summer from neighbouring gardens – lawnmowers, children's shrieks, laughter, a dog barking. All those regular garden sounds that I don't ever remember hearing in our harbourside home.

I was upstairs with Emily and Josh when the police showed

up that day to arrest Marcus and Jonesy. Jonesy shot one of them in the shoulder, but thankfully the officer made a full recovery. I stayed with Emily when the paramedics arrived at the house to help her give birth in Josh's bedroom. She squeezed my hand throughout the whole thing and we both sobbed when little Bianca – Bee for short – finally made her entrance into the world, named after Emily's beloved godmother.

Poor Emily hasn't fared too well in the aftermath of all this. She's still carrying a deep sadness around with her. Not surprising, really, after what happened to Aidan last summer. I guess it will take a long while for her to recover from the trauma of those events.

Recently, I've been growing more and more worried about her state of mind. I've dropped heavy hints about her maybe needing to talk to a professional. But so far, she's pushed away all my attempts to get her some help. She does at least let me help out with Josh and Bee, which is something. Aside from absolutely adoring her kids, it also allows me to feel like I'm somehow atoning for my husband's terrible crimes against her family: robbing her of a husband and her children of a father.

Frustratingly, Emily refuses to ask her parents for any sort of emotional or financial aid. In fact, I don't even think they've come over to see her after her ordeal, which is just plain weird if you ask me. It sounds like her godmother has offered to help, but Emily says she feels like she's already caused Bianca enough grief, what with her property turning into a crime scene and all. Bianca tried to assure her that it wasn't in any way her fault and said she was welcome to stay on at Briar Hill Farm, but Emily understandably doesn't want to go anywhere near the place. I think she's needlessly punishing herself.

To make matters worse, Emily's currently living in emergency housing – a grotty B&B in Poole – which is really no place for a single mother with two young children. I've offered to help so many times, but she keeps cutting me dead, so I finally figured out a way to make her accept.

I've decided that once Lydia's a little older, I'm going to train to be a counsellor. To try to help people with their problems. Obviously, now that I have a young child, it's going to be a challenge to embark on a career. Mum said she'd help me out with childcare, but I can't rely on her all the time. So I asked Emily if she would move in with me rent-free in return for some help with Lydia. My house has five bedrooms and two bathrooms, so there's plenty of room for us to have our own space.

I told her she'd be doing me a favour, helping out with childcare while I train – although the truth of the matter is that Emily's in no state to look after her own children at the moment, let alone the addition of my child too. More likely it will be me helping her. She's finally agreed to move in next weekend. Hopefully, once she's settled, she'll begin to get her spark back and her life will improve. Then, once we both have proper jobs, she can start paying rent or get her own place. But, for now, it's the perfect arrangement.

I gaze at Lydia asleep in my friend's arms and think to myself that, despite everything that's gone on, I really am very lucky. And I'm determined to help my friend get back on her feet. After everything she's been through, she deserves to be happy again.

FORTY-SIX

EMILY

I sit in Dani's garden with the sun on my face. With Dani and Marcus's new daughter Lydia in my arms, pretending to care. Pretending to engage. But in reality, my mind is a deep black void. I keep it that way on purpose, because as soon as I allow any thoughts to enter, the memories all begin to jostle for space. They cascade into the void along with a mountain of emotions, all too raw to process – guilt, fear, hate, misery, self-loathing. All the worst ones sit just on the edge of that void. And if I let them, they'll pull me into the pit and drag me down into the darkness until I can't even see myself any more.

Dani wants me to talk to someone about it. Well, that's never going to happen. In fact, I should never have let her befriend me in the first place. I should have cut contact with her the day after I gave birth to my daughter. I should have let her get on with her life without me in it. But she said she liked me, she felt like we were bonding. She said I was helping her get over the trauma. So who was I to tell her no? Who was I to deny her my broken friendship, if that's what she really wanted?

Dani, with her perfect little newborn and her perfect character house in Ashley Cross. The type of house that Aidan and

I should have ended up with. But instead, Aidan is dead and I have nothing. And yet, I can't even allow myself the luxury of self-pity, much as I'd like to.

Because it's my fault.

The whole thing.

All of it.

Of course, everyone says I'm lucky. It could have been so much worse. At least I survived, right? At least I have my beautiful children. In a way they're correct – Josh and Bee are probably the only reason I haul myself out of bed each morning. But wouldn't it be so much easier if I didn't have them? If I could just step into the void and be done with it?

I wonder what Dani would say if she learned the truth. If she discovered that I, Emily Graham, the woman she now calls her friend, once had an affair with her husband, Marcus Baines.

I wonder what Dani would say if she knew that my daughter, Bianca, is also Marcus's daughter.

I wonder what Dani would say if she knew that the reason Marcus took on Aidan's gambling debt was so he could force him to hand over his newborn child without having to tell Dani he'd had an affair. The baby would be simply a miracle baby that he had adopted for them. An incredible surprise gift for his perfect little barren wife.

I wonder what Dani would say if she knew that Marcus had threatened me. Told me that if I didn't let him have custody of his baby, he would slit Aidan's throat.

I wonder what Dani would say to all that.

I glance over at my friend. At her calm, beautiful features as she sits in the sun, gazing at my children as they play on the grass, one of them a half-sister to her own daughter.

My affair with Marcus didn't last long. A couple of months at most. He initiated it when we bumped into one another at a dry cleaner, of all places, and got chatting. He was charming and flirtatious and I somehow let myself be swept away in the lust and excitement of it all. I'd never done anything like that before, never imagined I was the type to cheat on Aidan. But Marcus had this magnetism, this way of making me feel like I was the most important person in the world.

I had romantic notions of him leaving his wife and begging me to leave my husband so we could be together. But then, just as quickly as his infatuation sparked, he lost interest in me. Told me he would never leave his wife. That he loved her. That what we'd done was just a bit of fun and that he'd thought I'd understood that. I was devastated for a while. I felt rejected and stupid. Like I'd jeopardised my marriage for nothing. Until I discovered that I was pregnant.

The dates matched my affair with Marcus. At that time, Aidan and I weren't sleeping with one another – probably due to my tiredness and his gambling addiction – so I knew without a doubt that the baby wasn't his. I initiated sex with Aidan as soon as I discovered I was pregnant in the hope he wouldn't remember actual dates.

But then Marcus found out. He slotted the pieces together and realised the baby was his. And that's when everything started to unravel. When he concocted his ridiculous plan to take my baby. My little Bee. He threatened to hurt Aidan if I didn't give him custody of our child, even though I lied and told him it wasn't his. But he didn't believe me. And I never believed he'd actually go through with his threat. I thought it was just an angry reaction. When he kept sending those threatening text messages, I tried to ignore them. I had no idea that Aidan and I were running from the same person.

When Marcus started making those demands, that's when I realised how stupid I'd been. How gullible. Falling for all his lies. I'd jeopardised everything for some great love affair that had never really existed. When Aidan and I left town and moved to the country, that's when I started to truly appreciate what I had. I began to fall in love with my husband all over again, wishing more than anything that I could rewind the clock and erase that stupid affair with his awful boss that led to us having to uproot our lives and live in fear. But now Aidan's gone.

And the greatest irony is that Dani – the woman I betrayed – is now trying to help me. Trying to fix me. Taking me in as her lodger when she has no idea what kind of person I really am. What I did. I give a small, strangled laugh as she reaches across to give my knee a reassuring squeeze.

She's the innocent party here. I know that and yet my blood still burns with resentment at the fact that Marcus didn't want Bianca and me. He wanted Bianca for *her*. Perfect Dani with her huge house and her kind heart, being so charitable towards poor old traumatised Emily.

I suppose there's nothing stopping me from telling Dani what really happened. I could open my mouth right now to tell her that Marcus is Bianca's daddy. Watch her reaction. Shatter her world even more. After all, it will most likely come out in the end anyway. These things always do. But I just can't bring myself to do it. So the whole ghastly truth sits on the tip of my tongue like a cyanide pill. And I stay silent. For now...

A LETTER FROM SHALINI

I just want to say a huge thank you for reading *A Perfect Stranger*. I hope you enjoyed it. If you'd like to keep up to date with my latest releases, just sign up here and I'll let you know when I have a new novel coming out. Your email address will never be shared and you can unsubscribe at any time.

www.bookouture.com/shalini-boland

The inspiration for the novel came a few years ago when I suggested to my husband, Pete, that we rent out the spare room to make some extra money. He looked at me in horror, and that was the end of that.

I love getting feedback on my books, so if you have a few moments, I'd be really grateful if you'd be kind enough to post a review online or tell your friends about it. A good review absolutely makes my day!

When I'm not writing, reading, walking or spending time with my family, you can reach me via my Facebook page, through Twitter, Goodreads, my website or mailing list at http://eepurl.com/b4vb45.

Thanks so much,

Shalini Boland x

KEEP IN TOUCH WITH SHALINI

facebook.com/shaliniboland

twitter.com/ShaliniBoland

goodreads.com/shaliniboland

ACKNOWLEDGEMENTS

Thank you to my amazing Bookouture editors Natasha Harding and Ruth Tross for making *A Perfect Stranger* the best it could be. I'm so grateful!

Thanks also to the rest of the wonderful team at Bookouture for your talent, expertise, promotion and support. Jenny Geras, Peta Nightingale, Richard King, Sarah Hardy, Kim Nash, Noelle Holten, Jess Readett, Alexandra Holmes, Saidah Graham, Aimee Walsh, Natalie Butlin, Alex Crow, Melanie Price, Hannah Deuce, Occy Carr, Mark Alder and everyone else who helps to make my books fly.

Thanks to the lovely Lauren Finger for your superb proof-reading skills. Thank you to designer Lisa Horton for yet another eye-catching and evocative cover.

This novel started life as an Audible Original, so I'd like to thank the team at Audible for such a great opportunity. Thanks to Andrew Eisenman for getting in touch and overseeing the whole shebang. Thanks to my talented editor Katie Salisbury. Thanks to Harry Scoble for taking over the reins and being so lovely. I'm in awe of Arran Dutton at Audio Factory for creating such a great production with superb narration from Alison Campbell, Tamsin Kennard and Ciaran Saward. Thanks also to Alys Hewer, Khadija Roberts and everyone at Midas PR, especially the lovely Amber Choudhary, Camilla Mosley and Ben McCluskey.

Special thanks to Teresa Harden for doing a super-speedy emergency beta read. You're the absolute best!

Endless thanks to all my lovely readers who take the time to read, review or recommend my novels. It means so, so much. Thanks also to all the fabulous book bloggers and reviewers out there who spread the word. You guys are the absolute best!

As always, I want to thank my family for being such awesome human beings. Not forgetting my woolly writing companion Jess, who's a truly awesome little pup.

Made in the USA
Middletown, DE
16 February 2023

24991781R00156